HEAT OF BATTLE

Angel's mind was spinning. Just a little while ago, she had been in a hospital room locked in harsh debate with Dr. Carl Lenzini over whether a terminally ill patient should be allowed to have his wish and die in peace without another useless operation.

Now she was in Lenzini's office, sharing a hastily assembled "picnic" meal.

It was his peace offering, he said. But it was turning into something else.

There was nothing peaceful in what she felt when his lips came to meet hers. Sensation flooded her and she pulled back, breathless. She tried to look away from his eyes but he called her back. "Look at me, Angel. You're so lovely."

His hand had come to pull her closer to him. His tongue was exploring the velvet recesses of her mouth. Then his lips were on hers and then . . . Her heart beat wildly.

Now was the time to pull back, Angel knew. Now was the time to show Dr. Carl Lenzini she was not as vulnerable to his appeal as he thought. Now was the time—but that time was running out fast. . . .

HEART CONDITIONS

HEART CONDITIONS

Elizabeth Neff Walker

A SIGNET BOOK

SIGNET
Published by the Penguin Group
Penguin Books USA Inc., 375 Hudson Street,
New York, New York 10014, U.S.A.
Penguin Books Ltd, 27 Wrights Lane,
London W8 5TZ, England
Penguin Books Australia Ltd, Ringwood,
Victoria, Australia
Penguin Books Canada Ltd, 10 Alcorn Avenue,
Toronto, Ontario, Canada M4V 3B2
Penguin Books (N.Z.) Ltd, 182–190 Wairau Road,
Auckland 10, New Zealand

Penguin Books Ltd, Registered Offices:
Harmondsworth, Middlesex, England

First published by Signet,
an imprint of Dutton Signet,
a division of Penguin Books USA Inc.

First Printing, December, 1994
10 9 8 7 6 5 4 3 2

PUBLISHER'S NOTE
This is a work of fiction. Names, characters, places, and incidents either are
the product of the author's imagination or are used fictitiously, and any resem-
blance to actual persons, living or dead, events, or locales is entirely coinciden-
tal.

BOOKS ARE AVAILABLE AT QUANTITY DISCOUNTS WHEN USED TO PROMOTE PROD-
UCTS OR SERVICES. FOR INFORMATION PLEASE WRITE TO PREMIUM MARKETING DIVI-
SION, PENGUIN BOOKS USA INC., 375 HUDSON STREET, NEW YORK, NEW YORK
10014.

With very special thanks to David Pepper, a real family-practice doc with a talent for plotting. Thanks also to Chuck Gherman and Morley Singer for infusions of their doctorly knowledge. If I didn't get it right, well, that's a lay person for you . . .

Chapter One

The operating room was more crowded than usual. Angel, holding a retractor rather than performing the surgery, felt decidedly annoyed. It should have been her operation. The next torsed ovary was supposed to be hers, and it probably would have been if Dr. Williams hadn't been trying to placate the general surgeon, a wild-eyed, unruly-haired behemoth who glared at everyone because it hadn't been an appendix after all.

That's how it had started—a sick teenage girl who was taken to the operating room because the surgeon suspected a ruptured appendix. When he'd opened her up, he had found a perfectly normal appendix but a decidedly inflamed and torsed ovary. Now, any general surgeon worth his salt could have removed an ovary, but the rules of the game call for a specialist in gynecological surgery to be called in to perform the task.

Though Angel wasn't precisely a gynecological surgeon, she was an M.D. in the family-practice residency at Fielding Medical Center, and as part of her training, she had pushed to learn gynecological surgery. This would not have been the first ovary she had removed, and she felt perfectly capable of doing it in the present instance.

What was so galling was that Dr. Williams, her supervisor, had been perfectly willing to let her do the surgery until the maniac with the black hair had glared at him and said, "Not in my operating room, she won't. No one has proved to me yet that a family-practice resident knows how to do proper gynecological surgery, and until they do, she can hold a retractor."

Williams wasn't supposed to back down under that kind of pressure, of course. The man was a wimp as far as Angel was concerned. She had said quite firmly, "I've removed several ovaries before, Dr. Lenzini."

"Well, you're not doing it on my patient," he informed her bluntly. And Williams had just let him get away with that nonsense.

The family-practice residency was not quite two years old at Fielding, but the other doctors already showed some respect for it. Not Lenzini. You'd have thought Angel was a medical student from his attitude. He stood away from the operating table, his wild hair barely contained by the scrub hat, his mouth and nose covered with a mask that merely heightened the effect of his demanding eyes and disordered eyebrows. Lenzini watched every movement Williams made, and looked as though he wouldn't hesitate to criticize, even though the older man probably had twenty years of experience more than he did.

Angel wasn't sure why the male doctors found it necessary to make derogatory remarks about their unconscious female patients. Possibly it was to embarrass the females in the operating room—including doctors, nurses, and technicians. Possibly it was to make themselves seem more in charge. But it was a very annoying habit that she had noticed routinely on the gynecological service. Dr. Williams had not seemed particularly egregious on other occasions, but perhaps he felt it incumbent on him now, under Lenzini's glare, to be one of the boys.

For whatever reason, he said, "These girls are so stupid to get pelvic inflammatory disease, putting out for every Tom, Dick, and Harry who will have them."

Before she could slip a rein on her tongue, Angel heard herself saying, "Men think with their dicks."

Williams stopped what he was doing and stared at her. In his coldest, most hostile voice he said, "I beg your pardon."

Something strange was happening to Angel. Though she would have bitten her tongue to prevent the remark, now that she had made it, she refused to take it back. "I said," she said, remembering that it should have been her operation, "men think with their dicks."

There was a muffled snort from Dr. Lenzini that might have been amusement or fury. Angel didn't know or care which it was. Everyone else in the room seemed frozen in place. After a lengthy pause, Dr. Williams bent to his task again, saying, "You can't talk like that during surgery."

"Well, I thought that's what was expected," Angel remarked sweetly. "Making sexist comments. I've been feeling a little guilty about not joining in when I scrub on GYN operations."

"I don't make sexist comments," Williams snapped. "We'll discuss this later."

This was supposed to intimidate her, of course. As a resident, she had to cater to all the doctors higher up, the attendings and the people in her department. If they didn't like the way a resident talked to them, or disagreed with them, they could write her up and give her a bad evaluation. Angel was amazed that anyone came away from being a medical student and a resident with an ounce of backbone left. She had begun to feel her own backbone soften over the years, and recently it had begun to seriously worry her.

Williams was finished with removal of the ovary and, stripping off his gloves, he turned to Lenzini. "If you'll close, I'd like to have a word with Angel."

"Angel." The behemoth laughed and cocked his head at her. "Now there's an inappropriate name." When she turned to leave, he said, "No, don't go. I'm going to let you close. I want to see if you're as good with your hands as you are with your mouth."

Sexual innuendo was as rampant as sexism in the medical world. "Men think with their dicks," Angel muttered, stepping back to the table.

"I know," he said. "It's only when you forget that that you get in trouble."

Angel refused to look at him. The door closed behind Dr. Williams, and she accepted the suture the scrub nurse held out for her. Dr. Lenzini stood close beside Angel, watching every move with hawk eyes.

When she had finished, he shrugged. "Not bad. Of course, any general surgery intern could do that."

Angel snapped off her gloves and struggled to remove her surgical gown on which the larger men, like Lenzini, merely hunched their shoulders to break the seals. He seemed about to lend her a hand when the circulating nurse deftly stripped her of the disposable item and tossed it in the waiting plastic bag.

"Thanks, everyone," Lenzini said, as if it were his ritual close.

And a nice ritual, Angel thought, not remembering ever having heard someone say it before. Somehow it made them feel like a closer team, and appreciated. She would have to remember it for when she was in a position to be in charge of an operating room.

"Not so fast," Lenzini ordered, catching up with her as she started down the hall. He was truly a large man, six-four or six-five, with more the build of an orthopedic surgeon/former football star than a general surgeon. He had not removed the scrub hat, but his mask was gone, and Angel was confronted with what she could only describe as a smirk. "I think, since I was captain of the ship, that I should get to be there when Williams bawls you out."

"I doubt if he'll want an audience," she said, pulling off her own scrub cap. The women almost always chose the bubble caps, which left their hair relatively unscathed. Angel gave her head a slight shake, and her auburn tresses flowed down to her shoulders. She'd been on call the night before and had gotten almost no sleep. Her body ached with exhaustion, which only intensified after having to be particularly alert during the oophorectomy just now. She wanted nothing more than to find a bed and fall into it, but Beth, the circulating nurse, had whispered that Dr. Williams expected her to meet him in the residents' lounge. "And you probably have a lot better things to do than follow me around," she added to Lenzini.

Dr. Lenzini seemed unimpressed with her attempt to shake him off. He strode along beside her at a pace that showed he was attempting, barely, to match her stride and not overtake her in his usual impatience to get where he was going. "I don't have another operation until this afternoon, and I can't think of anything I'd rather do than watch him try to ream you out."

Angel wasn't sure how to take this, so she said nothing. The residents' lounge was deserted except for Dr. Williams, who stood in front of a set of windows that glared with March sunshine. Angel had almost forgotten that it was turning spring outside in the real San Francisco world. Williams looked disconcerted by the appearance of Dr. Lenzini behind her, but the younger doctor just grinned and said cheekily, "Thought I should see how an old pro handles this kind of situation." He immediately plopped down on one of the two orange plastic sofas and cocked his head attentively.

After waving her to the far end of the other sofa, Dr. Williams adopted one of those hurt, puzzled expressions people use when they're trying to pretend they aren't madder than hell. He marched back and forth across the room in front of the glaring windows.

"I can't believe you did something that stupid," he began. "That was just plain nuts, saying something like that. You know what hospitals are. It will be all over the place before noon."

Angel knew that was quite likely. She also knew he thought he'd look like a fool if he let her get away with it. Lenzini merely regarded her inquiringly. But Angel wasn't ready to say anything.

"I don't think you understand how serious this is," Williams insisted. Probably not serious enough, on the face of it, to throw her out of the program, especially since it was March and most of her evaluations for the year had been excellent.

"Sure I do," she said. "Day after day I get to stand there and hear women abused by the male doctors. If I know what's good for me, I keep my mouth shut. Of course, the doctors aren't aiming any of this abuse at me. They're just making routine comments about how inferior women are, which I shouldn't take personally, even if I am one. Because, of course, they don't mean it about me, or any of the other women in the room, or even any women they may be married to or associated with. Men think with their dicks."

"Stop saying that! It's a crude, childish, abusive thing to say."

"I know."

"Then why are you saying it?"

"Because it's the kind of thing I hear all the time. See one, do one, teach one."

Lenzini laughed. "She's got you there, Williams."

Dr. Williams glared at him but addressed Angel. "Don't be flip. Do you really feel that way about men?"

"Well, no, but then every man I've ever heard say something sexist has assured me that he isn't a sexist. Apparently you don't have to be sexist to say sexist things."

"It's a matter of opinion, what's a sexist remark."

"Yeah," Lenzini chimed in, mocking one or the other of them. Angel couldn't be sure which. He lounged easily on the orange plastic, making it squeak as he shifted his long legs. "Some women are too sensitive."

Dr. Williams, ripe with avuncular sorrow, moved away from the windows and came to loom over Angel. "I've invested a lot of time in your career, Angel. I thought you were serious about medicine."

Angel refused to take that bait. He wanted her to grovel, and she wasn't having any of it. She was overworked, underappreciated, and regularly humbled. For this she should apologize? No way! Behind Williams she could see Lenzini, who grinned at her, raised his eyebrows, and winked. Really, the man was impossible.

The tension in the room increased as her silence lengthened. Color rose from Dr. Williams's neck to his face, and he looked as though he were about to explode. Just as he opened his mouth to speak, Lenzini rose and said, "That's the problem with letting women into the operating room. They think they should be treated fairly. Where did they get an idea like that? Tell me, *Angel*, why you think women should be treated fairly in the operating room?"

Angel didn't know if it helped that he was making a mockery of the whole subject. Williams looked ready to throttle him, and she had no simple answer to such a ridiculous question. Lenzini watched her patiently, thrusting a hand into the back pocket of his scrub pants and withdrawing a stick of chewing gum, which he proceeded to unwrap and stuff into his mouth. After a minute he said, "Well, I can understand your hesitancy. There isn't any reason we should treat women fairly in the operating room, is there? They aren't treated fairly anywhere else. Why should we be the exception?"

Obviously Dr. Williams objected to this line of reasoning. "You're confusing the issue with your jesting, Dr. Lenzini. I'm sure there's not one woman on the house staff who finds our program sexist, or any of the attending doctors particularly sexist. Angel is way out of line."

Lenzini snorted. "Angel is just the only one who's spoken up. Of course your program is sexist. Mine is." He bowed in Angel's direction. "It's not, young woman, that we intend them to be sexist, it's just a long line of tradition in medicine. It's changing, but slowly. And having most of the women buy into it doesn't help."

"Blame the victims," she retorted. "You're asking the women to be stronger than the men."

"Hell, it's for their benefit."

"It's for everyone's benefit."

Lenzini shrugged. "Maybe." He turned to Dr. Williams and said, "Let's forget it, shall we?" Peering at Angel's name tag, he added, "Dr. Crawford made a joke in the operating room. We misunderstood her."

Williams frowned. "We can't have the residents trying to make fools of us. The whole system would break down."

"I don't think Dr. Crawford is capable of making a fool of me," Lenzini protested. "Or you either," he added as an afterthought. "Bet she was on call last night."

"I would have said it if I hadn't been," Angel insisted.

Lenzini laughed. "Sure you would have. Come on. I'm taking you to lunch at the cafeteria."

"Why?"

"Because then it will be obvious to everyone that I knew you were joking and that I forgive you."

"Oh, wow. That's really generous of you."

"Just smart," he replied, reaching down to grasp her hand. "You coming, Williams?"

"No." Dr. Williams still wore a prodigious frown. "I hope you realize we've been lenient with you this time, Angel. A repeat of this kind of behavior could be damaging to your career."

Threats always rubbed Angel wrong. But Lenzini had a firm grip on her hand as he pulled her out of the mushy sofa and his eyes challenged her to make a wrong move.

"Yes, Dr. Williams," she sighed, pulling her hand from Lenzini's grip. "I understand."

"Good. Don't forget to look in on our patient this afternoon."

"I won't, Dr. Williams."

Satisfied, the older doctor left the room, and Angel stood staring after him.

"You can stick your tongue out if you like," Lenzini offered. "I won't snitch."

Angel would have liked to tell him to go to hell, but his suggestion of being seen with her at lunch was actually eminently sensible. "You're all heart."

Though it was shortly before noon, the cafeteria was already crowded. Fielding Medical Center was a large complex, and the cafeteria served a vast population, so there were extensive seating arrangements, indoors and out. To one side a segregated area for doctors and their guests was beginning to fill as well. Angel was still in her green scrubs, and Dr. Lenzini still had his scrub hat over his dark hair. She preceded him in the line for a choice of chicken or barbecue. Thinking he would choose the chicken, a much more medically correct choice, she picked up the barbecue. He followed suit, but in addition accumulated an extra potato salad, a square of cornbread, and a piece of cherry pie.

"I'm a growing boy," he informed her lightly.

Angel paused at the cashier to present her card, but Lenzini waved it aside, saying, "I'm getting both of these."

"Thanks, but I'd rather get it myself," she said, again presenting her card to the cashier, who, after a brief glance at Lenzini, accepted it.

"You women," he muttered. "What the hell am I supposed to do with all the money I make if I don't buy some poorhouse officer lunch every once in a while?"

"You could contribute something to a battered women's shelter."

"Actually . . ." But he changed his mind and nodded toward the doctors' dining area. "We'll be most effective over there, I think. That is, if you aren't going to object."

"I appreciate what you're doing," she replied, weaving her way behind him past a dozen tables.

"I love a grateful woman."

Lenzini surveyed the doctors' area carefully before edging toward a long table with three other people. One of them, Roger Janek, had been the anesthesiologist on the case that morning. The other two were an older neurologist and a middle-aged orthopedic surgeon. As he set his tray down, Lenzini said, "I don't know if you all know Angel Crawford, a family-practice resident here."

"We've just been hearing about her," the neurologist, Ben Taylor, admitted. "Roger was unfolding the saga for us. He tells a good story, Roger. Exaggerates sometimes."

Lenzini laughed. "Probably not this time."

The orthopedic surgeon, who had sat silent until now, demanded, "Did you really say men think with their dicks in an operating room? That sounds pretty uncalled for to me."

Angel had never met this man before, but his disapproval was palpable. She intended to point out to him Dr. Williams's sexist remarks, but before she could open her mouth, she felt Lenzini nudge her toward a chair.

"I thought it was a really astute observation," Lenzini remarked as he claimed his own chair beside hers. He dug right into the potato salad. "You're a surgeon, Doug. And what do we say about surgeons? They've got to have balls, right? That's what we say."

"These days," Roger pointed out, "we say they have to have a fire in their bellies."

"Yeah, well, it's the same thing, isn't it?" Lenzini stabbed the air with his fork to make his point. "We're saying they have to be men, or think like men, or act like men. Now, Angel here is a woman. And it irritates her that we think only men can really be surgeons."

"Who thinks only men can be surgeons?" protested the orthopedic surgeon, Doug. "There are plenty of women surgeons. It's hard for them to be orthopedic surgeons, of course, because of the physical strength involved, but . . ."

Lenzini and Roger burst out laughing.

Dr. Doug looked offended. "Well, it's true. When a woman tries to enter the program, we point out to her the necessary physical force needed on some of our cases because she should know about that up front."

"So she'll know she has to get help from her techs once in a while, like everybody else," Lenzini concluded. "So even more often than most, so what?"

"What if there aren't any techs around?" Doug demanded. "What's she supposed to do then?"

"The same thing you'd do, Doug," Roger suggested. "Find one. Techs are everywhere."

Angel was taking this all in as she forced down her lunch. Apparently Dr. Lenzini wasn't going to make her defend herself. In fact, it looked as though he weren't going to let her speak for herself at all. She waited until she had his attention by smiling kindly at him, then asked, "So why wouldn't you let me operate, Dr. Lenzini?"

Rhetorically he asided to Roger, "Have you ever encountered such an inappropriate name? Well, Angel, my guess is that there were three or four things at work here. First, I've never been much of an advocate of the family-practice residency in a city like San Francisco. We're specialists here, not generalists. Second, Williams didn't stand up for you when I challenged him. That didn't say much for your experience. Third, I was annoyed that I'd misdiagnosed the kid as having appendicitis and wanted to take it out on someone. You were by far the easiest."

The neurologist shook his head. "I guess that about covers it. Too bad we can't have this much clarity on everything."

"Wait a minute, wait a minute," Lenzini protested. "I said there were four reasons."

The others regarded him with mock expectancy.

"And fourth, I remembered my own residency and how character building it had been. We tend to forget that," he told his fellow attending doctors. "Residency is a period of your life when just about anyone can dump on you, and there's very little you can do about it. Isn't that so, Angel?"

Angel wiped barbecue sauce from her fingers. "Yes, that's true, Dr. Lenzini."

"You see?" he said triumphantly. "Now here was a perfect opportunity to build this young woman's character. She didn't avail herself of the opportunity, of course, but that may be because her character is already well enough built. Who is to say? Well, perhaps Dr. Williams. Dr. Williams knows her better than we do. He told her that what she said was crude, childish, and abusive, and she agreed with him. He demanded to know why she would say such a thing, and she said, 'See one, do one, teach one.' He asked her if she really felt that way about men, and she said sexists don't think they're sexist, or something like that. He said he'd invested a lot of time in her career."

His companions, unsure at first of where he was leading them, were now openly amused, except Dr. Doug who took these matters very seriously. Dr. Doug said, "It's a matter of opinion, what's a sexist remark."

The others howled. Lenzini confided, "That's what Williams told her. And I told her that women were too sensitive."

While the others laughed, Dr. Doug looked perplexed. "But that's true," he insisted. "Women read too much into casual remarks."

"Like men think with their dicks," Lenzini concluded. "It's all the same, isn't it? Hey, Roger, did you have to intubate Mrs. Helvici in the ICU?"

And the conversation about Angel was over. She didn't quite feel a part of their discussion of other hospital happenings, but Lenzini turned to her occasionally to include her in the group or to learn if she'd heard a particular bit of gossip. As soon as she had finished eating, she excused herself, pleading pressing patient matters on the sixth floor. The men each acknowledged her departure with a nod or wave. Lenzini rose, his mouth curved ruefully. "Watch your step, Angel."

"I usually do, Dr. Lenzini." She turned to go but paused to say, "And thanks."

"My pleasure."

Angel received a number of censorious looks during the afternoon, but for the most part she was too busy to pay any heed to them. It could have been much worse, and probably would have been without Lenzini's assistance. She had five postoperative patients to see and three new admits on whom to do history and physicals, plus a trip to radiology to go over the results of a CT scan on an outpatient of hers. Several of the doctors and nurses teased her about what they'd heard, but she pretended surprise at their thinking it was anything more than a joke. At any moment she expected a call from the head of the department, but it never came, and at seven she escaped to her flat two blocks from the hospital.

Exhausted, she climbed the two flights of stairs and leaned heavily against the door as she tried to unlock it. Her eyelids were so heavy she could hardly keep them open now that she was minutes away from her bed. The door opened into an entry hall that, like several of the rooms in the flat, had dark-stained wood wainscoting and hardwood floors. If Angel had spent more time there, she would probably have made some effort to lighten the place up with spring flowers and colorful prints. As it was, she mostly slept when she was at home, and the curtains were seldom even open on daylight for more than a few hours.

Her roommate, a resident in the neurology department, spent even less time in the flat, but only because she spent so much time with her male friend. Each of the women had her own bedroom; Angel's was in the back overlooking a scraggly garden two stories below. All three flats theoretically shared the backyard, but it got little use, perhaps as much because of the fog as that the tenants had so little spare time.

The building was a three-flat Victorian, newly painted in one of the three-color schemes that had become so popular in San Francisco. Angel herself doubted that the original paint job had been so flamboyant, but had to admit that the navy, burgundy, and dark gray brought out the wonderful detail around the doors and windows and under the eaves. Convinced that she would one day have the time to properly decorate her flat, she had originally bought plants that died from neglect and prints that were never framed. Instead she had learned to do the minimum in tidying of her own room, and managed to buy thick shades that made her bedroom perfectly dark even when the sun was still out. Not that it mattered. As soon as she hit the bed, she was sound asleep, whether she had remembered to brush her teeth or not.

Unfortunately, on this occasion when she walked into the flat, her roommate Nan was standing in the arched entry to the living room eager to talk. Nan was a tall woman, two or three inches taller than Angel's five-seven, and she had ash blond hair, which she wore in a French braid pinned loosely to her head. Nan's eyes were dancing with humor when she confronted Angel.

"I've heard nothing but your antisocial remarks in

the operating room since the middle of the day," she said. "At least half a dozen people who know we room together made sure I heard what had happened. Geez, Angel, were you trying to get kicked out of your program or just out of the OR?"

Angel slumped on the overstuffed sofa and let her backpack fall to the floor. "They didn't let me do the oophorectomy. I was tired. Williams said how stupid women were. I don't know. It just got to me."

"Who didn't let you do the oophorectomy? You've removed ovaries before."

"Yeah, I know. Well, Dr. Lenzini said I couldn't, and Williams didn't argue with him. Both of them are jerks."

Nan laughed. "Hey, they're both surgeons. What do you expect?"

"Well, I'm going to be qualified to do some surgery, too, and I'm not going to be a jerk."

Nan's eyes twinkled. "I'm not sure that's possible, Angel."

It was a standard joke between the two of them, never more than lightly touched on. Non-surgeons thought surgeons were arrogant; surgeons thought non-surgeons were wimps who deliberated rather than acted. Neither could have done without the other, though both groups would have been willing to try. Neurologists were non-surgeons as were family-practice doctors. But because family-practice physicians had to know OB/GYN and its complications, some learned surgery, peripherally.

"I heard Dr. Lenzini took you to lunch with him."

Angel folded her arms on her chest and said

crossly, "He wouldn't have had to if he'd behaved properly in the first place, would he?"

"He didn't have to anyhow." Nan dropped into an armchair opposite the sofa. "I've met him. It probably whizzed him off to misdiagnose that patient as an appendectomy. He hates being wrong."

Curious, Angel asked, "How do you know?"

"I was doing a neurological exam on a patient who shared a room with one of his. He couldn't believe the woman was still on an IV a week after her cancer surgery. He walked out muttering about cutting the umbilical cord. I was in and out of the room a lot around that time, and, I want to tell you, this woman gave the nurses no end of trouble about her pain after the IV was taken away because she'd had a patient-controlled analgesia machine with it. She got hysterical once, screaming until her roommate buried her head under the pillow, and no amount of medication seemed to calm her down. Lenzini was fit to be tied, but he finally agreed to let her have the IV and the machine back."

"He was probably right to take it away in the first place. You have to wean patients at some point."

"So he said, at some length, to the patient. Who was not intimidated, by the way. I can't imagine why not, when here's this irate bear of a man with his hair springing out from under his scrub cap, his eyes snapping like electric sparks. I think they called him from surgery to placate her."

Angel shook her head. "I'm not surprised he has a temper. On the other hand, he obviously has a sense of humor. He thought my situation was funny as hell."

"But he tried to rescue you."

"Just another one of those surgeonly attributes—doctor to the rescue stuff." Angel picked up her backpack and rose from the sofa. "I'm exhausted, Nan. If I'm not in bed in two minutes, I'll fall asleep right here."

"He's not married."

"Lenzini? No wonder."

"He lived with someone for a long time, years maybe. I don't know what happened with them."

"Did I ask? Do I care? The man is a jerk." Angel trooped to the hallway leading back toward the bedrooms. She turned to add, "A sexist jerk," before she disappeared into the rear of the flat.

Nan sighed.

Chapter Two

Clifford Lenzini did not think of himself as a jerk, sexist or otherwise. Supremely confident at thirty-three, he enjoyed almost every minute of his life. He worked long and hard, played almost equally hard when he had the time, and would have missed having a woman in his life if he'd had time for one. But with ten and twelve hours of surgery several days a week, as well as seeing new patients and postoperative patients, to say nothing of his research activities and the time he had to spend training the surgery residents—well, it hardly left a yawning gap in his life.

He had not given a thought to his unusual behavior regarding Angel Crawford in the month since it had occurred. If he had seen her around the medical center, he might have been reminded of it, but that had not happened, and it wasn't unusual that it had not happened. Fielding was a large hospital, exactly the type he had expected to end up in. Cliff's father was an orthopedic surgeon in San Diego, and Cliff's whole life had been geared toward his going into medicine.

Though he had gone to medical school in the

Northeast, he had chosen to train on the West Coast. He wasn't sure why he'd taken a fancy to Fielding, and it certainly hadn't been his first choice. But then, he didn't get his first choice in the match that occurred for every medical student in his senior year of medical school. It was, perhaps, the first time he'd suffered a disappointment of that magnitude, and he was proud of himself for never having let it slow him down for a minute. Broken eggs were for omelettes, right?

San Diego had the more typically California climate. In San Francisco there was fog, and summer was more like spring, but Lenzini had adapted. He could play tennis year-round. He could bike and sail and run. You couldn't beat California for its climate. Sally had left him for New England. Who needed freezing snow and blazing heat? He'd choose California any day, especially in April.

A surgery consult had been requested for a patient on Fielding 6 East. Cliff's chief resident had gone to see the patient, but had paged Cliff urgently with what he'd found. Fielding 6 East was an oncology floor, and Lenzini was informed that the patient had advanced metastatic intestinal cancer. "So is there something we can do for him?" Cliff asked.

"I think so. I think we can clear the blockage and give him a little more time," he was told.

"So what's the problem?"

"The medical resident doesn't agree with me."

Cliff swore and glanced at his watch. These things were never cleared up at a distance. And they were only cleared up quickly if he put in an appearance. "I'll be right over."

He tossed a lab coat on over his scrubs and ran a hand through his disordered locks. Once, years ago, he had been told by the chief of the surgery department that a doctor was more effective when he looked the part. Cliff did not particularly agree with him, but, taking the hint, had always attempted a symbolic reorganization of himself before leaping into a diplomatic situation. He climbed two flights of stairs to the sixth floor and strode down the hall with determination. Room 686 was the farthest room from the nurses' station. Naturally.

There were three people in the room already, not counting the patient, who was a frail, elderly man sitting up in bed, though he was obviously in pain. The nurse was taking Mr. Edwards's blood pressure and unabashedly listening to the argument between the chief resident and—Angel Crawford.

"Oh, for God's sake!" he grumbled. "What is it this time, Angel? I thought you *liked* operating on people."

He knew full well that family-practice residents only operated (if they operated at all) on gynecological cases, but he could not resist baiting her. Unlike himself, she was not surprised by the encounter. Apparently the chief resident had already mentioned calling him. Her position shifted, however, toward the patient, whom she looked for all the world like she was protecting from the big, bad surgeons.

"Dr. Lenzini. I'm afraid there has been a misunderstanding. Mr. Edwards doesn't wish to have surgery."

"Oh, really," Lenzini replied, moving toward the old man. "You wouldn't mind my examining you, would you?" he asked Mr. Edwards, who stared at him without saying anything. "After all, Angel, someone did call a consult."

"That was the intern, who didn't bother to read my notes in the chart."

Dr. Lenzini, being a mammoth of a man, had no difficulty in maneuvering Angel away from the bedside. He rested a hand lightly on Mr. Edwards's wasted arm. "You've been in pain. Dr. Jones here believes that an operation would make you more comfortable. It wouldn't cure you. I'm sure you understand that. But it could make you more comfortable."

"No," Mr. Edwards replied, looking beseechingly at Angel. "Tell him."

"Mr. Edwards knows that his disease is fatal," Angel said, startling both Dr. Lenzini and the chief resident, Dr. Jones, with her bluntness. "He knows that surgery might prolong his life, but that ultimately it could not make him well. His pain is not unbearable. For the most part, we're able to control it with medication. He believes that surgery would merely prolong his suffering." At Dr. Lenzini's frown, she added, "It's his prerogative, Dr. Lenzini. I've explained this to Dr. Jones."

"Did you explain it to Mr. Edwards?" Lenzini asked. "Did you perhaps sway his thinking on the matter?"

Angel turned to the patient. "Mr. Edwards, we don't mean to talk about you as if you weren't here. Dr. Lenzini's concern is that I might have influenced you in your decision. He's quite correct in saying that an operation would probably help you temporarily. And it would certainly keep you alive for a few more days or weeks. Do you understand that?"

"No operation," the man said.

"He doesn't seem to be entirely oriented," the chief resident pointed out.

"He's perfectly cogent," Angel contradicted. "Mr. Edwards is not a man of many words, and frankly I think he's tired of saying the same thing over and over again. As you or I would be," she added.

The nurse, who had managed to remain in the room by straightening the patient's bed and organizing the various tubes coming out of his body, shifted her glance to Dr. Lenzini. Cliff sat down on the edge of Mr. Edwards's bed and looked the elderly patient directly in the eye. His hands remained folded in his lap, but there was a restlessness about his right foot, which he tapped against the metal of the hospital bed.

"Do you have family here?" he asked.

"My wife. She comes every day."

"That's good. I'm sure she's a comfort." Lenzini glanced at the row of cards on the bedside table. "She can't want you to be in pain. She probably wants you to stay with her as long as you can. She'd probably want you to have the operation."

"No," Mr. Edwards said. "We've discussed it. I'm not going to leave her with a pile of bills."

"I'm sure she's not worried about the bills," Lenzini protested.

"She'd be crazy if she wasn't," Mr. Edwards retorted, but he was visibly tiring. "Look. I'm going to die. If I die tomorrow or if I die next week, what's the difference? A bunch of money for the hospital and for the doctors. It's no big deal to me. I've lived my life. And now I'm ready to die."

He put his hand out to Angel, and she pressed it. "This one," Mr. Edwards said, "she understands. Don't know why the rest of you can't." He slumped back against the pillows with a wan smile. "Now go away, all of you."

Dr. Lenzini took Angel's elbow and propelled her out of the room and down the hall to the alcove off the nurses' station. "Sit," he said, but remained standing himself. "I thought I told you to watch your step."

"I have been," she protested, shaking back a lock of auburn hair that had fallen across her cheek. "I tried to tell Dr. Jones that this was the patient's decision, but he wouldn't listen."

Dr. Jones, ready to jump into the fight with both feet, was obviously surprised when Lenzini turned to him and said, "It's okay, Jake. I'll handle this. Why don't you finish what you have to do?"

The young man shrugged, frowned a surgeonly frown at Angel, and left. She grinned after him. "You teach them early how to do that, don't you?" she asked.

"Look like God, you mean?" He shrugged. "It comes naturally to the guys who choose surgery, I think."

"How about the women?"

He dismissed her question with a wave. "That's not why we're here. How long ago was it that we had that little contretemps in the operating room?"

"About a month ago."

"You've changed rotations?"

"Yes. I'm doing six weeks on oncology."

Lenzini was thumbing through the patient's chart while they talked. There was a long pause while he read the last few pages of notations and considered the various lab results. With a snap, he closed the plastic binder and regarded her thoughtfully. "Surgery is indicated. You seem to understand that."

"I do. But Mr. Edwards doesn't want surgery, and he's perfectly well aware that he wouldn't last much longer if he had it."

"I wonder who made that perfectly clear to him," Lenzini remarked.

Angel looked surprised. "You're not aged enough to be of the Old School who believed you didn't let the patient in on the facts. Mr. Edwards asked, and I told him. I didn't beat him over the head with it. His wife was there, and they both asked intelligent questions, and they both seemed determined not to prolong his suffering."

"The whole purpose of the operation would be to relieve his suffering."

"Yes, but only temporarily. You can't stop the progress of the disease."

Lenzini had wandered over to the X-ray view box. He seemed distracted for a moment by two X-rays left there for viewing. After a moment he said, "What he seemed most concerned about, Angel, was the money. Don't they have insurance?"

"Yes, pretty good insurance, but there's a co-payment that will keep adding up as long as he has care. Mrs. Edwards came to me and told me not to worry about the money. If it would do her husband real lasting good, she didn't care about the money.

But I couldn't really tell her that it would do more than prolong his life a week or two."

"Or maybe a month."

Angel sighed. "I did tell them the outside limits, Dr. Lenzini. You can't make a patient do what he doesn't want to do."

"That's not precisely true. Any effective doctor can influence a patient to do what he thinks is appropriate." He was bearing down on her, and he knew it, but he wanted to find out just where she stood. She was young and relatively inexperienced, and her judgment could not necessarily be trusted.

"He wants to die with some kind of dignity." Angel shrugged one shoulder helplessly. "I could, presumably, barrel over him and insist that he needs the surgery. But he doesn't. It wouldn't make his dying any better, just longer."

"That's only your opinion, Doctor. Older, wiser doctors might view the situation differently. They might think another week or two of relatively comfortable living is worth the effort and the money."

"He would be in pain again after a while. He can't avoid that." Angel leaned forward, her face intent, her gray-green eyes fervent. "Mr. Edwards has fought this a long time. You've seen his chart. He's been brave and determined. Now he knows he's reached the end, and it doesn't seem right to insist that he fight some more just because we don't want to give up. He hasn't given up; he's just accepted his fate. It seems to me that we should be accepting his decision, not fighting it. We should let him exit in peace."

"We don't do that until there are no options left, Angel."

Angel rose to face him. "You may not, Dr. Lenzini, but I do. I'm not going to be one of those doctors whose ego stands in the way of her letting a patient do what he knows is right for himself. I'm not going to play God in situations like this."

"Sometimes you have to play God, Dr. Crawford. Sometimes you have no choice. Maybe you can't handle that."

She actually squared her shoulders before she said, "I can handle it, Dr. Lenzini. This doesn't happen to be one of those cases."

"I'm not sure you're right. I'll talk with the head of oncology service, and we'll let you know our decision."

Dismissed, she turned and left the alcove without a word. Lenzini watched her go with a mixture of annoyance, interest, and grudging respect. She wouldn't back down, even when he pressed. That could be stubbornness or conviction. Hard to tell at this point. She was a cute thing, though, and he remembered their previous encounter with amusement.

It was a wonder he'd never heard of her before that occasion if she'd been going through the medical center propounding all these heretical views. Curious to find out more about her, he motioned the nurse Judy into the alcove with him. Judy had been in the patient's room with them and taken in the whole scene.

"How long has Dr. Crawford been the resident on

Mr. Edwards's case, Judy?" he asked, though the information was doubtless in the chart.

"I think she picked him up in her continuity clinic. Certainly she's had him since she came on the service. And she's been very good with him—patient about explaining things and ordering enough medication to keep him pretty comfortable." Judy ran energetic fingers through her short curls. "Not all of them feel comfortable doing that."

"I know." Lenzini flipped open the chart and tapped the last entry. "Her intern seemed to disagree with her about the possibility of surgery."

"Her intern is a jerk," Judy replied, uncompromisingly. "He doesn't read anyone else's notes, and thinks he knows everything."

Lenzini grinned. "I bet he doesn't think the nurses know what they're doing."

"You've got it." She turned to go. "She's good, Dr. Crawford is."

"She may be wrong in this case."

Judy shook her head. "I don't think so, Dr. Lenzini. Talk to Mrs. Edwards."

"I will."

Lenzini knew better than to run roughshod over people who knew a patient and a case better than he did. Given his way, he would have operated on Mr. Edwards, because there was a chance they could prolong his life for a few weeks. But it was major surgery, which in itself would be painful to recover from, and the aggressiveness of the tumor made it unlikely they could stem the tide for long. There was even a chance that when they opened up the abdomen, they would find things were too far along to make a difference. In that case, they would simply close the patient again and send him back to his room to die.

Still, most patients opted for even a few weeks' grace. Lenzini wondered if that was because the surgeons pressed them to accept the small palliation they could offer, or because the patients really clung to life so fervently. Perhaps a little of both. Certainly few surgeons could allow any chance for improving a patient's condition to pass by. It might have been one of the things that fueled the enmity between internists and surgeons.

Lenzini stood for a while after the nurse had left, going over the information in the chart. He could find no physical reason why Mr. Edwards shouldn't have surgery. With a grimace, he returned the chart to the rack. All he had to do was sort out whether Angel Crawford or the patient was the instigator of Mr. Edwards's decision. Something that would waste a good hour of his time, on a day when he really couldn't spare it. Lenzini, who had a tendency to express himself rather primitively, growled as he strode toward the office of the cancer-unit's director.

Angel was writing a note in the chart of another patient an hour later when a large shadow fell across the page. Without even turning to look, she knew that it was Lenzini. She could *feel* him behind her and an unfamiliar surge of adrenaline raced through her. This was a specialized form of the fight or flight response perhaps. She had no intention of fleeing from this wild man, but she was not in a position to fight him either. If he wanted to perform surgery on

Mr. Edwards, by heaven he'd find a way to do it. Angel continued to scribble in the chart.

"We need to talk," he said finally.

With her head, she indicated the chair beside her
and continued to write. "So talk," she suggested.

"I want your full attention, Angel."

He continued to stand over her, and she glanced
up at him to assess his mood. "Half a minute, then,
okay? Judy is waiting for these orders."

"I'll wait for you in the lounge."

Angel didn't particularly want to be alone with
him in the doctors' lounge. It would remind her of
the day she'd met him and he'd sat in on her reprimand by Dr. Williams. In all likelihood, she realized
with a sigh, she was about to suffer another reprimand. Apparently her evaluations were not going to
shine this spring, which was ironic since she was beginning to feel really competent, if nowhere near finished learning her craft.

At first she thought he'd fallen asleep. When she
opened the lounge door, he was sprawled on the
sofa, his eyes closed, his face lax, and his shoulders
slumped down. Surprisingly, he looked no less powerful this way, with his legs spread out and his arms
extended loosely at his sides. As usual, his disordered black hair needed a comb run through it. Angel hesitated before entering the room.

"Come in, come in," he growled, but took another
moment before opening his eyes. "Shut the door,
Angel. I don't have all day."

He rubbed a fist at his right eye and shook out his
shoulders. "Sit down over there where I can see
you."

Angel took the chair opposite him that he indicated with an impatient gesture. He stared at her for a long moment, wearing an aggravated frown. "I talked with the head of the oncology service, and I talked with Mrs. Edwards."

"Good," she said.

"Are you so sure they'd back you up?"

"Not at all, with you intimidating them. But under ordinary circumstances, yes, I believe they'd support my stance. After all, I didn't come up with it by myself as you seem to think. I was just trying to make clear what Mr. Edwards and his wife wanted."

"Patients don't always know what's best for them."

"Doctors don't always know what's best for a particular patient. Two people in the same situation might choose different routes for their care." Angel felt too restless to remain seated. She popped up from her chair and walked impatiently across the room. "We're not debating what the medical options are here, Dr. Lenzini. I know what the surgical indications are and for a patient interested in accepting them, I'm perfectly agreeable."

"That's big of you."

She snapped around to face him. "Why are you making such a big deal of this? It can't be the first time some patient of yours has refused recommended surgery. Is it me? Is it that you don't trust me just because I said men think with their dicks?"

He grinned. "Hell, I haven't given that a thought since the day you said it. Angel, it's my responsibility to make sure the residents don't overstep their bounds in matters like this. We had a request for a consult on your patient. He could use surgery. So I have to check it out."

"You heard him say he didn't want surgery."

Lenzini sounded irritated when he spoke again. "Listen to me, Angel. Everything depends on the way you present something to a patient. If I want a patient to have surgery, I present it as a foregone conclusion. The patient accepts that it's important, necessary even, and he doesn't give two thoughts to disagreeing with me."

"I know that."

He waved her to silence. "Conversely, if I have decided that a patient won't benefit from surgery, I present it in such a way that he won't want to have it done. I think it's entirely possible that you could have presented the idea of surgery to Mr. Edwards that way."

"Well, I didn't," she insisted. "There is also the route of presenting something in a neutral fashion, where you lay out the benefits and the disadvantages. I think a patient deserves to know as much as possible."

He grunted. "Obviously you do. Hell, Angel, if I told most of my patients *everything* about their surgery ahead of time, they'd run screaming from the room."

For such a big man, he certainly made it to his feet with a minimum of motion. He stood several feet from her, but he might as well have had her arm in a hammerlock from the way his eyes pinned her. "We don't do unnecessary surgery here. We don't need to. There are enough diseased bodies to fill our beds and keep us busy."

"I didn't say surgery on Mr. Edwards would be unnecessary. He simply doesn't want it."

"Yeah, I know. But I'm not sure you're getting the point, Angel." He ran a hand through his hair, which made it no worse. "Sometimes you have to sell surgery. You internal-medicine types don't like doing that. Yes, yes, I know you're in family practice, but you're basically internal-medicine people, and you resent surgeons and surgery. So it's not easy for you to sell surgery when the benefits are marginal." He cocked his head at her. "You see what I mean?"

"Yes." Her pulse had suddenly sped up. "I guess."

"Let me see your hands."

"My hands?" Puzzled, and slightly nervous, she extended them to him.

Lenzini held them casually, turning them over and back, before dropping them. "Yep, you have surgeon's hands, Angel. Better get used to it."

"There is no such thing as surgeon's hands," she protested. "You just wanted to see if they'd shake, if I was intimidated by you."

"You could do worse than be intimidated by me. You still have a lot to learn."

"I know that, but I don't let it intimidate me. What would be the point?"

"Damned if I know." He shrugged and laid a hand lightly on her shoulder. "Just keep watching your step, Angel."

"Yes, Dr. Lenzini," she said, with mocking servility. "Anything you say, Dr. Lenzini."

"The mouth on this one," he said, shaking his head. "They don't make residents like they used to."

"Thank God."

"So run along. I have important things to do, like surgery on people who want it."

Angel had the distinct feeling that he was appraising her as she walked from the room, but she didn't turn around to check. She couldn't tell quite why she felt so disturbed by her meeting with him. He had not, after all, been terribly hard on her. He had just been there, and his presence was somehow overpowering.

When he had touched her, her hands hadn't shaken, but she had felt electricity run through her. And she bet he knew it; bet he had taken her hands and touched her shoulder to create just that reaction. Angel was sure Dr. Lenzini knew that his virile stance, his bristling masculinity disturbed susceptible young women. Probably older ones, too. But she didn't plan to be susceptible to anything other than learning good medicine. If he could teach her better medicine, she was more than willing to learn. That was the only role he would play in her life, and she felt certain even that wouldn't be a particularly uncomplicated one.

Chapter Three

Between the last two surgeries of the day, Cliff relaxed in the lounge off the dressing room. He was tired but not exhausted. A cold soda rested between his knees as he stretched to get the kinks out of his shoulders. He was alone in the room for some time before the door opened. Roger Janek, the anesthesiologist who'd been working with him, wandered into the room.

"Damnedest thing, Cliff," he grumbled. "You know about the anesthesiology department bash tonight, right?"

"It would be hard not to have heard about it," his friend replied. "That's all you guys have been talking about for weeks."

"Yeah, well, we had this great idea, Kerri and I. It's not formal, you know, and we were both going in tuxes."

"It's been done before."

"Oh, shut up, you jerk. Of course it's been done before. But we thought it would be fun, and she looks smashing in this tux we got her secondhand."

"Great. I hope you'll have a terrific time."

"Cliff, that's the problem. She's sick as a dog with

the flu. I just talked with her on the phone, and she's too bad to even get out of bed. She said I should go without her."

Cliff regarded him impassively. "They never mean it."

"I know." Roger sighed. "But it seems such a waste, and I was supposed to be master of ceremonies and all that. Actually I have to go, whether Kerri can come or not."

"Then go alone. There'll be plenty of women there to dance with. They'll all make a fuss over you if you're alone."

Roger appeared to consider that for a moment with interest, but eventually he shook his head. "I'm at the head table, and I have to introduce all these people, and I need someone personable with me to do the chitchat stuff. Kerri's great at that. She remembers everyone's name and how many kids they have. She talks with the wives and lets us guys talk about what we want to. Hell, why did she have to be sick this one night of the whole year?"

"I imagine she did it on purpose to make you mad," Cliff suggested.

"Oh, buzz off. Anyhow, I don't know what to do. I really should take someone else. I suppose she could wear Kerri's tux if she wanted to. Just someone pleasant who wouldn't make a big deal out of it. You know anyone?"

Cliff felt an impish impulse rise within him. It was not a totally foreign urge for him to have. In his younger days, when he took himself less seriously, he had frequently played such a role. But he smiled pleasantly now and said thoughtfully, "The girl who got in hot water in one of our operations a month back," he said. "Angel Crawford. The one who says men think with their dicks. She sounds like just the right one for the occasion."

Roger stared at him. "You must be kidding."

"Not at all. She's about Kerri's size, could wear the tux, and would undoubtedly have no problem conversing with everyone from the head of your department down to the lowest drudge in the office. She doesn't wear a ring, but I suppose she might be attached to someone. I'm serious, Roger. You ought to ask her."

Roger looked undecided. He had a habit of tugging at the drawstrings on his scrub pants, and now he very nearly undid them with his unconscious fiddling. Tucking his hands carefully behind his back, he asked, "Do you have her number?"

"Of course not. Page her in the hospital. I doubt if she'll mind." Cliff finished his soda in one long pull. "And if you call her, *don't* tell her I mentioned her."

"Okay." Roger looked at his watch. "If I can get hold of her before I have to go to the OR, I'll ask her."

"Great." Cliff tossed his can into the trash. "Have fun."

"I scarcely remember which one he is," Angel confessed to Nan that evening as she worked on her hair. "And he's bringing a tux for me to wear. Really, though, it's been such a rough week, I couldn't resist going out, even to a department party. I've always heard anesthesiologists know how to have a good time."

"I've met Roger. He's a nice enough guy, I guess. A few nervous mannerisms that would drive me crazy, but hey. It's the perfect setup, too, if he's already going with someone and just needs you to fill in for an evening." Nan tucked a stray strand of hair against Angel's cheek. "Unless, of course, you're looking for Mr. Right these days and haven't mentioned it to me."

"Hardly." Angel glanced down at her bare feet. "What kind of shoes do you suppose one wears with a tux? Somehow heels don't seem appropriate."

"I think you ought to wear your Nikes," Nan teased.

"Not a bad idea." Angel rummaged in the closet until she came up with a glistening pair of white leather tennis shoes. She regarded them skeptically. "They'd be hard to dance in," she reflected, tossing them back in. "I guess it will have to be the standard black flats."

The doorbell rang, and the two women looked at each other. "You'll have to get it," Angel said. "When your date is bringing your clothes, he can't expect you to greet him at the door fully dressed. Give him a glass of wine and tell him I won't be long, okay?"

When Nan returned with the tux, she grinned. "He looks adorable in his tux. And I want to warn you, Angel, he didn't seem altogether sure I wasn't you when I answered the door. How well does this man know you?"

"Not at all, actually. I think he just remembered

me from the OR the day I got in trouble. Not much of a recommendation, huh?"

"Some men can't resist a challenge."

"I doubt if he's one of them." Angel had already begun to work her way into the unfamiliar garments. Over the years of medical school, internship, and residency she had become adept at quick changes, and with Nan's help ("He didn't want any wine"), she was soon regarding herself critically in the mirror. "It'll never be my favorite outfit, but there's a certain charm about it. I feel like I'm going to a prom."

Nan straightened the bow tie and flicked a speck off the arm of the coat. "Goes great with that auburn hair. I think you'll knock 'em dead, kiddo. Off you go."

Angel, not quite remembering what Roger Janek looked like either, sneaked up the hall and peeked into the living room where he waited, studying a dead plant on the windowsill. "We're going to throw it out one of these days," she said as she came into the room. "But even dead, it's company."

Roger swung around and regarded her with appreciation. "Hey, that looks great. Kerri's going to really miss this; she would have been smashing."

Nan, who was right behind Angel, remarked, "The man is brimming with tact."

"I didn't mean that you weren't smashing," Roger protested. "I mean, you look great. Angel, is it?"

"And wait till you see his bad side," Nan muttered.

Unoffended by his ineptness, Angel marched up to her date and linked arms with him. "It's all right,

Roger. I insist that we talk about Kerri practically all evening. I'm sure she's a beautiful young woman, and I'm sorry she's sick and couldn't come tonight."

"Well, so am I, but you're a great sport to agree to go at the last minute." Roger gallantly raised her hand to his mouth for a kiss. He stood only a few inches taller than Angel, and was of a wiry build, with strong hands and a youthful face. His hair looked combed within an inch of its life, presumably to make it behave, though it was no more than a curly brown mass.

There was something dear about him, Angel decided. It was going to be a pleasant evening. "Don't wait up," she called cheerfully to Nan.

"As if I would," her roommate grumbled. "Have fun, you guys."

During the whole evening, Roger did not introduce Angel without first saying, "Kerri has the flu, so she couldn't come. This is . . ." She found that it didn't bother her in the least. He was actually refreshing with his total lack of polish. She had, after all, come from a midwestern family with no pretensions to sophistication. Roger's forthrightness was amusing and distressing by turns, and the nervous habits he had, like tugging at his cummerbund and twisting his left ear, were forgotten after the realization of what they were.

Angel had welcomed the opportunity to sit down to an amazingly good dinner with people from Fielding whom she'd only noticed around the medical center. Roger was wont to tell the story of her outburst in the OR and, though there were some frowns and looks askance, most of the doctors and their partners, being in a party mood, accepted the incident for what it was—a light mocking of the sexist attitudes sometimes found in the OR.

As master of ceremonies, Roger was particularly appealing, describing the head of his department as "our very favorite anesthetic," and assuring the assembled throng that "Without our specialty, they'd all have nightmares instead of sweet dreams." He introduced with personal anecdotes each of the residents finishing the program that spring, and he led everyone in a cheer of his own devising (on the order of "Wipe 'em out, wipe 'em out, waaaaay out"), which left his audience roaring.

"So dance now," Roger said at the conclusion of the program. "That's what we have a band for." He reached down a hand to Angel. "We'll get you started, this Angel and I."

He was a good dancer, though he didn't talk much while he danced. Angel felt comfortable with him, as though she'd known him a long time. "You did a great job of emceeing," she congratulated him. "How did you get chosen for that?"

"I lost a draw," he admitted. "There were three of us in charge of the entertainment, and I lost."

"It's a real shame your Kerri was sick. She'd have loved it."

But Roger had been distracted by a newcomer. "Well, look who's here. Who let you in? We have to kowtow to surgeons all day long; we certainly don't need them at our socializing."

Even before she turned to see him, Angel knew it would be Lenzini. He seemed to keep popping up like a bad penny. Lenzini was dressed in a sport jacket and slacks, and though a little more casual than most of the guests, looked strikingly attractive.

"I just did an emergency case with Chuck," Lenzini said, indicting an anesthesiologist who had arrived late. "It was rough, and he suggested I come along to lighten up. You think anyone will mind?"

"Hey, you're the five-hundred-pound gorilla, as far as I'm concerned," Roger assured him. He went into his usual routine about how Kerri couldn't come and this was Angel Crawford, a family-practice resident.

"We've met," the two of them said together.

"Oh, sure, you would have," Roger agreed, looking a little self-conscious. "What you need, Cliff, is a stiff drink. There's an open bar by the entrance."

"What I need," Lenzini corrected him, "is to dance with this woman. Someone soft and alive and pretty."

"Is that sexism?" Roger asked Angel. "He says it to all the ladies."

"I'm flattered that he noticed I was alive," Angel said.

"Alive and kicking," Lenzini complained as he held out his hand to Angel. The music had just stopped, and it was unclear whether the next dance would be fast or slow, but Lenzini held onto Angel's hand. "Nice outfit. I've made it a point of honor myself never to own a tux, but if one looked as good on me as this does on you, I might reconsider."

"It's not mine. Roger's friend Kerri was supposed to wear it, but she got sick."

"You don't say." His eyes danced, but he ducked his head as the music started, slow music, and he pulled her to him. "I've met Kerri. I doubt if it would have looked as good on her. She has dark hair."

He was talking into Angel's auburn hair at the time, moving easily with her. Angel wondered at the length of his body against hers, the feeling of fusion that had taken place the moment he claimed her. Bodies were a part of her work. She dealt with them every day, in all sizes and shapes. But not healthy, swaying male bodies that seemed a part of her and yet apart from her in a most disturbing way. He held her with casual grace, accessible but not proprietary.

If his hands had made electricity flow through her that morning, having his whole body fit to hers was overload. Angel felt a decided shortness of breath, which she would have diagnosed as pathological in a patient. It seemed important to conceal it from Lenzini because she had no intention of letting him see his effect on her. She wished he would say something, anything, because she certainly was not capable of doing so either physically or mentally.

Angel told herself that she could not possibly have formed an attachment for her overbearing companion, and lust was something she could not quite believe in from her previous tepid experience. Sex was, with the proper involvement and knowledge, a pleasant if somewhat overrated experience, in Angel's opinion. It could feel safe and comfortable, but hardly so earth-shattering as some people would have you believe.

Lenzini continued to say nothing, his arms around her and his head brushing hers. The music ended, and Angel drew back slightly, but he narrowed one eye at her and said, "I think we should have another one."

"Do you?" she asked, her breathlessness under better control now that she wasn't pressed against him. "Does it matter what I think?"

"Not particularly," he drawled, but asked, "Don't you want to dance again?"

"Well, I . . ."

The music started, and this time it was fast music. He grimaced but shrugged. "I'm good at this, too," he informed her.

"Is there anything you aren't good at?"

"Not that I've discovered so far. Woodworking, maybe."

She almost expected him to be one of those men who danced so energetically that they were embarrassing to be with. Or danced with such sexual innuendo that you wanted to walk off the dance floor. He was neither. He moved with a charming fluidity, sensuous in a joyful way, almost as though the motion itself were springing from his core. Though she occasionally felt self-conscious when she did fast dancing, Angel could not resist the delightfulness of Lenzini's performance. Once, from sheer exuberance, she laughed out loud, and he grabbed her and swung her around in a jitterbug movement that again left her breathless.

His eyes seldom left her face. Angel wasn't sure whether he was trying to convey something to her or not. He looked amused, and intrigued, and curious by turns. Like flames burning at a distance, she could feel the heat of his desire, but it was tempered by caution, under an easygoing control. Surgeons were decisive but not impulsive. They knew what they wanted, and surprisingly, many had the control to wait for it.

Angel was not sure that he wanted her, specifically. He might have been horny. He might have been lonely. He might have been frustrated or sad. She couldn't tell. She didn't know him well enough, and he had a well-defined mask that would not easily have been penetrated. She was, perhaps, a game for him, a challenge to his hunter instincts.

It was with something like relief that she was approached by another man at the end of the dance. Lenzini let her go without protest. She saw him dancing with other women as she herself changed partners after each dance. Roger danced with her again, and several of the men she'd worked with on gynecological operations during her last rotation. They talked shop, or they talked about sports or the theater or San Francisco. As a group, the anesthesiologists were certainly the most personable men Angel had met in the medical profession. Roger himself was as friendly and eager to please as a puppy.

To her, Lenzini seemed very different from the anesthesiologists. He radiated energy; they exuded calm. He burned with passion and pride and power; they emanated charm and confidence and even a quiet courage. Angel admired the anesthesiologists. She wasn't sure how she felt about Lenzini.

Toward the end of the evening, he appeared in front of her again, neatly outmaneuvering a young man from her own Wisconsin class in medical school. "I think she's promised to me," he said, grasping her hand. She could have denied him, but smiled her regret at the young man instead. Angel didn't want to go home without being in Lenzini's arms again.

"I think dancing is *almost* the perfect activity," he whispered in her ear, holding her firmly against the length of his monumental body. "Two people joined together in rhythmic, invigorating movement, lost in the joy of the moment. Want me to take you home?"

"How far did this line get you with all the other women you've danced with tonight?" she asked, lifting her face to watch his expressions.

"Not far, as you can see, since I'm back here with you."

"Well, it's not getting you anywhere with me, either."

"Actually, I didn't ask to take any of them home."

"I'm surprised. Not because most of them were married, I imagine."

"No, because I was waiting to ask you," he said, unabashed. "It's my contention that you should always go home with your first partner at a dance. Don't you agree?"

"If I did, that would be Roger in my case. And I certainly intend to have him take me home."

"But he wouldn't mind if I took you," Lenzini assured her. "He has made it clear, after all, that you were not his first choice of a date tonight."

Angel laughed. "He does have a tendency to be frank, doesn't he? I find it refreshing."

"Unlike my own underhanded technique of rampant seductiveness."

"Is that what your technique is?" she asked, leaning back from him to allow her the pleasure of watching his reaction. "I couldn't tell, Dr. Lenzini."

He bent down swiftly and planted a kiss on her forehead. "Oh, you could tell all right, Angel. My name's Cliff."

"Well, I'm not going to call you that. I'm watching my step."

"Are you sure?" He swung her around until both her feet were off the floor, holding her against him as if she were no more than a pillow-weight. He danced in wider and wider arcs along the edge of the dance floor, moving them away from the others.

"Put me down, you gorilla!" she insisted, laughing.

"Only when you say you'll let me take you home."

"I'm not going to let you take me home. I am not a birdbrain, Dr. Lenzini."

"No, you're a bright young doctor who probably works too hard and doesn't play at all."

"I suppose," she said as he allowed her to touch ground again, "that really describes you better than it does me. You don't know anything about me."

He shrugged, but his eyes were intent on hers. "I know that you're pretty and soft and alive."

Roger had appeared at her elbow and shook his head wonderingly at Lenzini. "This is where we came in, I think, Angel. Has the man been repeating himself all evening?"

"Something like that," she said, taking the arm Roger offered. "Good night, Dr. Lenzini."

"Good night, Angel."

In the men's dressing room the next morning, Cliff looked up from his seat on the bench to find

Roger Janek staring down at him. "Great party last night, Roger," Lenzini said. "I hear you were quite a hit. Sorry I missed that part of the show."

"It was fun. But Kerri didn't seem any better when I called this morning." Roger's brow was uncharacteristically furrowed. "I wish I weren't scheduled for the OR all day today."

"It's always a good distraction."

"I suppose."

When Roger looked as though he would wander off to change from his street clothes to his scrubs, Lenzini reached up to stop him. "What about Angel Crawford? Was she," he searched for the appropriate words, "a satisfactory fill-in?"

"She was nice." Roger regarded him with curiosity. "You know, Cliff, it was a little strange your showing up there. And coming immediately to dance with Angel. And winding up with her at the end of the evening."

"Yeah." Lenzini snapped a mask over his face. "The subtleties of my mind astonish even me."

Chapter Four

Because she didn't know what to make of her evening, Angel refused to think about it at all. When she had gone to bed, she had pushed visions of Lenzini from her mind, only to awaken in the morning knowing that she had dreamed about him. She was not, she decided, responsible for her unconscious mind. Still half-asleep, she had seen the tux on its hanger suspended from the curtain rod, and she had wondered what it would have been like to have been in a filmy dress instead in his arms. And immediately chased the thought away.

Every time she allowed her mind to wander, it ended up at the same place. Angel had eventually climbed out of bed in something of a snit, determined to concentrate on her work. Which should have been easy in the ordinary course of a day, but a strange thing began to happen. When she was writing notes in a patient's chart, suddenly Lenzini would be there on the floor. He didn't always speak to her, though he usually acknowledged her presence with a friendly wave. When she went to the cafeteria he would be there, surrounded by a group of doctor friends. He didn't ask her to join them, and she would usually scurry past hoping he didn't think she was following him around.

Had he always been so prominent in her world? Surely she would have noticed. Even when she decided, quite uncharacteristically, to take in the movie at the medical center theater, he appeared, alone, and he nodded to her but made no effort to claim a seat near her. What was happening here? Angel felt confused and slightly paranoid. She began to see Lenzini in figures of large men at a distance before she could recognize who they were. His presence wasn't in any way ominous, just distracting and worse, frustrating. Angel wanted him to talk with her. Maybe she even wanted to go out with him; she wasn't sure.

Two weeks after the anesthesiology party, she had called a psych consult for a patient who seemed to be having more than ordinary difficulty in adjusting to her diagnosis of esophageal cancer. The patient's operation had gone well, and her chances of a five-year survival were almost even. Angel had been careful to be very clear with her about the encouraging facts, but her patient had become more and more depressed. When the psychiatrist, Dr. Stoner, came out from his interview with Mrs. Ramirez, he sought out Angel in the charting room.

Dr. Stoner was a forty-seven-year-old man with longish hair, showing some gray, brushed back to fall low on his neck. Angel thought he looked like nothing so much as an aging hippie, but she had heard that he was a very effective doctor, empathetic and a good diagnostician. Dr. Stoner slid onto the low counter to talk with her.

"Mrs. Ramirez is obviously clinically depressed and should be started on a course of antidepressant medication," he said, frowning slightly at the chart he held in his hand. "I'll leave an order for it. But look, the thing is that she needs more support than we can give her on the floor, so I'm enrolling her in a cancer support group that meets twice a week in the outpatient clinic." His pen ran out of ink as he wrote and he made a tsk of annoyance. Angel handed him another one from a drawer under the counter. "Thanks. If that doesn't work we'll try a new plan, okay?"

"Sounds fine," Angel replied. "Um, Dr. Stoner, can I ask you a question, sort of a personal question?"

"About you or me?" he asked with a laugh. "Shoot."

"Well, I've been having this feeling that I'm being . . . not followed exactly, but this one person, another doctor in the hospital actually, seems to keep showing up where I am. Only sometimes it's not him, when he gets closer. But usually it is, if you see what I mean."

"Residency is a tough time," he offered sympathetically. "Do you think of this guy as persecuting you?"

"No."

"Maybe harassing you?"

"Not exactly."

"Hmmm. So are you worried about him or about you?"

"I'm kind of worried that I'm obsessed with him or something."

"Are you attracted to him?"

Angel shrugged. "Maybe. Only I'm not like that usually, you know? I'm just an ordinary person, and I don't obsess over men. But I never saw this guy until we had a run-in or two, and now I see him all the time. He doesn't try to talk with me or anything. He just shows up where I am. Only sometimes I just think it's going to be him and it's not."

Dr. Stoner nodded his understanding. "That's natural enough under the circumstances, Dr. Crawford. If you think the guy's trying to intimidate you or something, just tell me who it is and I'll talk with him."

Angel hastened to say, "Oh, no, I wouldn't want that. I'm sure he doesn't mean any harm. And I suppose it could just be coincidence."

Dr. Stoner tucked the chart under his arm and hopped down from the counter. He caught a glimpse of her name tag and said companionably, "I bet you get as much teasing about your name as I do."

"Only from Dr. Lenzini," she muttered absently.

Stoner cocked his head, suddenly alert. "Is Cliff the one wandering around where you are?"

Angel flushed. "I didn't say that."

"No, but the two strains of thought seemed to come together." Stoner grinned at her. "I wouldn't worry about Lenzini, you know. He's harmless, well, after a fashion. We're good friends. I'll talk to him."

Angel grabbed his arm. "Oh, please don't. I . . . It was just that I thought I'd gotten paranoid or something with him popping up everywhere I went. I don't think he's following me or anything."

"Oh, he probably is," Stoner grumbled, his warm brown eyes sympathetic. "The man has no sense of proportion. To him, if he wanted to catch a glimpse of you now and again, he'd just arrange it so that he could. It would never occur to him that you might find it odd."

"Why not?"

Stoner shrugged. "He doesn't realize that the rest of the world pays attention to what the people around them do. *He* doesn't, so he can't quite picture that anyone does, on an ongoing basis. When he takes an interest in something, he pursues it in his own idiosyncratic way." The psychiatrist regarded her with curiosity. "I wonder what it was that made him take an interest in you. Other than the obvious reasons, which are never obvious with Cliff."

"Does he do this often?"

"Oh, no, I didn't mean that." Dr. Stoner extended a hand for her to shake. "I've said quite enough. If you want me to do something about Cliff, let me know. It would be better, though, if you confronted him yourself. I'm sure you'll find he's perfectly unconscious of what's happening."

Angel accepted his hand easily, but watched him walk away with a certain amount of trepidation. She had certainly not meant to reveal Lenzini's identity to the psychiatrist, and was horrified to find that the two of them knew each other well. Feeling both foolish and distressed, she turned to her medical duties with a firm resolve to simply forget Lenzini, whether he appeared in her vicinity or not. What difference could it possibly make if he wandered past her? It seemed highly unlikely to her that the surgeon had developed an "interest" in her in any ordinary sense of the word—like a normal person who would ask her for a date. So what was the point of paying any attention to him?

Like most intentions, Angel's plan to ignore Lenzini completely fell apart when she accidentally ran into him at her corner grocery. Surprised into speech, she exclaimed, "What are you *doing* here?"

"Um, buying a half gallon of milk," he said, holding up the container.

Angel glared at him. "This is *my* corner store."

Lenzini looked perplexed. "Well, hell, Angel, it's on my way home, and I'm out of milk."

"I don't believe you."

"No?" His eyes danced. "Come home with me, and I'll show you."

"I am *not* coming home with you."

It was Angel's turn to produce her purchases for the cashier, and she set them down firmly on the moving rubber counter. In a whisper that carried considerable force, she said to Lenzini, "You have got to stop doing this."

"Doing what?" he asked innocently. "I buy milk all the time. I'm a growing boy, remember?"

"When was the last time you bought something in this store?" she demanded, feeling sure this would trap him.

"I don't know. I don't pay much attention to where I shop." He raised his brows at her. "What's your point?"

The clerk asked her for $8.72, and before Angel could dig in her wallet Lenzini had flipped a ten-dollar bill on the counter. Angel very nearly tore it in half, she was so mad. "Don't you *dare* try to pay for my groceries!"

Lenzini and the clerk shared a comradely male look that made Angel want to punch one or both of them. With what dignity she could muster, she proffered the correct amount of money, accepted the paper bag the clerk handed her, and left the store. She heard the two of them chuckling behind her. Before she had gone more than fifty yards, however, Lenzini had caught up with her, his half gallon of extra light milk cradled in his right elbow.

"What's going on, Angel?"

Angel refused to speak to him. She trudged on up the hill, ignoring him. When she got to her building, he was still trying to cajole her, saying, "Come on, say something. What have I done? How am I supposed to know what's the matter if you won't tell me?"

There were ten steps up to the main entry, and Angel ran up every one of them. The three doors, each painted a burgundy color, were arrayed across a landing crowded with two huge pots of impatiens and several hanging baskets of fuchsias. Angel put her key in the lock of the door on the far right, and it opened into a small entry with stairs leading directly upward. She slammed the door behind her. Lenzini hammered on it.

"I'm not going to go away until you talk to me," he announced loudly enough for her to hear him through the door.

Angel climbed the stairs, two flights of them, still mad as a wet hen. When she got to her front door, she unlocked that as well and stormed into the flat, knocking the door shut behind her with an elbow.

"What's all the ruckus?" Nan called from the living room.

"That jerk followed me home."

"What jerk?"

"Lenzini."

Nan appeared in the entryway and watched Angel disappear into the kitchen. "You can't seriously mean you left an attending surgeon pounding on your front door."

"Of course I can mean it," Angel assured her stoutly, banging cabinet doors and the flatware drawer.

Nan warily followed her and found Angel digging into a container of yogurt. Angel's temper always made her exceedingly hungry. "What if he doesn't go away?" Nan asked Angel.

"We'll call the police."

Nan rolled her eyes. "Sure we will."

"Well, we will. *I* will. He has no business following me home." Angel spooned another bite of yogurt into her mouth. "God, I was hungry."

"You want to tell me what's going on?"

Angel hadn't told Nan about Lenzini's appearance everywhere she went. It had sounded just too preposterous. "He's been following me," she said now, waving her spoon. "Well, not exactly following me, but I run into him everywhere."

Nan looked shocked. "You mean he's been harassing you?"

"No, I don't mean that. I mean he pops up when

I'm on a floor at the hospital, when I'm in the cafeteria, when I go to a movie at Baker Hall. And," she declared dramatically, "just now he showed up at the corner store."

Her roommate looked at her suspiciously. "Do you think you're having some kind of breakdown, Angel?"

"Certainly not. Look, Nan, I never used to see him anywhere. I would have remembered."

"So what does he do when you see him?"

"Oh, nothing much. He says 'Hi' sometimes. I told you he wasn't harassing me."

They could hear the knocking at the street door continuing. Nan looked nervous. "I think you better go talk to him."

"He tried to pay for my groceries," Angel wailed.

"Now there's an arch-villain for you," Nan muttered, walking out of the room.

Angel ran after her. "Where are you going?"

"I'm going to let him in."

"But why? I just told you what he's been doing." Angel folded her arms across her chest, the yogurt container thrust into her shoulder. "I won't talk to him."

"You sound like a five-year-old." Nan was at the console buzzing the street door unlocked. She opened the front door of the flat and stood there as they heard steps spring up the two flights. Lenzini appeared with his container of milk and his usual unruly black hair. Nan offered her hand. "I'm Nan LeBaron, Dr. Lenzini. I'm going to leave you and my nutty roommate alone to sort this out."

Their visitor shook hands with her, smiling his most charming smile and thanking her for her intervention. Angel frowned at her, but Nan merely pointed to the living room and gave her a shove in the right direction before disappearing into the back of the flat. Because there seemed little help for it, Angel walked with dignity into the sun-drenched room. She graciously indicated the sofa for her visitor and chose a chair in front of the window, which would make it irritating for Lenzini to face her.

"Could I put my milk in the fridge?" he asked with mock humbleness.

"You're not going to be here that long."

Lenzini merely looked at her, and she eventually shrugged with assumed negligence and said, "Go right ahead. The kitchen is the second door down on the left."

When he came back, it was with a poured glass of milk and a package of cookies that she had just bought at the store. "Well, help yourself," she muttered.

"Thanks, I did." Lenzini pulled a chair up beside hers. "Since you were eating the yogurt, I didn't think you'd mind. They're my favorite cookies. We have that in common."

"We have nothing in common," she retorted. "I bought them because they're *Nan's* favorite cookies." This was not precisely true, but she had no intention of agreeing with him about anything.

He crunched enthusiastically on the first of many cookies. After a moment he said, "So tell me, Angel, why you're so annoyed with me."

"I just hate it when men pretend not to know

what's going on." She felt barely able to keep her seat. "I do not for one minute believe you aren't conscious of what you're doing, and if you are, you need your head examined. And I wouldn't try Dr. Stoner because he seems to accept your idiosyncrasies with no more than a shrug."

"Jerry? What the hell does Jerry have to do with this?"

"Nothing, absolutely nothing." Angel tried to organize her thoughts so that she could present her case concisely and tellingly. "You've been following me."

With a cookie halfway to his mouth, he paused and frowned. "No, I haven't."

"Yes, you have. You've been showing up all over the place wherever I go."

"That doesn't mean I've been following you. We work in the same place, for heaven's sake."

"You're a surgeon!" she cried, indignant. "You have a busy schedule. How do you explain that we keep seeing each other all over the hospital? I see you at least twice a day. That didn't used to happen."

"I suppose it's because we know each other now," he suggested, the picture of innocence.

"And I suppose it is that you arrange it that way. Do you deny that?"

Lenzini stared at the ceiling for a while, and then at a stain on the side wall, his lips pursed. After some time he ate another cookie and drained his glass of milk. Finally he looked back at her. "Look, Angel, it's not as if I'm following you. I just like knowing you're around and not getting into trouble. I worry about you."

"You *worry* about me? she asked, unbelieving. "Why the hell would you worry about me?"

"You're young," he answered, sounding immensely philosophical.

"I'm not that much younger than you are. Maybe four or five years."

"Yes, but you're a woman, and you don't have the kind of experience I do."

"Thank God."

"Well, yes, but it's a tough time, residency, and you've gotten into trouble more than once. It could happen again."

"And what if it does?" she demanded. "I'll get out of it, too. You can't do anything to change that, and why would you want to?"

"I don't want you to get kicked out of your program."

"I'm not going to. Lenzini, I'm a good doctor. For the most part I've gotten good evaluations. It's very unlikely that I would be kicked out of my program, and even if I were, what's it to you?"

She seemed to keep coming back to this point, and he seemed not to answer it. This time Angel repeated herself. "What's it to you, Dr. Lenzini?"

He shrugged his great bear shoulders uncomfortably. "I don't know. I just feel somehow responsible for you."

Angel stared at him. "Responsible for me? You hardly know me. I'm not even in your department. Go mentor some poor woman resident in surgery who *needs* a little male support on her side." But this thought gave Angel a clue to what was going on. "It's the sexism, isn't it? The sexism is beginning to bother you a little now that you've seen someone stand up against it. Well, I wouldn't worry about that. I'm not likely to stand up against it again any time soon."

"I'm going to get another glass of milk."

"Oh, for God's sake," Angel snapped, before following him to the kitchen. He opened the refrigerator door as though he'd done it a hundred times. When he had poured the glass of milk, he said, "The refrigerator's almost empty."

"We don't eat here very often."

"I could take you out to dinner."

"No, you couldn't."

He gave an exaggerated sigh. "You're just being contrary now, Angel. It wouldn't be any big deal for me to take you out to dinner."

"You're simply avoiding the subject again," she scolded. "You can't seem to give me a straight answer. What is it that bothers you about my situation?"

"You just seem vulnerable."

"I'm no more vulnerable than anyone else. And if you mean as a woman, well, we get used to that. We don't like it, but we don't have much choice, do we?"

"I don't think of the nurses as vulnerable that way."

"The men aren't in the same competition with the nurses. You don't seem to understand, Lenzini, that men use sexism to put women in their place. The nurses are already in their places, as far as you're concerned. It's the women *doctors* who aren't."

"You sound like a feminist."

"Well, of course I'm a feminist. You expect me not

to want to have equal rights with men? To not get the same salary for the same work or have the same opportunities for the same talent? Where in the hell are you coming from, Lenzini? Where have you been for the last twenty years?"

"Twenty years ago I was thirteen."

"Exactly. You're far too young to have this kind of mentality. I could expect it of some of the older doctors, but you grew up with the women's movement. Where were you hiding?"

"My dad's a surgeon, too. My mother stayed home to take care of us. That's just the way it was." He waved a hand with negligent grace. "A lot of women believe that raising children is the most important thing a woman can do."

"Oh, just go away, Lenzini. I'm not going to try to educate you on a woman's right to choose for herself what she wants to do with her life. I pity the poor women in your department, but they'll just have to stand up for themselves." Angel opened the refrigerator door, took out his half-empty container of milk and thrust it at him. "I can take care of myself. You don't have to haunt me like a guardian angel. If you really want to do some good, take a hard look at your sexism."

Reluctantly he accepted the milk. Angel herded him toward the front door with little shooing movements of her hands. He paused with his hand on the doorknob, asking, "Don't you like me?"

"As much as I can like any sexist jerk," she assured him.

"Don't you think we could go out sometime?"

"No, I don't think we could go out."

"But I stood up for you with Williams, and in the cafeteria."

"Only because you can laugh at sexism so easily. Not because you disapprove of it, or even recognize it, for that matter. Good-bye, Dr. Lenzini."

He had opened the door and was about to step through the portal, but seemed unable to leave. "Tell me again what Stoner had to say to all this."

"I didn't tell you the first time. Now go away, and don't pop up on the oncology floor twice a day, or at the movies or in my corner grocery, okay?"

"I can't promise I won't run into you every once in a while, Angel," he said earnestly. "We both work at Fielding."

"Fine. Dandy. We'll run into each other occasionally. Good-bye."

With decided emphasis, she pushed the door closed behind him. For a while she heard his footsteps, first inside the stairwell and then outside going down to the street. Angel did not go to the front window to see him actually descend the hill. He had left, and she was relieved. Wasn't she?

"I see the coast is clear," Nan remarked, startling her.

"Yes, he's gone."

"So what did he say about following you?"

Angel dug a hand into her hair, shaking it free of her neck as she walked into the living room. "Oh, I think he had some crazy idea about protecting me."

"From what?"

"Men like him, I guess." Angel shook her head

wonderingly. "Don't ask me, Nan. That's as close as I could come to what was going on."

"I think you ought to go into psychiatry. All the strangest ones do."

Angel threw a sofa pillow at her.

Chapter Five

Lenzini sought out Jerry Stoner the next day. The long-haired psychiatrist regarded him with amusement when he appeared at his office door. "Upsetting the next generation of physicians, are you?" he asked, waving Lenzini in.

Cliff took the chair facing Stoner's desk. The office was cramped, the bookshelves that lined the walls were overflowing with texts, and there was a sound-deadening carpet of truly appalling hue on the floor. "They might as well have put you in the basement," Cliff commented.

"Tangentiality," Stoner proclaimed, "Maybe avoidance. Tell me what's going on with you and this young woman."

"How do you know about her?" Cliff demanded. "She mentioned your name and refused to say one word more."

"She consulted me casually about the feeling she was having of being followed, wondered if she was obsessed or something."

"I wasn't following her."

"What *were* you doing?"

Lenzini shrugged. "I don't know. She's cute. I just like seeing her."

Jerry Stoner regarded him skeptically, but said nothing.

"Yesterday I ran into her at a corner grocery store."

Jerry rolled his eyes. "Right."

"Well, I saw her go in, and so I parked and went in, too. I needed milk."

"Naturally."

"She got upset."

"Wow. How surprising."

Lenzini frowned. "Well, why should she get upset just because I show up? Anyhow, I followed her home, but she wouldn't talk to me. Finally her roommate let me in."

"Did it occur to you that this young woman might call the police, Cliff?"

"Why should she? She knows who I am. She knows I don't mean her any harm."

"How does she know that?"

Lenzini growled. "It's obvious! I don't go around hurting women." He stared at the framed photo of Stoner's grown sons on the desk. "She understands now that I was trying to protect her, at the hospital."

"Interesting." Jerry's eyes narrowed. "From what?"

"Oh, I don't know. She seems vulnerable, that's all."

"What is it you were trying to protect her from?"

"Geez, Jerry, what is this, an interrogation? Or do you think I've become one of your patients?"

"How about answering me?"

Cliff made a face. "She claims it has something to do with sexism."

"Really? Another surprise." Stoner was mocking him, of course, but he went on to add, "Dr. Crawford seems to know you a bit better than I had suspected."

"We've had a couple of run-ins." Cliff gave a brief, humorous account of the operating room fiasco and its aftermath. Jerry Stoner listened attentively, but didn't seem to find it as amusing as his companion. Finally, Cliff said, "We danced a couple of times at an anesthesia party. There seemed to be," he said, "something going on between us."

"Men often think there's something going on when the women don't," Jerry retorted. "And vice versa, I suppose. Look, Cliff, I want you to think about Sally."

Lenzini's body became unnaturally still. "Why?"

"I want you to think about why she left."

"She got a job in New England."

"You couldn't hear her then, and you can't hear Dr. Crawford now." Jerry rose. "I've got patients to see, Cliff. Think about it."

"You psychiatrists are full of it," Cliff grumbled as he swung out the door.

"Yeah, full of wisdom, insight, helpfulness," Jerry called after him.

Angel hadn't seen Lenzini for a week and a half. Only once since he'd been at her flat had they run into each other, and then it was obviously by complete accident, as Lenzini had seemed as much in a hurry to get away from her as she was from him.

Not that her heart didn't speed up; not that she wasn't struck by the way his unruly hair escaped his scrub cap and his surgeon's hands laid claim to a patient's chart. She smiled pleasantly, but took an abrupt turn down a different corridor just as he attempted to do the same thing.

"Don't bother," he grunted. "I'll be off the floor in two minutes."

Angel had nodded and gone straight to the patient's room. She hadn't seen him since, and perversely she missed him. Maybe his appearance here and there really had been a comfort to her, knowing he was around and that he was around because he "worried" about her. Not that she needed that kind of paternalistic concern, of course, but it had been nice to know that *someone* cared.

Her life was too busy at the moment to leave much time for such mulling over of what was or wasn't happening. During her six weeks on the oncology floor, she had to learn a great deal about treating cancer in adults. Her experience on the pediatric floor had been different. The children hadn't quite conceived of what death was. How could they? But these adults knew, and some of them knew they were about to die.

Angel was constantly astonished that nurses could work on the oncology floor for years, finding it in themselves to give again and again to these suffering patients. They spent much more time with the patients than the residents or attending doctors did. Angel had seen doctors bypass rooms in which a patient was dying, pleading there was nothing further they could do for them. A poor excuse, she thought. She could certainly do better than that.

But then something happened that she had not

anticipated. Weeks before, she had discharged Mr. Edwards with his medication adjusted so that he could spend his few remaining weeks at home with his wife. Paged for a new admit, she found him in the emergency room, without his wife, in dire straits. Angel came to the side of the examining table where he lay and took his hand.

"You don't look so great," she said, trying to rouse a smile from him.

"Ah, Dr. Crawford. Thank God you're here at least." He clung to her hand desperately. "She died, my wife died. Her heart gave out. I never knew she was sick. One morning I couldn't wake her." Tears slipped down his sunken face. "I wasn't there to hold her hand when she died. And she won't be here to hold mine."

"I'll hold it," Angel assured him. "I'm so sorry about Mrs. Edwards. But I'll be here."

"Thank you. Thank you. I didn't know she was sick. It was too much for her, taking care of me. I didn't know."

"No, of course you didn't." Angel wondered if she should have noticed some sign of Mrs. Edwards's cardiac problem. But there wasn't time to thrash that out now. She needed to get Mr. Edwards to the oncology floor.

"No heroics," the old man was saying. "Nothing like that. Just let me die. The sooner I die, the sooner I'll be with her again."

"We'll get you a bed and try to make you comfortable," Angel told him.

An hour later she had seen him on the floor, and the nurse Judy had agreed with her he didn't have much time left. "I'll page you when the time is near," Judy promised. "He's sleeping now, and we'll monitor him."

It would have been all right if he'd died in his sleep. Angel could have handled that. But he hadn't. Judy had paged her, saying he was in extremis and in pain and asking for her. And Angel had just gotten to his room when a Code Blue was called. Judy slipped into the room and whispered, "It's Mrs. Leong, Dr. Crawford. She's arrested. Room 644."

Torn between her two patients, Angel had automatically done what she was trained to do—save life. She reached Mrs. Leong just before the crash cart came whipping through the door, and she called the code as she watched the nurses and doctors perform their functions with the precision of a ballet.

"We have a pulse. We have a pressure."

There was relief and congratulations all around, but Angel suddenly felt overwhelmed with dread. As soon as she was able, she returned to Mr. Edwards's room, but there was no life left in the poor shrunken body. His eyes were still open, and they seemed to plead for help. From all she could see, he had died alone, save for an unfamiliar aide wide-eyed with terror in the corner of the room. The code had drawn everyone away from his bedside, since there was everything to be done for Mrs. Leong and nothing they could do for Mr. Edwards. Nothing but hold his hand and comfort him. She had promised. She had meant to be there. And she had failed him.

"I'm so sorry, Mr. Edwards," she whispered, smoothing back the strands of hair on his scalp. "I'm so sorry."

Angel found her way to the on-call room by instinct. She hadn't known where to go to be alone, to try to sort out what had happened. It was considered weak and inexcusable to cry if you were a doctor. But Angel had to cry. She was filled with agony and disappointment, in herself, in the cruelty of fate. All he'd asked was for her to be there with him, for God's sake. And yet she hadn't done the wrong thing. There simply had been no choice.

When the storm of her tears had abated somewhat, she heard a tap at the door and Judy calling softly, "Are you okay, Dr. Crawford? Like me to bring you a cup of tea or something?"

"Thanks, no, I'll be fine. I just need a little longer if there's no emergency.'"

"We'll need you to sign the death certificate, but that can wait for a few minutes."

"Sure. I'll be out soon." But even as she said it, a fresh bout of tears flowed down Angel's cheeks. Would it always be this way? Too many demands on her, choices that weren't choices at all, no chance to do what her heart dictated? Angel mopped at the tears with a tissue, which she stuck in the pocket of her lab coat. For several minutes she pressed cool fingers against the lids of her closed eyes, concentrating on regaining her equilibrium. She could do it if she didn't think of Mr. Edwards. After a while she stuffed a few more tissues in her pocket, ran a comb through her hair, and left the security of the on-call room.

This was not the time to run into Lenzini, and yet she very much feared that it was he striding up the corridor toward her. She had been mistaken on a few occasions, but his height was almost unmistakable. He came abreast of her and swung around to walk beside her toward the nurses' station.

"Judy said Mr. Edwards died. I'm sorry." He peered more closely at her. "What's the matter?"

Angel was afraid to say anything for fear the tears would start again. She bit her lip and made a dismissive gesture with her hand.

"Have you been crying?" he asked, incredulous. "This can't possibly be your first patient to die."

"Go away," she said.

They had reached the nurses' station where Judy regarded Angel with concern. "You didn't have to come yet. The death certificate could have waited."

"What the hell is the matter with you two?" Lenzini grumbled. "You aren't neophytes. I swear women are too emotional for their own good."

"And you'd know what's good for us, wouldn't you?" Angel shook her head with annoyance. "This has nothing to do with you, and if you don't butt out, I'm going to complain to the head of your department."

"Now there's a threat." Lenzini towered above her, glaring. "That will certainly get me a blot on my record."

"What kind of threat could I possibly pose to you, Dr. Lenzini?" Angel asked, her eyes hard. "You have all the power in the situation, and by God, you intend to use it, don't you?"

Judy blinked at her; Lenzini backed away. "I'm not using any power," he protested. "I told you I was sorry your patient died. You're just overreacting, and I pointed it out to you."

"Well, I'm very grateful for your help, and I hope you'll go help someone else now. I have a death certificate to sign."

The forms had been spread out for her in the room behind the nursing station, and she moved there to concentrate on them. She was vaguely aware of Judy talking with Lenzini, but she refused to pay any attention to their interchange. The least she could do now was fill out the death certificate in a respectful way for Mr. Edwards, since she seemed to have let him down when he was dying. Angel sighed and rubbed her forehead.

"Why do I always screw up with you?" Lenzini asked sadly from behind her. "I'm really sorry, Angel. I didn't understand. You know, you were the only one who stood up for the old guy when he really needed it. He trusted you."

No matter how well meant, it was precisely the wrong thing to say just then. Angel dug in her pocket for one of the tissues to try to stem the tide of tears.

"Oh, hell." Lenzini nudged the door shut with his foot to give her some privacy. And then he talked while she cried, not precisely ignoring her, but trying with the flow of his words to give her some time and some room. "I know how awful it feels to let someone down. When I was your age, I had a patient who thought I was sliced bread. He thought the sun rose and set on me. It was flattering, but mostly it was a huge responsibility, because he was a very sick kid. His folks had been killed in the car accident that he was injured in, and he had just latched on to me like I was Mom and Dad and everyone else important."

Angel drew great breaths of air to calm herself, never turning to look at him. As he continued to talk, she started to fill out the form again, slowly, precisely.

"He was in the hospital for a long time. Everything had to be repaired, not once but several times. And he took it all and never lost hope. Then he began to bleed internally, and we just couldn't stop it. I told him he'd be all right. I tell them all that," he admitted, "because I can't bear to think beyond fixing them. I took him into the OR and went over everything, inch by inch. We were pushing blood in like mad, and he was losing ground. I finally tried an endoscopic examination of his esophagus and found something way up, most likely a clot." Lenzini sighed. "Well, anyway, he died. Just like that. We couldn't revive him, no matter what we did."

He squeezed her shoulder gently and turned to go.

"Thanks, Cliff. I'm okay now."

"Good."

As much to her surprise as to Lenzini's, Angel said, "I'll probably get out of here about seven tonight. If you're interested in dinner . . ."

"Come to my office whenever you're ready."

Long before the end of her day Angel regretted her impulsivity. Several times she considered calling and saying she couldn't possibly get away, or even that she had simply changed her mind. Instead she continued to work steadily until she could conscientiously sign out to the doctor on call. In the locker room, she disposed of her lab coat and straightened the plaid skirt and red blouse she was wearing. There was no one else around at the moment; it was ten after seven. She made a face at herself in the mirror, took her jacket from its hook, and banged her locker door shut. There were maybe a dozen reasons not to meet him, but it didn't matter. She was going to do it.

The surgery department was located on the fifth floor in the east wing of Fielding. Angel had looked up his office number in the medical center directory and found her way there without difficulty. There were still people in some of the offices, with lights on and conversation carrying out into the corridor. Angel stopped in front of a closed door with Lenzini's name on it. Her heart was annoyingly beating rapidly, and she took a moment to try to calm down. Eventually she knocked on the door.

"Come in."

He was seated at his desk, apparently absorbed in a journal article in front of him, but he looked up immediately and smiled at her. "I wondered if you'd change your mind," he said.

"Several times," Angel admitted as she pulled the door closed behind her. It was only a moderate-size room, very pleasantly furnished with oak furniture and an Oriental rug. There were various models of body parts and an old-fashioned teaching chart in one corner, a small love seat in another. But he dominated the room, as he seemed to dominate any room in which she saw him. Angel took the chair facing his desk.

He slouched down in his seat, crossing his arms on his chest. One of the things that Angel could hardly bear to see was the dark hair on his arms. It made her insides do somersaults for some stupid reason. She wanted to feel that hair on her bare skin. Her gaze shifted to a framed photograph of a cottage in the mountains. "Is that someplace you go?" she asked.

"A couple of us share it. I get July this year. You could come up there with me." He responded to her frown by adding, "It's a great place, three bedrooms, away from everything. Sometimes groups of us go together to swim and bike and hike. You'd like it."

"I'm not that athletic."

"You don't have to be athletic to enjoy it. Look, Angel, I didn't tell you I was on call tonight because I didn't want to give you a chance to change your mind about our having dinner together. I only have to take call once a week, but I have to admit I almost always get paged. Usually I just stay in the hospital until late."

She shifted in her chair, ready to get up. "We can do this some other time."

"That's not what I'm saying. I had my secretary send out for a picnic meal. It's all in the fridge in the lounge. I didn't want to bring it in here until you came."

"In case I didn't show?"

"That, or something spoiling. So will you stay put while I get it?"

He had moved from behind the desk to a position beside her chair. Angel could feel the tension in her body rise just with his nearness. It was not smart of her to be there in this frame of mind, but she nodded. He rested a hand briefly on her shoulder and said, "Great. I'll be right back."

When the door closed behind him, Angel took another deep breath. Madness. He did things to her that she didn't want to think about. She found herself on her feet, hanging her jacket over the back of the chair. There were journals scattered on a coffee table in front of the overstuffed love seat, and she stacked them on the floor to make room for the picnic. *Of course* she shouldn't sit that close to him, but there was really no other option, the desk being so full of charts, journals, and unsigned correspondence.

Lenzini returned with several boxes of supplies. "I'm going to lock the door," he said. "Not because I'm going to attack you, but because I have some overly enthusiastic house officers who don't always remember to knock when they get excited about something. Do you mind?"

Angel felt a shiver run through her. "I guess that's okay. Not that it would be so awful to have them interrupt our meal."

"If you'd rather I didn't . . ."

She couldn't bear the way his eyes drilled into her. "No. I don't mind."

The lock clicked over with a satisfying thump. Angel felt momentarily breathless, and blinked uncertainly at Lenzini as if she weren't sure what to do next.

"Why don't you spread out the food, and I'll open the champagne."

"I don't drink much," she informed him, taking one of the boxes.

There were attractive containers of cold chicken, pasta salad, raw vegetables with dips, fruit, and an assortment of petits fours. "This is gorgeous." Angel accepted the glass of champagne he offered her. Meeting his eyes was more difficult.

"To a harmonious evening between us," he toasted.

He was mocking her, but lightly, and his eyes captured hers with playful intensity. "To harmony," she agreed, taking a sip. Ice-cold, it was perhaps the best champagne she had ever had. Angel smiled hesitantly and concluded, "Between us."

"We need music." He slipped open a drawer in the wall cabinet where a CD player rested. "I'm not going to ask you what you like. You can choose next time."

She watched his arms as he switched on the music. The dark hair bristled with life and filled her with desire. Abruptly, Angel sat down on the love seat and helped herself to an assortment of picnic items. When Cliff joined her, strains of classical music in the background, he sat so that his thigh was touching hers, lightly but definitely.

"If I'd taken you out to eat, we'd have had to decide if we wanted Chinese or Mexican or Thai or some such thing. And there would have been people around, and maybe so much noise we couldn't hear each other talk. It's kind of nice this way, don't you think?"

Angel could feel the pulse beating in her throat. His nearness was disorienting. "Hmmm," she said, having forgotten what he asked. They reached for their glasses at the same moment, and their arms brushed. Angel reacted as though she had been shocked. Lenzini cocked his head at her questioningly.

"Do I make you nervous?" he asked.

"I guess. I'm sorry."

He grimaced. "Sometimes it's annoying being so gigantic. It intimidates people."

"I imagine most of the time you don't mind that."

"Angel, Angel. The things you say." He seemed to study her mouth for a while, but then continued to eat. "Where do you come from?"

"Wisconsin. I'm planning to go back there to practice."

"Don't you like San Francisco?"

"I love it, but there are plenty of doctors here. A lot of the people in my program are interested in working in the inner city, working with underserved people." Angel wiped her fingers on a large napkin. "But I like the idea of being the old family practitioner."

"You don't *look* like the old family practitioner." Lenzini's brows drew together in a frown. "I don't really like the idea of family practitioners in the city. There are a lot of specialists around. Why should poor people have to put up with generalists who don't know as much?"

Angel raised her brows at him. "I don't think this is the way to promote harmony, Dr. Lenzini."

"All right," he grumbled. "But I have a right to my own opinion."

"I'm sure no one would think of denying you."

"Oh, people deny me all the time," he retorted, allowing a sexual innuendo to creep into his voice.

His wild hair had been lightly tamed for their encounter. He wore green scrubs and tennis shoes. His hands and arms were well tanned, as though he'd managed to be outside more than in an operating suite. And the suggestion in his eyes was almost palpable. Angel's hand paused as she raised her glass to her mouth. His hand came to cover hers, guiding it back down to the table. His face was suddenly inches from hers, a question in his eyes. Angel was not aware of answering. His lips came to meet hers. Sensation flooded her, and she pulled back, breathless.

He ran a thumb along her brow, gently sliding it down along her cheek to her lips. First along the upper and then the lower lip he rubbed his thumb. Angel tried to look away from his eyes, but he called her back. "Look at me, Angel. You're so lovely. Your lips are so soft and yielding." He pressed against her lips, and his thumb slipped inside. Angel captured his thumb with her mouth and sucked on it, her eyes closing with pleasure.

His other hand had come to pull her closer to him. She could feel the pressure on her back, the fingers kneading against her blouse. And then his thumb was gone from her mouth and his tongue was there, and he was exploring the velvet recesses, rubbing, licking, sucking against her own tongue. Angel was responding to him, timidly at first and then more boldly, wanting more and more. His tongue was gone and his lips were on hers, and then on her neck and then on her blouse where her heart beat wildly.

And then above her nipple, sucking the nipple, blouse and bra into his mouth. Drawing on her, urging and teasing. Her body was alive to the touch of him, thigh to thigh, his hands on her back, his mouth above her breast. She felt rich with desire, her body puffed with it, her breasts bursting with the need for his mouth. He slipped a hand to her front and began to unbutton the red blouse. Her breath was coming in quick, deep pants, her eyes on his now, but unsure of what to do. She wanted him to touch her. She wanted this to progress. But she wasn't sure, even caught up in the heady desire, that she was ready to make love with him.

In a whisper, she said, "I don't think I can, Cliff. It's not that I don't want to. I don't think I should. I don't know you well enough. It's just not right."

"Hmmm." His lips came to hers again. "It's all right, Angel. We'll stop where you want to stop."

"That doesn't work. It's better to stop now." His fingers had found their way under her bra to the skin on her breast, to the sensitive nipple. Her breath drew in with a sharp exclamation. "Oh! Please. It would be better to stop now."

"Not for me. Not for you. Angel, I promise I'll stop anywhere you ask me to." He withdrew his hand from her breast. "I can stop now. Hell, I'm a surgeon. I have incredible control. But I think we don't need to stop now. We can go a little further, enjoy touching a little more." He had allowed his fingers to slip under the blouse again and rub against her nipple. "Let me please you for a while."

Angel could barely stand the pleasure. It coursed through her body, down her trunk, and into her groin where the ache was sweet misery. Lenzini finished unbuttoning her blouse and tugged it out of her skirt. His fingers deftly unfastened her bra and, holding her eyes with his, he removed it. Long before his eyes found her breasts, his fingers were there, stroking, rubbing, tempting. Angel groaned and leaned against him for a moment, trying to clear her mind enough to know what to do.

Suddenly the sensation on her breasts changed, and she saw that he was rubbing his arm against the bare skin, just as she had imagined. The nipples stood out hard as brass, and yet her whole body trembled. "I . . . I don't. Yes." The bristling hair against her breasts made her burn with need, the need for him to continue touching her and the need to touch him. Angel lifted his scrub top and allowed her hands to massage him, running them over his chest and down to his waist, but no farther.

The love seat was too small for them to lie down beside each other. Cliff shifted her with ease, however, so that she was lying on him, her breasts above his mouth. Gently he nibbled at her, licking her nipples and running his tongue around her breast. And then he took the nipple in his mouth and drew her into him. When he sucked on her nipple, the fire raged down to her groin, lighting it with desire, calling forth an ache so incredible that she could hardly believe she didn't explode.

Her own fingers slipped beneath the waist of his scrub pants. First the flat of his belly, then the wiry hair, and finally they reached his swollen penis. As he drew on her nipple, she encircled his member, wanting to give the kind of pleasure she was receiving. But she was distracted by his finger between her legs, slipping inside her panties, rubbing against her swollen lips. "Oh, God."

His mouth on her breast, sucking, tugging, swallowing her inside him. His finger sliding moist within the recesses of her body, reaching, stroking, soothing, stimulating. Touching her everywhere that mattered, teaching her the excruciating excitement of her body with his. Another stroke, higher, higher. Another sip at her breast, calling, calling. And suddenly she exploded, her body racked with spasms, arched, crying out.

And with the release came tears. Unexpected, unstoppable tears. Angel lay against his chest and sobbed even as her body's release continued. Lenzini held her against him, rocking her gently until the sobs slowed down. "I'm sorry," she choked out. "I didn't know that would happen."

"Hey, it's okay," he whispered near her ear. "It's been a rough day for you. We'll . . ." His pager went off. "Perfect timing. You okay?"

Angel nodded and rolled away from him. "Go ahead and get it."

When he stood up and went to the phone, Angel quickly slipped on her bra and blouse. He hung up while she was still buttoning. "I have to go straight to the emergency room. Damn. It doesn't sound like I'll get away any time soon."

"That's okay. I'll straighten up here and go home." Angel was having trouble looking at him.

Lenzini came to stand beside her. With a finger

he tilted her chin so he could see her face. "We'll get it sorted out, Angel. Take the stuff home with you so you and your roommate won't starve, okay? You're not going to be all jittery when you see me next time, are you?"

"Probably."

"Well, don't be," he said gruffly. "Look, I've got to get down there. You understand."

"Of course I understand." She sat on the love seat until the door closed behind him. Then slowly she began to pack up the remains of their picnic.

Chapter Six

W here did all this come from?" Nan asked as Angel unpacked the box she had lugged up the stairs.

"Dr. Lenzini and I had a picnic, in his office, but he got called away. He told me to bring it home."

"You had a picnic? With Lenzini?" Nan regarded her with astonishment. "I thought he got on your nerves."

Angel sighed. "He does. Unfortunately, in more ways than one. Don't ask. Are you hungry?"

"I'm starved." Nan sat down at the kitchen table and helped herself to the chicken and pasta salad. "I think you better at least clue me in on what's happening so I won't hang up on him if he calls."

"You know you wouldn't hang up on him. You're the one who let him in here." She dipped a radish in the tangy dip and popped it into her mouth. "Something happened at the hospital today. A patient died when I wasn't with him, and I'd promised. I felt like hell, and then Lenzini was rude to me, but he apologized and told me a story. Oh, God, Nan. I don't know. Maybe I'm crazy. And more likely than not, he knows just how appealing he can be when he opens up."

"I'm surprised more of them haven't figured it out," Nan remarked, reaching into the box for the last item. "Wow! He knows his champagne. You guys didn't get through half of this."

"No wonder."

Nan smiled coyly at her but politely refused to ask any questions. "My dad says he's going to serve this champagne at my wedding."

"Does he know something I don't?"

"No. He's planned it for a long time. In fact, he's been putting cases of it down for a few years just in the hopes."

"Parents are such a source of entertainment," Angel teased. "Especially yours."

"Hell, you're the one who wants to go back to Wisconsin. I don't think it would be smart for me to be in the same state as my family."

Reaching down to slide a container closer to Nan, Angel noticed that she'd missed the lowest button on her blouse. Surreptitiously she attempted to button it without Nan noticing.

"I already saw that," Nan said. "I'm sure you're responsible enough to have insisted on protection."

"It didn't come to that," Angel admitted.

"Ah, I see. Well, in that case I suspect we'll hear from the dedicated surgeon within a short time, a matter of days. But, Angel, you know you might never hear from him again after that, don't you?"

Angel kept her tone light and teasing. "Are you suggesting that this is a matter of pure and simple conquest? I know they have a reputation, Nan. And Lenzini certainly fits the stereotype perfectly. He's just so physically attractive to me. Sometimes I forget that I don't like him. Actually, I do like him . . . occasionally."

"You are one messed up woman," Nan proclaimed. "Have a glass of champagne."

"That's certainly guaranteed to clear my head."

"We're not trying to clear your head. We're trying to loosen your tongue."

Angel put her elbows on the table and rested her chin on her locked fingers. "You know me, Nan, I'm a solid sort of person. I don't jump off the deep end. For the most part, I've been perfectly willing to leave men out of my life while I've been in training. But this guy. My stomach does somersaults."

"The worst kind of symptom." Nan looked sympathetic as she helped herself to a large strawberry. "Fortunately it goes away after a while."

"Yeah, I suppose. It's just . . ."

"What?"

"It hasn't ever been like that before."

"Really?" Nan considered her with a sad expression. "Then it's going to be rough for you, Angel. I wish there were something I could give you to clear it all up."

"I don't think I want it cleared up," Angel admitted. She rubbed a finger across the design on the petit four, tracing the green and pink pattern to the edges. "He feels very special to me."

Nan shook her head sorrowfully. "Poor dear. I feel for you."

* * *

Cliff was not entirely disappointed by the abrupt ending to their first "date." Certainly Angel's desire had seemed to match his own, but he recognized her vulnerability and her hesitation about a full sexual encounter. Her spate of crying had surprised but not shocked him. He just hoped she wasn't one of those women whose ordinary response to an orgasm was tears. He far preferred laughter himself.

Angel had certainly disoriented him for a while there. He was glad for some perspective on the situation. She was, after all, a woman like other women, susceptible to the call of her body. Lenzini had begun to think that she really *wasn't* interested in him, something that he found more or less intolerable when he himself had taken an interest.

It seemed to him that it wouldn't be a bad thing to leave Angel hanging for a day or two. To build up the suspense, so to speak. To give her time to adjust to the idea of their being lovers. Besides, it was a particularly busy time for him. Due to some medical-center budget cuts, he was forced to abandon his research lab to do more operations for the time being.

So the day after their picnic, Lenzini had paged Angel, who returned his call promptly but sounded slightly nervous. He had adopted his most courtly behavior. "Thanks for getting back to me right away, Angel," he said. "I just wanted to tell you how much I enjoyed being with you last night. I wish I hadn't been called away."

"That was okay," she replied. "I . . . had a nice time, too. Nan said to thank you for the great food. We even finished off the champagne."

"Good." Lenzini glanced at his calendar, which

was full but not impossible. "I want to see you again soon, but they've got me scheduled up to my neck."

"No problem. You know what it's like with residents," she said lightly. "We hardly know whether it's day or night most of the time."

"Yeah, I remember." Lenzini could tell she was trying to match his casualness. "I'll give you a call in a day or two when things calm down, okay?"

"Sure. Take care."

And she hung up, just as though he were a medical call that was over. Lenzini remembered that residents got into a habit of doing that, handling calls in the briefest possible time so that they could get on with what they were supposed to be doing, but his was not that kind of call. With a shrug, he dropped the phone into its cradle. He had plenty to do without trying to second-guess Angel Crawford.

Angel was not satisfied with the phone call, but she had no time to think about it. When she turned to head down the hall, she saw Roger Janek walking toward her, looking like hell. He was unshaven and there were dark hollows under his eyes, meaning, from Angel's experience, that he'd been awake for more than forty-eight hours. His distraction was apparent when he passed her without noticing. Angel laid a hand gently on his arm to stop him.

"Roger? Is there something the matter?"

The anesthesiologist blinked at her, and sighed. "Angel. Sorry. I didn't see you. You're on oncology right now, aren't you?"

"Um-hmmm." Angel had a sinking feeling in the pit of her stomach. "Why are you here?"

"Kerri. She's back on the floor." He rubbed his unshaven chin with restless fingers. "It wasn't the flu, back at the anesthesia party. The cancer has come back, big time."

"I'm so sorry. Who's her doctor?"

"Hazen. He's good, I know. But he's not very hopeful."

Angel walked with him down the hall, wishing she could think of something helpful to say. "How old is Kerri?"

"Thirty-five." Roger paused outside a door where the patient inside was sleeping. "That's her. She was up almost all night last night vomiting. She can't keep anything down. You know, when they operated on her last year to remove her uterus, they thought the ovarian cancer hadn't spread beyond that, so she had a good chance."

The woman in the bed looked pale and uncomfortable, even asleep. She had brown hair pushed back from her face and wore a hospital gown that looked too large for her. Angel turned her gaze back to Roger.

"How long have you known her?"

"A year. I did her anesthesia when she had surgery last time. When I came for the pre-op visit, she just bowled me over. She was so up, so sweet. You wouldn't believe how dear she is, Angel. Naive and kind and generous." His eyes gleamed with moisture. "I keep thinking someone's got it wrong. It can't be Kerri who was meant to be sick."

"I know what you mean. But they don't get sick because they deserve it. It's just an awful accident of fate."

"Well, I hate it," he said, uncharacteristically vehement, pounding an impotent fist against the door frame. "I'd take her place any day. She should be running around and laughing and having a good time."

"I wish she were." Angel saw that Kerri had opened her eyes. "You'll want to go in to her now. I'll talk with you later."

"No, come in and meet her. You can keep an eye on her for me," Roger suggested, "when I'm working and can't be here." He took her by the elbow and pulled her reluctantly into the room.

A smile spread across Kerri's face when she saw Roger. "Hi. Anyone would think you were the patient," she teased him. "You need a nap and a shave."

"Hi, yourself," he said gruffly. "Kerri, this is Angel Crawford, who wore the tux to the party when you couldn't come. She's on an oncology rotation right now."

As though she were anywhere but a hospital, Kerri thrust out her hand. "Hi, Angel. Roger said you were a great substitute that night."

"I never said that!" he protested.

"It was a great party," Angel said, taking the small hand and pressing it gently. "What a shame you couldn't be there."

Kerri scrunched up her nose. "Yeah, after all the planning we did. And everyone's told me what a super emcee Roger was. I wish I'd seen him." Then, in case this seemed like self-pity, she hurried on. "He's making a nuisance of himself here with my doctor, Angel. Pestering him with all sorts of questions. Maybe you could get him to just relax a little. Take him to lunch or something."

"I'm eating here with you," Roger insisted, pulling a granola bar from his pocket. "I don't have to be back in surgery for another half hour."

Angel had picked up real concern from Kerri's eyes and nodded her understanding. "I'll talk with you later. You two enjoy a few minutes together."

Roger was oblivious to what had passed between the two women, but Kerri said, "Thanks, Angel. Nice to meet you."

When Angel passed Kerri's room later that afternoon, she decided to drop in to say hello. Thinking herself unobserved, the young woman was staring out the window, a tear creeping slowly down her cheek. At Angel's footsteps, she quickly brushed the moisture away and attempted to smile.

"It's not so much that I feel sorry for myself," she explained. "Though I guess I do. But Roger just won't accept it. He wants me to believe I'm going to live. Does that make any sense to you?"

"In a doctorly way. But for Roger it's more personal. He can't bear the idea of losing you."

"It would be easier for me if he could."

Angel nodded. "I know. I'll see if I can talk with him about that. It's especially hard for doctors to admit there's nothing left that they can do. We're very much take-charge people, Kerri."

"Yeah. Heaven knows, I'm not too keen on the idea of dying myself." Kerri patted the side of her bed. "Tell me about the party. Do you have time?"

"Sure. I have time."

Why was it, Angel wondered later, that patients

seemed willing to broach the subject of death with her? She certainly had no more answers or comfort to offer than any other doctor around. But the subject of death itself held a little less terror for her perhaps than it did for some of them.

Angel tried to talk with Roger that evening when Kerri had fallen asleep. Exhausted, he had slumped down in a chair in the lounge, planning to spend the night there again. Angel perched on the arm of the sofa across from him.

"Kerri and I had a talk this afternoon," she said. "She wanted to hear more about your emceeing the anesthesia party."

"If I'd known she was really sick that night, I wouldn't have gone. I bet she knew all along what was happening."

Angel lifted one shoulder in a gesture indicating lack of knowledge. "But she wanted you to go, Roger. So, if she knew what was happening and she told you, she would have defeated her purpose."

"What's your point?" He didn't ask it sharply, as someone else might have, but with curiosity.

"When we love other people, sometimes we get selfish on their behalf. Like, you could have said that Kerri needed you because she was sick and you'd have stayed with her. But that's not what *she* wanted, was it?"

"No."

"And now she wants you to understand that it would be easier for her if you could accept that she's dying."

"No." He shook his head, slowly, for a long time. "She can still beat it. Hazen said there are some drugs that might slow the progress. And maybe by that time, they'll have found something new."

"You're believing our own lies, Roger."

"They aren't lies, Angel. Anything is possible."

"Well, no, they aren't lies, but they're a bit of false hope, aren't they? Nothing cures her kind of advanced cancer, and the radiation would be very hard on her. Do you think it's fair to ask her to go through that for nothing? I've worked with Hazen. He doesn't recommend external irradiation or radioactive implants for someone in Kerri's condition."

"But he'd do it."

Angel put a hand on Roger's knee. "For who? Not for Kerri. She doesn't want it. If she did it, it would be for you. And I think that's really more than you should ask of her."

Roger grimaced. "You don't know her. You've just seen her now, when she's sick. She wouldn't think that way if she weren't sick."

"But she is sick, Roger. And she knows she's dying."

"I don't want her to give up hope."

"Hope of living? But that's impractical. She can hope for a peaceful death, but only if you'll come to terms with it, too." Angel stood up. "I'm sorry to butt in. And I'm sorry about her condition. I'm telling you what I think she wants you to know, but only you can decide what you're going to believe. One thing I can tell you is, that she wants you to go home and sleep tonight and come in shaved tomorrow when you see her before you go to the OR."

"What if she has another night like last night?"

"She'd rather you were at home in bed. Roger, that's what Kerri wants."

He chewed at his lip for a moment, tugged at the loose belt around his waist, and rose. "Okay. I'll just tell the resident on call to ring me if there's an emergency."

Angel nodded.

Over the next week, Angel got in the habit of dropping in on Kerri when she had a free moment. It might only be for a minute or two, or she might bring a tray of food for the two of them to share. She didn't come when Roger was there, but they talked about Roger a lot. Kerri was deeply in love with him, and wished that he'd been able to meet her aunt.

"She raised me, all by herself. My folks died in a car accident when I was little. She was so sweet, my Aunt Sophy. She would have loved Roger."

And they talked about her friends, who found it hard to come to visit in the hospital because they were young and afraid of death.

"I've taught kindergarten in city schools for more than ten years. They call, all my teacher friends, and the women I've met over the years, and they send cards, but some of them can't bear hospitals. Facing death is too much for them. I can understand that. It's awkward for them to know what to say. They don't want to skirt the subject, but they're afraid anything they say will sound like a platitude."

They talked about Roger's newest flight of fancy, that they would be married, soon. As soon as she got out of the hospital, they would go to city hall. Or have a judge come to her house. Why shouldn't they get married?

"I understand why he wants that," Kerri said. "Actually, I want it, too. He's trying to make me get better by holding out that temptation. He's saying that if I can just get out of the hospital, we'll be all right. Angel, maybe you could talk to him again."

"He's still in denial, Kerri. I'll try, but he hasn't developed any defense against his pain and fear. Do I sound like a psychiatrist? I talked with Jerry Stoner casually yesterday. He said we just have to keep working with Roger."

But Angel was beginning to wonder about herself. In the short time she'd known Kerri, the older woman's sweet nature and ingenuousness had captivated her. Kerri had come to seem like the sister Angel had never had, and the possibility of losing her so soon had prompted Angel's appeal to Dr. Stoner, not just on Roger's behalf.

In the midst of all this subtle trauma, there was a lack of Cliff Lenzini. He had called, twice, sort of teasing her along, she felt, and she did not need his game playing just then. Not that she would have welcomed it at any time in her busy life, but it seemed particularly out of place just then. When he called for the third time, a week after the picnic, she was short with him.

"Look, Cliff, you don't have to call me. I'm busy, you're busy. Let's not worry about it, okay?"

"But I want to take you out, Angel. There just hasn't been a minute."

"Right. I understand." Angel could hear the impatience creeping into her voice. "Maybe this just isn't a good time in either of our lives."

"Wait. What are you saying? That you don't want to go out with me?" He sounded incredulous.

Angel remembered his hands on her body, the hair on his arms rubbing against her. Her throat tightened. "No. I'm not saying that."

"So maybe this weekend?"

Angel was standing at the nurses' station, her back to the counter, staring at the chart rack. "I'm on call."

"Damn." She could hear him growl. "I'll call you next week."

"Okay." And she hung up.

For some reason Lenzini had gotten it into his head that the call was from Angel, and he had to adjust his mind when he heard his sister's voice. "Hi, Catherine. What's up?"

"I bring you a message of relief," she said with a laugh. "I know you weren't happy about the prospect of going to San Diego for Dad's sixtieth. Well, he insists he doesn't want a party, and Mom can't change his mind. So you're off the hook."

"Terrific. Actually I'm not surprised. Having a party would only remind him he's getting older."

"Oh, sure. He wouldn't have noticed it otherwise," Catherine teased. "He'd just go on operating with stronger bifocals."

"Hey, we wear those cute little miners' lamps on our heads," Cliff reminded her. "Maybe I'll send him a singing telegram."

"Don't you dare. Mom specifically told me to keep

you from doing that this year. Just send him a card, Cliff, and call him on his birthday, which is two weeks from Wednesday."

"I know when it is."

"Yes, but if you put it on your calendar now, you might remember to call."

Lenzini growled and drew his calendar toward him. "Okay, Catherine. I'm writing it down right now. Hear my pen scratching?"

"I thought you had fleas," she said, echoing their insults from childhood. "Everything okay with you, Cliff?"

"Always." His pager went off, and he automatically glanced down at the number. "I've got to go, Catherine. Thanks for calling. Say hi to Mark."

Lenzini was not at all happy with the way things were going, as far as Angel was concerned. He could probably have found a time for the two of them to get together this week if he hadn't wanted to heighten the suspense. Apparently Angel wasn't feeling the suspense, and it looked very much like he was going to lose her interest if he didn't actually get them together some time soon. He hated that it had been she who couldn't make it this weekend.

Well, probably she was toying with him, playing hard to get. Not about being on call, there could be no doubt about that. But in her suggestion that they should forget about getting together at all. Because it really had sounded for a moment as though that was what she was saying.

And she had sounded irritable with him, another trait that was hard for him to accept. Lenzini could remember being irritable ninety percent of the time he was a resident, what with the lack of sleep and the constant demands. But he was not in the habit of courting women who were short with him. There were plenty of well-rested women who would give their eyeteeth (whatever they were) to be seeing a surgeon.

Lenzini would have pushed all of this from his mind and gotten on with his own work if he hadn't happened to have a disjointed talk with Roger Janek after a sigmoid colectomy they had just done together. Roger was a conscientious anesthesiologist who had excellent concentration for what Lenzini could only regard as the most boring job in medicine. To sit there hour on end, doing almost nothing but making minor adjustments, watching dials and gauges. Hours of boredom and minutes of sheer terror, as Richard Selzer had suggested.

Not the kind of crises that showed any genius, either, from Lenzini's point of view. Intellectual exercises rather than creative adventures, such as a surgeon might contrive. Under the circumstances, Roger's concentration was remarkable, since Lenzini knew that his woman friend was back on the oncology floor in desperate straits. Cliff did not find it possible to say much to Roger on the subject, other than a subdued wish that Kerri was doing okay.

"She's getting worse," Roger admitted, stripping the mask from his face and disposing of it along with his gloves in the bin. "Hazen doesn't think radiation is realistic when there's obviously so much metastasis and scarring."

"I'm sorry to hear it."

"Kerri wants me to accept that she's not going to

get better, and she's got Angel convinced that she should just let things take their course."

Lenzini's head snapped up from where he was bent over his operative notes. "Angel?"

"You see, Kerri's such a sweet person. She doesn't want to give anyone any trouble. I think she should force someone to do something for her."

"Do you mean Angel Crawford?" What other Angel could there be?

"Angel's really good with her. She stops in to visit Kerri all the time, and you know how little time you have when you're a resident."

Lenzini knew. "I didn't know Angel knew Kerri."

"I introduced them. Don't you think Kerri should fight this thing, Cliff? Don't you think she should be pushing for some kind of treatment, even something experimental?"

"Hazen's pretty good. Um, is Angel her resident?"

"No. But Hazen says they don't have anything more they can use for her ovarian cancer. No new protocols, nothing." Roger stopped as he was about to push open the door to the corridor. "Do you think there's anything you could do surgically?"

"Hey, I'm not her surgeon."

"Bailey's on vacation. He did the original surgery and thought the cancer hadn't spread. Obviously he was wrong. Otherwise, why would it have recurred so fast? You could take a look at her, couldn't you?"

"If there were any indication for surgery, they'd have called for a consultation, even with Bailey away."

"You could just check her out, as a favor."

"Rog, that wouldn't be smart. You know that."

Roger ran a hand distractedly through his hair. "Just as a favor. She's really special, Cliff. I can't bear what's happening." His voice had gotten rough with the sound of suppressed emotion.

Cliff squeezed his shoulder. "I'll look in on her, but I can't promise anything. Maybe I'll just have a word with Angel about her impression."

Roger's eyes lit up. "That's a great idea. Angel's been a brick. I think she's gotten really fond of Kerri."

Just when she's dying, Lenzini thought unhappily. All doctors were warned to maintain a distance from patients so that they could treat them with objectivity. Lenzini could just hear Angel say, "She isn't my patient." And naturally she had jumped right into the situation. No wonder she seemed especially irritable these days.

Obviously it would behoove him to stick his own oar into this particular muddle.

Chapter Seven

On Saturdays things were always quieter at the medical center. Quieter, that was, in terms of personnel bustling about. Angel never found being on call on the weekend particularly quiet in terms of her own work. This particular May Saturday, however, had been relatively uneventful, so by early evening Angel found herself paying a visit to Kerri.

Evening light filtered into the room, softening the harsh lines of doors and windows, bed and stand. The IV pole with its bags of fluids hanging down looked almost festive. Kerri glanced up from her book and smiled at Angel. "This is the perfect book," she said. "Thanks."

"Sure." Angel perched at the foot of the bed. "So where's your constant companion?"

"I made him go out for a real meal. One cannot survive on granola bars alone."

Angel considered Kerri's pale face and distended abdomen. Fluids were infiltrating her belly now, and she was growing weaker from lack of nourishment, the disease robbing her of any sustenance she could handle. And yet Kerri seemed perfectly composed.

"He'd shaved this morning, too," she said. "I was impressed. You have a good influence on him."

Kerri scrunched up her nose. "Sometimes." Her gaze wandered to the window, which looked toward the hills of Marin to the north. "I'm glad we have a minute alone, Angel. There's something I wanted to say to you."

"Sure."

"You know, when I'm gone, Roger is going to be really lonely for a while. Maybe even for a long time. But eventually he'll start to feel human again and be interested in things around him." Kerri glanced quickly at Angel, and then away again. "What I mean is, he might notice then what a terrific woman you are. And I wanted you to know that I think that would be great, if you and Roger . . . um, hit it off."

Angel giggled. "Oh, Kerri. I don't feel like that about Roger at all."

The other woman frowned. "I don't actually understand how you couldn't, I guess. He's so very dear. Sometimes it seems to me that anyone who spent any time with him at all couldn't help but fall in love with him."

"Yes, I see what you mean." Angel's lips twisted ruefully. "I guess some of us are just too perverse to fall in love with the most logical person, someone warmhearted and considerate."

"Well, remember what I said. You might change your mind." Kerri sighed. "But to tell the truth, I guess I'm relieved. It's hard for me to think of him loving someone else. Even in the future. You know?"

"Yeah, I know." Angel pressed Kerri's hand. "He

loves you now. That's what's important, for both of you."

The door to Kerri's room was open, and Angel heard someone come in but she assumed it was Roger. Kerri turned her head, but her expression was more curious than pleased.

"You don't remember me," the voice said, amused. "I'm Roger's friend Cliff Lenzini."

"Of course I remember you," Kerri contradicted him. "I just didn't expect to see you here."

Angel shifted on the bed so she was facing him. "Kerri has become as blunt as Roger recently."

"Sometimes that happens," he said, his eyes glued for a moment to hers. Then he turned to Kerri. "Roger wanted me to sort of check on you. In case there was anything I could do."

Kerri looked at Angel. "Does that mean surgery?"

"Yes, I think so. Dr. Lenzini is definitely a surgeon."

"Hey, I'm just doing what I promised Roger," Lenzini protested, pulling a chair closer to the bed and sitting down. "I'm not here officially."

"Good." Kerri smiled and offered her hand. "I don't need a surgeon. I've already done that."

"Some people do it lots of times," Lenzini teased, shaking her hand. "And sometimes it's useful."

Angel knew better than to say anything at this point. Kerri merely agreed with Lenzini and then asked if he still lived in the house on Twin Peaks.

"That's right, you've been there," he said. "Yeah, I'm still there. I haven't done anything to it, though. I always intended to add a deck off the bedroom."

"That would be perfect."

The two of them talked for a few minutes, mostly on harmless topics. But gradually Lenzini brought the conversation around to Roger. "He'd like you to do anything you can to get better. He's very fond of you."

Kerri looked him straight in the eyes. "I'm not going to get any better. Roger knows that; he's just not able to admit it quite yet."

Lenzini met her gaze without hesitation. "Sometimes we can buy a little time."

"I know, but I don't think it's possible in my case. Dr. Hazen has been very open with me about what's happening. The disease has spread too far."

"Would you mind if I checked your abdomen? Just to tell Roger that I'd done it."

Kerri looked to Angel for advice. Angel could only shrug her shoulders. It wouldn't do any harm, but she knew it wasn't what Kerri wanted.

"Okay," Kerri agreed, reluctant.

"I'll try to check in later," Angel said, getting up to go.

"I wanted to talk to you, Dr. Crawford," Lenzini said. He wasn't looking at her, but at Kerri as his fingers probed her abdomen. "If you have a minute when I'm done here."

Angel rolled her eyes at Kerri, who grinned. "Okay. I'll be at the nurses' station unless there's an emergency."

She had only been sitting at the counter writing in a patient's chart for a few minutes when he appeared. He pulled Kerri's chart and quickly paged through it, reading what he needed to know. When he had slipped it back on the rack, Angel was finished and waiting for him to speak to her.

"Walk with me back to the elevator, will you?" he asked. She fell into step beside him, and he asked, "What's the situation here?"

"I'm not her doctor, Cliff. Apparently Dr. Hazen believes he's done everything reasonable for her. She'd be at home except for her instability and her constant vomiting. She'd going downhill quickly now. Kerri accepts the fact that she's dying."

"And Roger knows it, but he can't accept it." Lenzini paused in the hallway outside a treatment room. "You didn't know her before this admission, did you?"

"No. Roger introduced me the second day she was in."

"Do you think it was smart getting friendly with someone so sick, Angel?"

Angel debated whether she needed to answer the question, which seemed remarkably insensitive, intrusive, and paternalistic. "Yes, I think it was. You don't get many opportunities in life to know someone as special as Kerri. If you're smart, you grab them when they're available. And, Cliff, I don't think it's any of your business."

"I'm just concerned about you."

"I want you to let me take care of myself," Angel said. "I wouldn't think of sticking my nose in your business."

He grinned. "Wouldn't you? Hell, I wish you would."

"No, you don't. You'd consider it unmitigated gall if I said something like that to you." She mimicked a childish, squeamish voice saying, "Oh, Cliff, do you think you should do that icky operating stuff? I mean, there's blood and all that. You'll get your hands dirty."

His eyes gleamed with good-natured humor. "I'd just laugh," he said.

Her eyes narrowed. "Not if I said, 'Cliff, do you think you should be doing favors for Roger Janek? He's imposing on you.'"

Lenzini was silent for a minute, regarding her seriously. "Okay, that would be none of your business. But, Angel, Kerri's going to die, and she's going to die pretty soon. The closer you get, the more pain that's going to cause you."

"Unlike a lot of the people around here, I expect some patients will die. We treat them because they're sick. It shouldn't come as such a surprise and with such a sense of failure when some die." Angel leaned back against the doorway to ease her aching neck. It was tough looking up at him when he was standing that close to her. "We can't save all of them."

"We try."

"Sure we try. But it can't be done." Angel leaned her head back and shrugged her shoulders. "I think that may be the most useful attitude I came to medicine with—not being terrified of death. Because then I don't have to harden myself every time it approaches. I don't feel like I have to keep the same distance for protection."

Lenzini looked skeptical. "You're probably just fooling yourself."

"Yeah. I bet I am." Angel straightened up and

backed away from him. "Look, I've got things to do. I'm cross-covering on Six East. Roger will be glad you looked in on Kerri. See you around."

"Now wait, Angel," he said, putting out a hand to stop her. "I didn't mean to insult you."

Angel shook his hand off her arm. "Right. I'll bear that in mind." She turned with a tiny wave of her hand and headed back to the nurses' station, leaving him to stare after her.

Prickly, prickly, Lenzini thought. He might have gone after Angel, but he heard her pager go off and knew she would indeed be busy with work. Also, he was not at all sure he needed to pursue someone who didn't appreciate his well-meaning concern.

His evening was entirely free. No reason not to have dinner out, take in a movie . . .

"Hi, Dr. Lenzini."

He found he'd wound up at the bank of elevators where he was being addressed by a nurse with her purse over her shoulder. Probably just off duty, he thought automatically. And he knew her, a pretty young woman named Jessica. No ring, a decided smile on her full lips, something about her eyes that suggested she was free. Maybe he should . . .

"Hi, Jessica. Busy day?"

"Not too, but I'm glad it's over. Weekends always seem like they should be for parties, don't they? You know of any tonight?"

He could very easily have said, "How about you and I making our own party, Jessica," but he shook his head, almost reluctantly. "Haven't heard of any.

You might check on the fourth floor. They're the real partiers."

"Good idea." She stepped onto the elevator that was going down. "You coming?"

"No, I'm going up. Good luck."

"Thanks."

Lenzini stood in front of the elevators for several minutes more, interrogating himself about why he had let this opportunity slip through his fingers. Nurses made much better dates than other doctors. Their hours were better, they were used to taking care of people, and they had a tendency to respect doctors—a winning combination as far as Lenzini was concerned. They also often settled into married life with a homemaking vigor that astonished him after seeing some of them party just as vigorously. No doubt about it, nurses had the upper hand where accessible women were concerned. Too bad Angel wasn't a nurse.

He was still standing there trying to decide where to go when Roger came off the elevator. "Did you see her?" Roger asked, and Lenzini only just stopped himself from doing something foolish like assuming he was talking about Angel. "Yeah, I checked her over."

Roger looked pathetically eager. "And?"

"There's nothing I can do, really. It's spread too far, Rog. I'm really sorry."

"Look, Cliff. I've been thinking about this for weeks. It sounds crazy, I know, but I just have to marry her."

Lenzini's jaw dropped. "Marry her? But, Roger, she's . . ."

"I know." Roger tugged at his belt. "It's not that I don't know. But you see, I'll always have that then, that she was my wife. Not just my girlfriend, or someone other people can dismiss."

"Rog, you know you love her, and she knows it. You guys are the only important ones. You don't need to be married."

Roger ignored him, drawing a small box from his pants pocket. "I bought her a ring. Maybe it's stupid, Cliff, but I wanted her to have it. I want someone to say that we're husband and wife. I want you and Angel to be our witnesses. That's not asking so much, is it?"

Lenzini wanted to tell him it was far too much, that it just wasn't done. But there was something so compelling about Roger's need that it silenced his protest. "When?" he asked.

"As soon as we can. How long does it take?"

"Don't ask me." Lenzini thought about the matter. "One of the nurses might know. But wait. You've got to see how Kerri feels about it. It may not be what she wants."

Roger looked dumbfounded. "Why wouldn't she want to get married?"

"I don't know. I just think you ought to ask her before you get carried away."

"All right, I will." Roger turned to leave him, tossing back over his shoulder, "I'll expect you to be available to be my best man at any time in the next two days."

Lenzini climbed onto the next elevator, shaking his head.

* * *

The nurses on the floor completely adopted Roger's cause. In no time, they assured Kerri, they could get the blood tests taken care of, find someone to marry the couple, produce a blouse of shimmering satin for the bride, see that the groom was suitably decked out in his tux, and any other detail that might seem impossible to her.

Angel wanted only to know what Kerri wished for herself. "Roger is important," she said, seating herself in the chair Lenzini had used the previous day. "But you're the one who should have the last word. Is this what you want?"

A flush of color rushed to Kerri's pale face. "Actually, Angel, it is. I would never have said. It didn't seem fair." She held out her hand with the diamond ring for Angel to admire. "It's absurd, isn't it? Getting married when you're dying. But it's like a symbol. Like I will always be important to Roger, even when time has passed and he gets on with his life. I'll have been his wife."

"I'm happy for you." Angel smiled a little tearfully. "You put us all to shame, Kerri. All our stupid little worries and irritations. You're like pure sunlight."

"Oh, hush! I'm no different than anyone else. You'll be my witness, won't you? Roger has asked Cliff Lenzini to be here, too. The nurses are going to take pictures and have a little celebration for us. Then I've asked Roger to take me away."

"Will he?"

"Yes, he's promised. He has a cottage in the mountains that he shares with some other people. I guess Lenzini is one of them. I've been there, and that's where I want to die. Not in a hospital, but out there where the air is fresh and you can hear the running water."

Angel squeezed her hand. "That sounds lovely. I saw a picture of it once. I'll think of you there."

"If I don't make it, if I don't get there, would you go for me? And sit on the rock by the stream and watch the birds soar over the woods?" Kerri cleared her throat and rubbed a fist at her eyes. "I'm getting all sentimental, aren't I? I didn't mean to do that. But I'd like you to go there. Roger would give you his key. I know it's asking a lot."

"You ask so little of anyone," Angel said. "Of course I'll go there if you don't make it, but I'm sure you will. Roger will find a way."

Kerri's eyes danced. "He's going to rent one of those campers, so I can sleep the whole way up. Which is probably a good idea. He's not much of a driver."

"I remember."

Cliff could not believe that the whole wedding had been arranged in such short order. He was literally paged from an operation to come to the ceremony, leaving the closing to his assisting resident. It did not occur to him that he should take the time to change into his suit and tie, so when he arrived he regarded the rest of the party with a decided chagrin.

Kerri was in bed, but in a beautiful blouse with a garland of flowers in her hair. Roger stood beside her, dressed in the tux she hadn't seen him in for the anesthesia party. And Angel. Angel had disposed of her lab coat and wore a simple blue-green silk dress that flowed over her body like water. It wasn't exactly sexy. Well, it was sexy to Lenzini, but he could see that you could argue that there was nothing particularly revealing or provocative about it. The dress elegantly illustrated that this was a woman of excellent taste, perfect figure, and simple grace. Not bad for one four-ounce item of clothing.

Slipping up beside Angel, Lenzini grumbled, "Why didn't anyone tell me this was formal? I'd have put on clean scrubs. I figured it was come as you are."

"No one expected you to dress," Angel said. She seemed a little stiff to him, as though she hadn't forgiven him for their encounter a few days previously.

"Well, look at you. You didn't fish that out of the dirty laundry this morning."

He'd surprised a laugh out of her. "No. I don't usually fish things out of the dirty laundry. Do you?"

"When I have to. There's no shame in it, you know. It's not like I need to join one of these dysfunctional groups, dirty-laundry wearers anonymous. I send all my stuff out to the laundry, but I'm sometimes too late to pick it up. There are women who do that for their men."

Angel raised her brows at his teasing. "I don't know any. You better latch onto one if you find her."

"Hell, I'll hire someone," he retorted. Then he turned to Kerri, Roger, and a judge who had been deep in conversation. "Do you want me to take the time to change?"

Roger assured him it wasn't necessary. Kerri said his scrubs were appropriate to the setting. The judge suggested that he might get rid of the ridiculous scrub cap. Lenzini stripped it from his unruly hair, and the judge muttered, "Maybe it would have been better if you'd left it on."

"No one's ever satisfied," he sighed to Angel.

The judge indicated they were ready to get started. Roger leaned down to grasp Kerri's hand, and she smiled tenderly up at him. The service was short but not abrupt, with the judge saying a few words about the beauty of a love so strong it surmounted all obstacles. When Roger kissed Kerri at the end of the ceremony, there were few observers whose eyes weren't moist.

Lenzini was, of course, one of them. But even he felt a catch in his throat, which he attempted to hide by saying offhandedly to Angel, "What's this husband and wife stuff. Whatever happened to the old man and wife?" But his voice caught on the last word, and Angel regarded him suspiciously before stepping forward to hug the bride and kiss the groom.

A gurney was wheeled into the room piled high with food and drink. One of the nurses kept clicking away with her camera, getting shots of everyone doing everything. Lenzini made sure she got one of him with Angel, though he had to maneuver very carefully to manage it. Angel was still not precisely welcoming him with open arms.

The two of them, however, had been chosen as witnesses for the marriage license, and because of the specialness of the occasion neither was going to appear anything but cordial with the other. How would it have looked to the bride and groom? Lenzini naturally capitalized on his opportunity.

Roger was seated on Kerri's bed, his arm around her waist. He looked terribly proud, and she looked ethereally happy. Each of the observers in turn came up to congratulate them, and then moved away to allow someone else to approach. Lenzini planted himself beside Angel to watch the progression.

"I thought Roger was crazy to suggest their getting married," he admitted. "I'll bet you didn't discourage them."

"Well, I had to be sure it was what Kerri wanted. She was my first concern."

"Like a patient."

Angel hesitated. "Like family, Cliff. Like someone important to you. And yes, like a patient, too, because she's so sick."

Lenzini watched Roger adjust the flowers in Kerri's hair with gentle fingers. Even now, when she was so happy, you could see that she was sick. Her face was thin and pale, lovely but haunting. "I don't know what he'll do when she dies."

"He'll mourn her. And he'll want to talk about her, Cliff. Not avoid the subject, as so many people believe. He'll want to tell you about things they did together, and the best thing you can do for him is listen and remember things, too. That's how you'll help him, if you can."

Lenzini realized she didn't totally believe he could or would be there for his friend. "Why wouldn't you think I'd help him, Angel? Do you think I'm some kind of monster?"

"Of course not. I didn't mean that at all." She stood for a moment considering, her left hand clasping her right elbow, a strangely defensive posture.

"I'm sure you'd always help where you knew how. You'd jump in and try to fix something if it was possible. But this won't be able to be fixed, and it will make you feel helpless."

"How can you possibly know that?"

She looked puzzled. "Because that's how we'll all feel, Cliff. At least, most of us. Your friend Dr. Stoner, the psychiatrist, he'd feel a little more comfortable in that situation probably, because he's used to dealing with people and their emotions. You and me . . ." She shrugged. "We'd just bumble along."

Lenzini grunted. "*You* wouldn't. You'd know the right thing to say."

"Why would you think so? I don't say the right things to you, do I?"

He looked slightly amused. "That's because you don't want to say the right things to me, Angel. Not because you couldn't."

She shrugged. "Maybe."

But Lenzini was picking up a message here, at least he thought he was. She was so damn difficult to understand. Right this moment it seemed like she was saying she'd like to talk to him and have things go smoothly. Was that possible? "Could you have dinner with me tonight?" he asked abruptly.

Angel blinked at him. "Tonight?" She looked a little panicky, her eyes flitting off toward the window and back. "Um. Not in your office."

"In a restaurant. You choose."

She bit her lip. "I just don't know if it's a good idea. I'd like to but . . ."

"Nothing heavy," he assured her, not sure himself what that meant. "Just dinner. To talk. You know."

The unusual wedding party was beginning to break up. Roger was approaching them with the license to be signed. Angel sighed and said, "Okay." Lenzini grinned.

Chapter Eight

A ngel chose a quiet Thai restaurant not far from the hospital. Lenzini consulted her desires as far as ordering went and then sat back and studied her. "How come you changed your clothes?" he asked.

"I didn't want to outclass you," she said, smoothing the collar of her gray suit. "This is what I wore to work today."

"It's not what you wore to the wedding."

"No, that was too fancy for dinner here."

"I liked it. I was hoping you'd be wearing it tonight."

Angel leaned back in her chair, head cocked to one side. "Is there some reason we're discussing my dress?"

"It seemed a safe topic. I guess it wasn't."

"Medicine is a safe topic. If you want safe, we can discuss medicine, like every other two doctors when they get together."

He eyed her curiously. "You know what I really want to know?"

"What?"

"Why you're named Angel."

She smiled. "Well, I had three brothers, all older than me. Apparently even when they were young they were hellions, and my folks thought that if they named a girl something really sweet and saintly, she'd toe the line."

"So did you?"

"No." Angel tossed back her hair, a look of reminiscence creeping into her eyes. "I was raised in a small town in Wisconsin, and with three older brothers there was no way I could behave like an angel. I liked to play ball and build tree houses. Sometimes we went on adventures, my brothers and I. They didn't seem to mind if I tagged along."

He leaned toward her and took a sip of the beer the waitress had brought. "What kind of adventures?"

"Oh, we went on hare-and-hound hunts, leaving paper trails. And we had a club on an island where we dug up pirate treasure." Her cheeks colored with embarrassment. "You know how kids are. We scouted Indian burial grounds and deserted churches."

"I didn't do things like that when I was a kid." He frowned. "I grew up in San Diego. My father is an orthopedic surgeon. Doctors' families lead a more structured life. We went sailing and horseback riding, and took gymnastics classes. It was a city. We didn't have room to roam like you did."

"You missed something, then. The freedom of going where you want and the excitement of not knowing what you'd discover next—they're great. I'm going back there when I'm through with my training.

Even if I don't have kids of my own, I'll want to see how my two brothers' kids grow up."

"I thought you said you had three brothers."

Angel hesitated before saying, "Brian died."

"God, I'm sorry. What happened?"

She drew a deep breath and looked down at her hands. "When I was fourteen and he was sixteen, he had a motorcycle crash. He wasn't wearing a helmet. They rushed him to the hospital and put him on a respirator. He looked okay, but he was brain dead. They did EEGs, but there was nothing."

"Poor kid. How awful for you."

"He'd been a terror, my brother Brian. And everybody's favorite. We all came to the hospital every day, and he looked alive to us. We couldn't believe Brian wasn't there anymore. He was a perfect donor for several organs that were desperately needed, and my folks didn't know what to do. He could have stayed that way a long time, on a respirator, but then his donor status would deteriorate."

Angel pushed her hand across the table, and Cliff clasped it tightly. "It was very difficult for us to let go of him. While he was there in that bed, we didn't have to admit that he was dead. We'd all start crying every time we tried to discuss what to do. Then our family doctor came and sat with us. He didn't say anything for a long time, just sat there.

" 'What you want to remember,' he said, 'is what you'd want the rest of the family to do if it was you.' He may have said other things. I don't remember. I just remember that. And it seemed very clear to us then, you know? Each of us would have chosen to have the machine turned off, to have our organs used to help someone who still had a chance. And our doctor didn't abandon us after telling us that, either. He stayed around through the whole thing. You don't find a lot of doctors like that. But I wanted to be one."

"God, Angel." He rubbed his thumb gently along the side of the hand he held. After a minute he said, "I'm glad you told me. It makes me feel like I know you a lot better. Well, a little better."

"That's why I wanted to go into family practice," she said, taking her hand back as plates of food were set in front of them. "And why it's important to me that people be allowed to die with dignity. Those people we keep alive by mechanical means who don't have a chance of living—we're not doing them any favors."

"It's hard to know when to quit hoping, Angel."

"I know. Everything isn't as clear-cut as it was with Brian. But we have to learn to look beyond the ends of our noses. Just because there's something more we can do, doesn't mean we absolutely have to do it."

Lenzini's brows drew together. "But we have to offer it, Angel. People have a right to know."

Angel nodded.

"Eat up," he urged. "This is great."

There was more she wanted to say, but she could tell he wanted her to enjoy her meal, so she smiled and changed the subject. Fortunately they discovered a mutual interest in movies, a subject that kept them in animated conversation for the duration of their meal.

Angel could feel a certain tension grow as Cliff

paid for their meal (refusing to let her pay her half) and directed her out of the restaurant. In a light but interested voice he asked, "Where to?"

"Home. I need a lot of sleep. I've got call tomorrow night."

"Home it is," he agreed.

"My home, alone," she clarified, just in case.

"Your home, alone." He looked down at her. "We could neck in your living room for a while."

"Nan would definitely be entertained."

"Maybe she won't be there."

Angel regarded him with serious doubts. "You haven't bribed my roommate to be out this evening have you?"

"Hell, I wish I'd thought of that. But I didn't. You give me far too much credit, Angel."

"Humph."

"What are the chances she'll be there?" he asked, hopeful.

"Oh, roughly even I'd guess. But that doesn't mean you can come in."

"I think we should be sporting here. Let's say if Nan's home, I'll leave immediately, but if she isn't, you'll let me come in."

"Pushy, pushy." Angel didn't know quite how to handle him, or herself. The more he talked, the more her body suggested she go along with him. "You said you wouldn't push me."

"I believe I said nothing heavy." He grinned. "That could be interpreted as almost anything."

"By you," she retorted. "By me it's interpreted as no pressure to pick up where we left off last time."

"I can accept that." He held the car door for her

and waited while she tucked her skirt under her. Then he bent down and touched the tip of her nose. "How about twenty minutes, if Nan isn't there?"

"You're impossible," she grumbled, her nose feeling all tingly and her lips positively parched. "All right. Twenty minutes. If Nan isn't there."

To the disappointment of both of them, Nan was at home. When Angel unlocked the door to let them in, the first thing she saw was Nan in the living room, wearing her scruffiest clothes and watching TV with a vacant stare.

"Hi, Angel," she called. "Long day, huh? How was the wedding?"

By this time she'd seen Lenzini behind Angel, and the look of chagrin that flashed across his face before being replaced by a polite smile and greeting. "Oh, dear. I can see I'm going to be *de trop*. I'll get out of here."

"No," Angel said firmly. "Cliff can't stay. He just wanted to make sure I got here safely. Didn't you, Cliff?"

"That's right," he agreed manfully. "Just wanted to see the little lady home."

Angel said to Nan, "You'll remember Dr. Lenzini, the sexist surgeon."

Nan ducked her head behind a pillow. "I'm not going to get in the middle of this," her muffled voice informed them.

"You see what you did?" they chorused. Lenzini drew her outside, calling to Nan, "She'll be in in just a moment," before closing the door. The stairway leading up was brightly lit, and there was very little space on the landing. It was hardly a romantic spot.

"Now," he said, ignoring his surroundings, "I think you owe me an apology, or a good-night kiss."

"You're impossible. You agreed to go away if Nan was home."

"You told her I was a sexist surgeon!"

"It wasn't the first time I've told her that."

"You're ruining my reputation," he groaned. "Angel, Angel, what am I going to do with you?" He drew her gently but firmly against his waiting body. "I just need to kiss you, all right?"

Angel could feel her heart speed up and the delicious longing sweep through her body. If she hadn't protested so much, and if she really hadn't needed the sleep, she would have gone home with him right then. She turned her face up to him and said, "I want you to kiss me, Cliff. I just want you to remember I'm going in there and going to bed in about two minutes."

"I'll remember."

His lips were warm and tempting on hers. His hands cupped her buttocks to lift her toward him. Every nerve in her body seemed to come alive and sing of erotic heights that begged to be scaled. Angel clung to him for dear life, allowing the excitement to fill her, hoping that he took pleasure from the simple, incomplete embrace. After a while she reluctantly drew back to rest her head against his shoulder. Her body felt shaky, her knees rubbery and uncertain. "I really have to go in now."

His voice was gruff with longing. "That's okay. Just promise me we'll see each other again soon."

Angel fumbled behind her back for the doorknob,

her eyes on Lenzini. The door opened, and she backed against it, allowing herself to move slowly away from him. Just as she was about to close the door after herself, she said, "I promise."

When his footsteps could be heard trotting down the stairs, Nan said, 'You two are something else."

Angel looked slightly abashed. "Yeah, I know."

"I hope you know what you're doing."

"You must be kidding." Angel stood in the arched entry, taking off her shoes. "If I knew what I was doing, I wouldn't be doing it, would I?"

"Hey, I'm a neurologist," Nan protested. "Don't ask me that kind of question. That's for Dear Abby."

Angel picked up her shoes and sighed. "He just gets to me, Nan. What can I say?"

"Go to bed. You're on call tomorrow."

"Right." Angel groaned, but a smile tugged at the corner of her mouth. "I'll probably dream about him."

"Lucky you."

Cliff had every intention of arranging to go out with Angel as soon as possible. But she was on call the next night, and his coauthor had only the next evening to go over the final draft of their research paper to be presented at a conference in Los Angeles the next weekend. And then emergency surgery made him cancel a date they'd arranged the third night. Which began the loop of Angel being on call again. It was a very frustrating week for him.

Though he seemed to spend half of his life on the phone, he didn't really like using it to talk with Angel. He wanted to be able to see her, and to touch her, and to pick up all the nonverbal clues she was so generous in sending out. Being on the phone robbed him, too, of his presence in a situation. Lenzini may have thought he took no advantage of his impressive size, but he was mistaken. He would not (naturally) use it to intimidate anyone, but he liked the stature it gave him, and the fact that most people literally had to look up to him. On the phone he didn't have this advantage. Which was all right, of course, but not his preferred style.

So when he talked with Angel, he had a tendency to sound a little overbearing, and he could feel her resistance immediately. He would try to back off, but she didn't seem aware of his compromise, keeping him at a distance by the impersonal nature of her exchanges with him. What Cliff needed was to see her in person, and he had hung up from finally arranging to do just that not ten minutes before he had Roger's call.

"Kerri died this morning," Roger said, his voice heavy with emotion. "She just died in her sleep. Just like that. I thought she seemed a little better yesterday. We were going to go to the cottage today. And she died."

"Oh, God, I'm sorry, Roger. She was a wonderful person. It's not fair she should die so young."

"No. She was really happy these last few days, though. Sort of euphoric. I'm not sure if it was the sickness or being married or what. Cliff, I hate being here alone."

"Of course you do." Lenzini glanced regretfully at the notation he'd just made on his calendar for that evening. "How about if I come over when I'm finished here?"

"You?" Roger sounded surprised. "Well, um, what I'd thought was that maybe Angel could come, but she said the two of you were supposed to do something and I said I'd call you and explain."

"I see."

"She's just so easy to be around, and she had gotten to know Kerri so well." Roger drew a shaky breath. "You don't really mind, do you?"

"Of course not." Lenzini leaned far back in his chair and stared at the ceiling. "I could come, too, if you think that would help."

"Thanks, but it's better if it's just Angel, I guess. You wouldn't really feel comfortable with me being upset and everything."

Lenzini wanted to argue with him, wanted to assert that he could be every bit as supportive and sympathetic as Angel, except that he knew it wasn't true. Funerals dismayed him, though he went when it was required of him. Naked grief was something he saw often enough as a doctor, but he was not comfortable with it, didn't know what to do or say beyond the very simplest of condolences. "Well, I'm really sorry, Roger," he said now, meaning it and wishing he knew what else to say. "Let me know if there's anything I can do to help, okay?"

"Sure. Thanks, Cliff. And thanks for being at the wedding."

Angel had heard from Kerri the night before she died. Despite Roger's insistence that she was better, Kerri had known her end was close. "You'll help

Roger, I know," she'd said. "I'm really glad we got married. I hope he won't regret it sometime later."

"He won't regret it."

"It isn't so awful, dying. What's awful is saying good-bye," Kerri whispered over the phone. "Thanks for not being afraid to get close to me, Angel. You've made my last few weeks very special, you and Roger."

"I'll never forget you, Kerri. You're one wonderful woman." Angel's voice cracked, but it didn't matter. "I just wish you could be here longer."

"Me, too. But I can't. If I don't talk to you again, well, thanks. And remember about going to the cottage. I don't think we're going to get there."

"I'll go. I promise."

She was not surprised the next morning by Roger's call, but grief flowed through her like fog, engulfing her emotions and obscuring for a moment the acceptance she had learned toward death. Torn between her commitment to Lenzini for the evening and her pledge to Kerri, there was really no choice, but she was relieved that Roger took the burden from her by calling Cliff himself.

As she was about to leave the hospital, Angel decided to slip up to Cliff's office to say hello if he was there. The door was closed and she tapped lightly, feeling slightly nervous, almost wishing she hadn't come. When he called to enter, she stuck her head around the door hesitantly. "Have a minute?" she asked.

Instantly he was on his feet and coming toward her. "Of course I do. You on your way to Roger's?"

Angel nodded and let him draw her into the room. "I'm sorry we had to postpone again, Cliff."

"Hell, I'm sorry about Kerri. You okay with that?" He studied her intently, pushing back the auburn hair from her face. His fingers lingered on her cheek.

"I guess. It's always hard. I never meant to give the impression it wasn't, you know." She smiled sadly. "But it was worth getting to know her."

"Yeah, a nice woman. I didn't know what to say to Roger."

"You don't have to say much. You just listen. He'll want to talk about her, not pretend nothing happened. At least I think he will."

"Is that what you did when your brother died?"

Angel was surprised and touched by the question. "Yeah. We're a really close-knit family, and we tried to help each other accept Brian's death. We talked and talked about him instead of pretending he hadn't existed. It helped."

"I guess I can understand that." Cliff ran a hand through his unruly mass of dark hair. "Death is just so final, Angel."

"I know." She hadn't taken a chair, not wanting to stay but a minute. He stood very close to her, almost as though he wanted to put his arms around her but was resisting the impulse. Angel appreciated his restraint but needed his comfort just then. "Cliff, I need you to hold me, just for a moment. If that's okay with you."

He silently wrapped his arms around her and hugged her to him. They stood that way for some time, neither of them speaking and Lenzini making no attempt to turn their closeness into a sexual encounter. Angel drew great support from his understanding, or at least his attempt at understanding. With a shaky breath she disengaged herself.

"Thanks. I needed that."

"Any time."

When she turned to go, he asked reluctantly, "Will you hold Roger like that, if he needs it?"

"Sure."

"I know that's okay," he said, frowning, "but it doesn't seem like it's okay. You know what I mean?"

"Yes, but it *will* be okay. He's just lost the woman he loved. He's not going to be thinking about sex, Cliff."

"Humph. Men always think about sex." He shrugged away his concern, squeezing her shoulder gently with his hand. "I know you'll do what you think is right, Angel. It's great you can be there for Roger. I offered but he thought I was nuts."

Half teasing and half seriously she said, "He just doesn't know your hidden depths, Cliff."

Lenzini growled, and Angel made a swift exit.

Her schedule was impossible for the next few days. In addition to the usual work demands, Angel spent as much time as possible with Roger, helping him adjust to Kerri's death and plan a memorial service. At the service in the hospital chapel, Roger told her that he was taking a few days off.

"To visit my parents in New York," he admitted. "I didn't tell them about marrying Kerri or about her dying. It all seemed too much to dump on them at once. I'm just going to explain and spend a few days there. Maybe it will help, maybe it won't. In either case, I need to do it."

"It sounds like a good idea," Angel said.

Roger dug in his pocket and pulled out a loose key marked with a red band. "This is the key to the cottage. It's my month there. Well, you know that because we were going to go. Kerri said you were going to make a little pilgrimage there for her."

Angel accepted the key, immediately attaching it to her key ring. "Yes, it's something we discussed. I think she felt I needed a break."

Her explanation seemed to relieve him. "Hell, it's the perfect place to get away for a few days, Angel. I bet you do need a vacation. Do you have any time coming?"

"Just this weekend. But that should be perfect."

Roger nodded. "Ask Cliff how to get there, will you? He has a map we made up. I couldn't find mine."

"Don't give it another thought."

But Angel was already giving it some serious thought. This seemed the perfect opportunity to spend time with Cliff, alone, away from the hospital, away from San Francisco even, with all their obligations and entanglements left behind. Roger wouldn't need her; she had the time. What could be more perfect?

"Oh, hell!" Cliff exclaimed when she presented the idea to him outside in the corridor. "This is the only weekend all month I can't get away, Angel. I've got a conference in Los Angeles, which I'd be happy as a hamster to miss except that I have to give papers both days. Next weekend?" he asked hopefully.

"Sorry. We'll be changing over, and I'm on call. I have an obstetrics rotation next, and it's the beginning of my third year. I can't try to rearrange that."

Lenzini raked his fingers through his hair in frustration. "This is simply extraordinary, Angel! I know you're trying, and I certainly am. How about the weekend after that?"

Her brows drew together in thought. "It would probably be all right, but I want to do this soon, this thing for Kerri. I just feel like I should. I'll go alone this weekend, and we'll find a way to see each other during the next week."

Lenzini's voice grew husky. "I'd like to be with you at the cottage."

"Another time. You have the cottage for August, right?"

"Yeah. Save me every weekend you have free," he insisted.

She laughed. "Well, the first one, anyhow. You might change your mind."

"I'm not going to change my mind."

Chapter Nine

Angel considered asking Nan if she'd like to come along for the weekend but decided she'd really enjoy the opportunity to be alone. In thinking back over the last few years, she could count on one hand the number of times she'd had a whole weekend to herself. Her only worry was that she would be too tired to drive the four hours to the cottage even with a night's sleep under her belt.

But when she woke up early on Saturday, she found it was a perfect day, sunny and breezy, with big puffy white clouds in the sky. Angel put the top down on her little red Rabbit and sang along with the radio as she sped over the bridge. Even without Cliff, it was going to be wonderful to be away.

Thoughts of Kerri intruded frequently on her mind, but they were thoughts about the young woman's life, not her death. They were stories Kerri had told her of her favorite times, some of them at the cottage in the mountains, some of them of her younger days in Montana. The farther Angel got from the city, especially when she started ascending into the Sierra, the more she dissociated herself from her contemporary life and remembered her own youth.

Going back to Wisconsin would bring her full circle to her cherished way of life.

There was just a year of residency left. In some ways it would be particularly demanding, in others the pattern had become so familiar that she felt almost comfortable with it now. And she would need to start planning for the time when she would carry her skills back to an area where they were needed. Not like in San Francisco where there was a doctor every square inch of the city. In Wisconsin, in some areas, her training would be extremely valuable since there weren't others to fill the gap. This is what she'd planned for for the last fourteen years, and it was about to become a reality.

A very poor time to be taking a man into her life.

There was still time to put the brakes on her relationship with Cliff Lenzini. They had both made good-faith efforts to get together. Perhaps it was Fate with a capital *F* trying to keep them apart. Angel doubted that. The lives of doctors had enough built-in emergencies, demands, and problems that it wasn't all that unusual they'd been unable to spend time together. But now, as her car roamed up the pine-scented roads of the mountains, Angel wondered if she should act more rationally than she was. No use setting herself up for a real heartbreak.

At a crossroads she finally pulled out the map Cliff had sent with her, unfolding it to find a drawing he had done of himself on the bottom of the page. Under an arrow reading "Los Angeles" he stood waving north, with a heart drawn on his sleeve. Angel laughed, and tsked, and drove on. There was just no way she seemed able to deny herself this relationship with him. Something about him drew her irresistibly, no matter what her head said, with all its good intentions.

The directions guided her to an unpaved road high on the side of a hill. She wove the car past streams and fields of wildflowers. Sunlight sparkled off the water and lit the golden poppy blossoms. One moment she was out in the open, the next passing under an archway of pine trees with shafts of light making patches on the road ahead. It was heavenly.

And then abruptly she reached the cottage. There hadn't been another dwelling for the last mile, and there it stood, a wooden cabin with a steeply sloping roof that the snow could slide from in winter. There was a woodpile under the overhang by the front door and a lean-to of a garage against the side of the building. Angel hadn't expected the cottage to be quite so old or quite so charming, despite the picture she'd seen in Cliff's office. No wonder Kerri had been so fond of the place. Angel fell in love with it instantly.

She hauled her suitcase from the back of the Rabbit and grasped the bag of groceries she'd brought with her. The key fit easily into the lock, and the door swung open on an open plan of living room, dining area, and kitchen that was furnished in a wonderfully eclectic style. Probably each of the members of the group had contributed something from their own places, and the result was chaotic but cozy. There was an overstuffed chair, a futon sofa, a burl-wood table, a Danish modern dining set, and a kitchen full of old-fashioned implements and tools that looked as if they must have come with the place.

Because all the owners were doctors, here in this isolated spot there was a phone, with an answering machine. And the message light on the answering machine was blinking. Angel set down her load on the nearest table and pressed the button for replay. Cliff's voice boomed out into the cottage.

"Hi, Angel. I'm in L.A. and I miss you and I wish I were there. We'd have a great time. Half the people here have never even heard of me. Can you believe that? Illiterates. I'll call you this evening if I'm not out having a wonderful time with some exotic dancer. Hope you find everything you need. Take care."

Angel saved the message, knowing she'd want to play it again. Then she wandered around the first floor, putting groceries away and inspecting the premises for mouse droppings as she'd been instructed. In which case she was to set the mouse trap. Right. Just because she was a doctor, she was supposed to regard that as of no particular consequence. When she made her way upstairs, she found that each of the three men had a bedroom that he'd furnished. She peeked into each of them.

Roger's room had pictures of him and Kerri on every surface in the room, bureau, night table, bookshelves. They were smiling and happy in most, though there were those moments Roger had caught of Kerri sitting thoughtful by the stream, or deep in a book on a hammock. It was a bright room, with yellow curtains and a yellow and white bedspread, with rag rugs on the wooden floors. Kerri had confessed to Angel that she'd been the one to furnish it, as Roger had very little interest in such things.

"We try to keep the rooms pretty much our own," Kerri had explained, "but when it's not your month, the other people can use them if they have guests and stuff. Mostly they put people on the futon downstairs."

Roger had told her she could use his room, their room, but Angel intended to use Cliff's. For a while longer, Roger could think of his room as his and Kerri's.

The second bedroom was Jerry Stoner's. It had come as a surprise to Angel that Dr. Stoner was the third owner of the cottage, but the room itself wasn't at all surprising. It looked like a Japanese meditation room, with *shoji* screens and clean, sharp lines in every piece of furniture. It had a view out over the valley and Japanese mats on the floor. Just as it was intended, it was a very peaceful room.

And then there was Lenzini's. Angel stood in the doorway shaking her head in disbelief. The blatant maleness of it made her want to laugh, or cry, with exasperation. There was one whole corner of the room filled with sporting equipment—a bike, skis, tennis racquets, golf clubs, a bow and arrows, fishing rods. The bookshelves had more magazines than books, and most of the magazines were ones like Playboy and Penthouse. The color scheme was roughly navy and maroon, in the faded curtains and vivid bedspread, on what was patently a water bed.

Angel shoved her suitcase into the room and followed it with a certain amount of caution. She was hoping there wouldn't be calendars with naked women on the walls. It had occurred to her already that if there were, she would take them down to the fireplace to burn, regardless of Lenzini's possible wrath.

But the only things on the walls were watercolors, rather good ones, that looked like they were of the surrounding area. On the bureau there was a photograph of what was obviously Lenzini's family. It would have been taken some years earlier, as Lenzini looked to be in his mid-twenties. He looked a great deal like his father, though his coloring was more like his mother's. Apparently he had a sister, somewhat younger, Angel guessed, an attractive young woman of queenly stature and mischievous eyes. Lenzini looked only slightly less imposing than his father, who stood like an old-fashioned patriarch with his hand on the seated Mrs. Lenzini's shoulder.

Angel knew she was storing up all this information in her mind, weighing it for and against Cliff. She would have been less than human if she hadn't. The magazines, the arrogant stance in the picture, spoke of a man she was not unfamiliar with, a man who had more than one sexist bone in his body. What alarmed her was not so much that she should be so attracted to him, but the possibility that she was attracted to him *because* he was so chauvinistic. Could she subconsciously be undermining her own values? Why didn't she fall for someone sweet and endearing like Roger?

She was about to toss her suitcase on the bed when one of the watercolors caught her eye. It was a fall scene of colorful trees and rushing water, but with a surprising melancholy about it. For some reason she could not begin to articulate, it reminded her of Kerri and of Kerri's death. Peaceful yet sad, the scene drew her closer, and she realized that it was probably the spot Kerri had described to her where she wanted to be remembered. And Angel's eye fell on the signature, which was without doubt C. Lenzini.

His signature was unfamiliar to her, but she didn't doubt it would be this bold sort of message. Still, Angel refused to believe he was capable of such work. As likely as not it was his sister's or his mother's work, done when they'd visited him at the cottage and kept because the watercolors were good and had sentimental value. Angel knew many doctors who were involved in the arts, especially music, not just attending concerts, but playing instruments, even composing. But this . . . No, she could not see Lenzini out in the countryside with an artist's easel, a brush, and a tin of watercolors. He was too big, too impatient, too cocky to put himself in such a vulnerable position.

Turning away, Angel noticed that Lenzini's view was up the mountain, where trees and sky and clouds predominated. Standing close to the window she could look down and see the stream, whose soft murmur reached the house at all times. Neither of these views were replicated in the watercolors on the walls, and she was relieved. Angel opened her suitcase and began to unpack.

After a sandwich and soda, she left the cottage to explore the area and find the spot Kerri had talked of. There were several trails leading in the direction of the stream, and she wandered down two before she recognized the clearing, not so much because of Kerri's description as because of the watercolor. A huge rock overhung the creek where a pool-like area had been excavated for depth. Birds soared over the woods, just as Kerri had said they would. Their cries mingled with the rush of the water and the cicadas in the warm grasses of the clearing.

Angel climbed on the rock and looked down along the stream where tree branches dipped down to the water and rocks made little cascades. For a long time she sat in the sun, remembering Kerri, and regretting that her friend had not had the chance to sit there just once again and smell the fresh, pine-scented air. She could think of Kerri's spirit soaring off with the birds or flowing down to the ocean with the stream. This was Angel's private memorial service for Kerri, and she allowed her tears to flow and relieve her of some of the ache she had been feeling. If Kerri had been able to accept her own death, Angel could do no less.

Eventually peace, or tiredness, overcame her, and she sleepily pulled a bottle of sunscreen from her shorts pocket. Stripping her clothes and leaving them on the rock, she sat on her towel to slather the lotion all over her body. Then she lay down on her towel on the grass. The sun toasted her body with its healing warmth. Angel lay on her back for a few minutes and then rolled over on her tummy, reveling in the sheer luxury of being lazy. She must have fallen asleep because when she woke the sun had shifted in the sky. Hot and greasy, she scooped up her towel and dashed to the stream, splashing into the hollowed out swimming hole with a whoop of delight.

Nothing, absolutely nothing felt like cool water on a naked body. Swimming was like moving through silk, feeling the water's caress on every part of her. Angel splashed her way giddily across the swimming hole, spurting water from her mouth and laughing with the sheer joy of it. Definitely she was going to begin swimming more often in the city; who could resist such refreshing sport? She would find a way, she decided as she paddled along, to fit in a swim at the med-center pool several times a week. Maybe at lunchtime, or even when she was post-call to relax her and bring her down from the nervous energy she had to generate to stay alert all those hours.

Sun gleamed through the water on her body, tracing her shoulders and breasts, tummy and hips, and her long graceful legs kicking in a sidestroke. God, I could swim forever, she thought, allowing herself to drift with the stream toward shallower water. I could float along down through the mountains, twisting past moss-covered banks and granite boulders. If I were a leaf, I could ride the water right down to the ocean, swayed along by the current, caught in the tug of the ocean's pull like a moon tide.

Angel hadn't received such bodily pleasure since . . . well, since she'd been with Cliff Lenzini. Which was what she was thinking of, so it took her a moment to realize that it truly was his voice speaking when she heard him say, "God, you're beautiful."

He was standing on the rock overlooking the stream, as totally naked as she was. He looked enormous against the sky, his head erect and his arms akimbo. "I see you weren't expecting me."

Angel tucked her feet under her and balanced on an underwater rock, only her neck and head above the water, as though that protected her from sight. "But you had a talk to give in Los Angeles."

"I gave it."

"But you had one tomorrow, too."

"My coauthor will give it. He needs the experience."

"But, Los Angeles, Cliff."

"A friend flew me up." He lowered himself into the water. "Wow! This is hardly warm water."

"It felt good after lying in the sun. You have to keep moving." Which she was not doing herself just then, and she began to feel the chill.

"Or," he said, his eyes not leaving her as he swam toward her, "you can share body warmth with another human being of the opposite sex."

Angel felt a shudder of anticipation rush through her body. "You could," she agreed. He was within reach now, and she folded her arms around his neck, her legs encircling his waist. Her wet lips found his. "You really are an outrageous man."

"Do you think so?" His hands had began to massage her buttocks.

"Yes." Her breath was already coming a little faster. She felt the hair on his chest against her breasts even underwater. The sensation was so exquisitely delightful that she grinned. "My body was feeling terrific even before you came. I'm not sure I'm going to be able to bear this excitement."

"Hmmmm. I think I can help you." His fingers

were exploring between her legs, and she purred with pleasure. "We'll have to devise a little water safety here, sweetheart. I didn't exactly come protected to the old swimming hole."

"I can't imagine why not," she teased. "You might have known what would happen."

"I might," he agreed, squirming with enjoyment as she ran her hands down his body. "I think we can probably find a very satisfactory solution to this very small problem, if you'll just let me adjust your position."

Angel allowed him to shift her so his penis was between her legs but not inside her. His rocking back and forth stimulated both of them slowly to a fine pitch of arousal. And then he kept her there, teasing and pleasing her, his lips locked on hers. The lotion had left her body slippery, and his hands slid temptingly over all of her. She clung to him, working her own magic with her legs wrapped around him, until he was the first to cry out his release. "Why, you angel," he groaned, rocking against her most vulnerable spot. "I do believe you're not a virgin."

"I learned it all in medical school," she protested, arching against him, aching with desire. His pressure on her nudged her over the line, and she gasped with the shock of the waves of delight surging through her. They clung to each other for long moments, with little nibbling kisses and watery hugs.

Angel sighed. "I'm glad you came."

"I should hope so."

"I meant to the cottage."

"I know what you meant, Angel." He wove his

hands through her wet auburn hair. "We're getting pretty close to the real thing. That's not going to be a problem for you, is it?"

She shrugged self-consciously. "I don't think so. But there are a lot of things I'm not sure about."

"Like what?"

"Like who you are and how I feel about you and how you feel about me."

He laughed. "Oh, that stuff. Well, I'll tell you something, Angel. You're the most adorable woman I've ever met, and I'm crazy about you."

Though he said it lightly, there was obviously a great deal of sincerity behind his words. They weren't a promise of undying love, but Angel wasn't sure she wanted a promise of undying love. "I'm kind of attracted to you, too," she rejoined. "You're so . . . impressive."

"I thought you were going to say interesting, like people say about something they're not even sure they like."

"Well . . ."

She snuggled close to him, and he nudged her with his chin. "Don't you like me, Angel?"

"As well as I like any sexist jerk," she quoted herself.

"I'm a reformed man," he insisted. "Ask anyone. I even gave a superior evaluation to a woman in the surgery residency this week. I mean, how unprejudiced can a man get?"

"Haven't you ever done that before?" Angel asked, horrified.

"For a woman?" He thought for a moment. "I

don't think any of them have been superior before, Angel."

She rolled her eyes. "You get superior women through your program every day, Cliff. They don't get chosen for it if they aren't superior."

"Well, I don't give many superior evaluations to men, either," he admitted. "I'm a tough evaluator. Everyone knows that."

"So this woman must have been flabbergasted."

"Hell, she almost burst into tears," Lenzini said disgustedly. "Imagine, a surgeon with great, dewy eyes. It's not done, Angel."

"What is it that's so scary about tears? I swear you guys would rather have someone pointing a gun at you than be faced with a little tear."

"This is far too philosophical a discussion for my taste."

With her holding on, he swam to the bank of the stream. The heat of the afternoon was fading, and Angel welcomed the towel he wrapped around her. He had brought extra towels and blotted her face and massaged her head with one while he stood naked before her. "Aren't you freezing?" she asked.

"Men are tough," he retorted, before finally winding a towel around his own naked torso. "Besides, I wanted you to have a chance to get used to me."

"You're so thoughtful. I don't know how I could have missed that before in you."

"You weren't looking." He kissed her lightly on the lips. "We'll bring our clothes up to the cottage. You'll want a shower before you dress."

"How do you know?"

Surprisingly, he flushed slightly, and shrugged. "Well, women do, don't they?"

Angel felt a small tick of warning or caution go off inside her. "Are we talking about any woman in particular?"

"No, of course not. Where the hell is this discussion going? I just suggested you might prefer to shower before you dress."

Angel decided to drop the subject, for the moment. "Yes, I would. I've got so much sunscreen on me, I'm likely to slide out of my clothes if I don't soap it off."

"I'd like to see that," he said, relaxed and amused again. "Your clothes sliding off. Preferably when we're alone in my room."

"I imagine you will." Angel picked up her discarded shorts and top, underwear, and tennis shoes. "So how come not everyone at the conference knew you?"

Angel had forgotten. With the hot water in the shower pounding down on her, she remembered Nan's original pronouncement on Dr. Clifford Lenzini. He wasn't married, but he had lived with a woman for a long time. How could she have forgotten that?

Simple enough to accept him at face value, she supposed. But he no less than she (probably much more) had a history. There hadn't, it was true, been any sign of a woman companion in his room. Angel didn't know any woman who would have tolerated sharing a room with a man whose girlie magazines were so aggressively strewn on the bookshelves. She had herself found them gone when she got back to the cottage, which had spared her the necessity of tucking them away in some closet.

Cliff had suggested that they share the shower, but Angel had begged off. She needed a few minutes to think about this new concept, that Cliff had been seriously involved with another woman, possibly not so long ago. As she shampooed her hair, she considered how she felt about that and found that it distressed her much more than she would have expected. She didn't want him to have been attached to someone else, and she certainly didn't wish to find that he still was.

This did not necessarily jibe with her image of herself as maintaining a calculated distance from him, of having a reserve where he hadn't invaded her mind. Angel turned off the water with a vigorous twist of the handle and stepped out of the shower. From the corner of her eye, she caught her image in the mirror and turned to see herself. This is what she'd looked like in the water, her hair plastered against her cheeks and drops running down her nose. But she looked sad now, concerned, and off balance. When Cliff had held her in his arms, she'd felt happy and safe and excited.

Angel turned away from the mirror and toweled her hair of the excess moisture. There were a lot of things she and Cliff needed to talk about, and she suspected he wasn't going to be easy to draw out on any of them. With the big fluffy towel, she dried off her torso and legs, remembering how cramped and uncomfortable it was showering at the hospital after a night on call. She would really benefit from this weekend of luxury, especially now that Cliff was there with her.

So did it make sense to push him on some of the issues that disturbed her? And possibly ruin her one chance for a weekend of true relaxation and enjoyment? Angel sighed and tossed the towel over the towel bar.

Getting to the cottage had required Cliff to exercise a great deal of ingenuity, planning, and resourcefulness. He had really wanted to give the research paper on Sunday, but allowing his coauthor, a chief surgical resident, to deliver it had been expedient and actually earned him points with certain people who thought he claimed too much attention for himself. Bribing a Los Angeles friend to fly him to the Sierra airport closest to his cottage had cost him a fair amount of money, and then there were the difficulties inherent in finding a ride to the cottage itself, some fifty miles away. If he had had anything less than Angel to look forward to, he certainly would never have attempted the feat.

But Cliff was looking to impress her, and he had decided to bowl her over by not only surprising her, but by making her dinner as well. His sister, bless her soul, had instructed him in the preparation of one meal only (she had a limited amount of patience), which he contrived to produce on any special occasion that presented itself—his parents' anniversary visit to San Francisco, the meeting of all the partners to the cottage for a holiday, etc.

It had not been easy finding Cornish game hens in Los Angeles between meetings, and he had certainly not welcomed their thawing in his luggage, but he was glad now that he had gone to the bother. While Angel showered, he dissected the little birds with surgeonly skill and set them to marinade in olive oil with garlic and lemon juice. He was still in the kitchen with his towel wrapped around his waist when Angel appeared in the doorway.

"Good heavens. You're going to fix dinner for me," she said, astonished.

"Of course. I'm a man of many talents." He reached down a container of wild rice from the unfinished wooden cabinet, shaking it to make sure there was enough. "Well, I'll need to bring more next time, but this will do. Keep an eye on it while I'm in the shower, will you?"

"Sure." Angel watched him dump the contents into a saucepan and add water. Then he placed it on a burner whose gas he had turned up as high as it would go. Angel maneuvered him out of the way and turned the gas down to a modest level. "Run along. I can handle this."

"And if you wanted," he said from the doorway, "you could make a salad. I brought some lettuce and tomatoes."

When she nodded, he turned to go up the stairs. Just before he disappeared from view, he released his towel so there was a split second of muscular legs and firm buttocks visible, if Angel happened to be watching still. He heard no gasps of astonishment from behind him, so he took the stairs two at a time for his shower.

Chapter Ten

Angel poured herself a beer and worked on a salad that included a great deal more than lettuce and tomatoes, since she'd brought various other veggies for such a dish. Standing at the chipped old sink, she could look out on a clearing of untamed grasses, with trees and rhododendron bushes beyond. In the kitchen itself, the pots and skillets hung from hooks that had obviously been there forever. It felt right, standing there, watching the light change to evening, knowing Cliff was overhead stomping around the bathroom.

The setting reminded her of Wisconsin, not because it looked much like her home state, but because of the rural, peaceful feel of the place. This was the atmosphere she missed so much in the city. The pace was slower, the air was fresh. It wasn't the responsibility in her daily life that stressed her as much as the feeling that the people around her had lost touch with this kind of tranquillity. They weren't only whirling on the outside, they were whirling on the inside. Heaven knew how they maintained their sense of balance; Angel didn't understand it. Without some stillness at their centers, how did they manage? And how would she manage if she got totally caught up in that kind of life?

Five years from now she expected to be in Wisconsin, in a house of her own. It would be in the country, or at least not in the city. There would be fields around, and farms within walking distance. There would be a pond to swim in and maybe a movie in the closest town. She would be the family doctor to the neighboring community; she'd know all of her patients and care about them. Wasn't that what she'd worked all these years for?

"Penny for your thoughts," Cliff said from the doorway where he had appeared without her hearing his approach.

"I was thinking about Wisconsin."

"Being out in the woods does that to you," he said. "Starts you thinking about all the remote places on Earth."

"I like being away from the city. Don't you?"

"If I didn't, I wouldn't have bought this place with the other guys. It's great for a break. I wouldn't want to live here all the time."

Angel sliced the last of the mushrooms and tossed them into the salad bowl. "I prefer the country."

"How come you did your residency here, then?" he asked as he opened the refrigerator and helped himself to a beer. "You could have listed only hick places."

"You know, you're very annoying when you do that."

"Do what?" he asked innocently.

"Refer to anything that isn't what you like in a derogative way, like hick places."

He came up behind her and put his arms around her waist, nuzzling her neck. "I just did it to get your goat."

"You're certainly good at that." She pushed him away, wagging the knife in her hands. "I thought I should have the experience of living in a city like San Francisco. Some place sophisticated and different from Madison. I put it at the top of my matching list, figuring if I got it, it would be right for me, and if I didn't . . ." She shrugged. "Then I could remain a hick forever."

With a bottle opener on the wall, he removed the cap from his beer and took a long sip. "Do you have to go back?" he asked after a while.

Angel looked puzzled. "What do you mean, have to?"

"Well, I mean, did you take loans from the government where they'll send you to the ends of the Earth to repay your obligation?"

"No, I don't have any obligations like that. I have loans, of course, but they're the usual kind that I'll pay back once I start practicing."

"So you wouldn't *have* to leave San Francisco."

"You don't listen very well, Cliff," she said impatiently. "I *want* to go back to Wisconsin. I want to practice out in the boonies where they don't have adequate medical care. That's what I've always intended doing."

"You can change your mind. People in the inner city need doctors, too."

Angel slid the salad tongs into the salad bowl and pushed it away from her. "What are you saying, Cliff? That I should like the same thing you do?

That I should want to practice in the city because that's where all the really sharp people are? I hear them all the time, laughing about local medical doctors as though they were country bumpkins who didn't know their ears from their elbows. What do I care? When I'm in Wisconsin practicing out in the backwoods, you can laugh all you want to at me. I won't hear you."

"You're a bit prickly about this, aren't you, Angel?" He lounged against the counter, his eyes locked on her face. "The reason I don't like your plan to go back to Wisconsin is that then you won't be in San Francisco to brighten my days. Not because you're going to turn into a bumpkin."

"I'm going to be around for another year, Cliff. I'm sure by then you'll have found someone else to brighten your days."

He shook his head. "Look, I'm a very straightforward kind of guy, and I'm not quite sure what's going on here. I don't know how long you and I are going to be together. Hell, you don't either. But there's something in your tone that says we won't be together because I'll be fickle or rotten or whatever."

Angel flushed and bit her lip. "I'm sorry. That isn't what I meant. I was just standing here thinking about where I'd be in five years, and it wouldn't be in California."

"Hmm." He took another sip of his beer and set the bottle on the counter. "I have to start the coals for the grill. Come outside with me. I don't think you've told me the whole truth."

The screen door banged behind them when they stepped down to the patio area. It reminded Angel of thousands of screen doors slamming in her past, of kids tearing in and out of the house, too impatient to close a door carefully, of summers full of youthful promise, of her three older brothers reluctantly agreeing that she could come along on their adventures.

Angel watched as Cliff unlocked the lean-to garage and opened a door off to the left. Inside were bags of charcoal, a large and a small grill, and shelves of canned goods. While he set up the grill, Angel wandered around the garage where a hammock was stored along with lots of well-worn sporting equipment. Obviously Roger and Jerry didn't find it necessary to keep their equipment in their bedrooms. There were inner tubes for the stream and faded purple wading shoes, torn fishing nets, and battered tackle boxes. Angel puttered around until she found some folding chairs, which she brought out and set up on the patio.

"I was never a Boy Scout," Cliff said as he stuck an electric starter on the grill and piled charcoal on top of it. "I hate the taste of lighter fluid on charcoal, but this way I always have to track down the extension cord, which is in the kitchen."

"I'll find it," she offered, getting up and starting for the screen door.

"It should be in the bottom drawer on the right, and you can plug it in above the counter. And would you bring our drinks?"

There were a lot of things in the bottom drawer on the right, among them an old phone book for San Francisco and a photograph of six people out in front of the cottage. It wasn't a good photograph, out of focus and not well positioned. Angel stuck the photo in her pocket and pulled the extension cord from the drawer. Juggling their drinks and the orange cord, she pushed her way back outside. Cliff smiled at her and finished setting up the coals.

"There. Now we can talk." After another long pull at his beer, he eased his large body onto the wooden-framed canvas-slung chair. "This wasn't made for a man my size," he protested, setting the beer down on a paving stone. "Now, then, my Angel, I think you have a more elaborate explanation to offer me for your—shall we say brusqueness?"

Angel pulled the photo from her pocket. "I think maybe she's the reason," she said, pointing to the woman around whom Cliff had his arm in the picture. "I'd forgotten about her. Not that I know who she is, but when I first ran into you, Nan told me you'd lived with someone, for a long time. Maybe until quite recently."

"I haven't asked you about your past, Angel. I don't really expect you to ask me about mine."

There was a stubbornness to his jaw that she hadn't noticed before. He didn't look angry, just determined. Angel studied the picture for a long time without saying anything. Roger was with Kerri in it, and Jerry with a woman she'd never seen before. Cliff's friend was an attractive blonde with a self-confident smile and very good legs. Her eyes were slightly narrowed against the sun, but even then they looked startlingly vivid.

As if she hadn't heard what he said, Angel continued, "I think it bothered me before that you assumed I'd want to come back to the house for a shower, as if that's what the *women* in your life liked to do. And it made me think about what Nan had said. All this time I haven't really thought about where you are in terms of relationships. For all you've said, you could be married and living apart."

"I'd have told you if I were married."

"Would you? You see, I don't know you well enough to know that, Cliff."

He growled. "No decent man would neglect to mention that he was married when he was starting a new relationship."

Angel slipped the photo back into her pocket, intending to return it to the drawer. "You've been around hospitals long enough to know there's a lot of interplay among the staff. Married, unmarried, long-term, short-term sexual encounters. Surgeons are particularly famous for their exploits. I hate sounding naive, but in some ways I am."

"I doubt that."

"You doubt a lot of things I say, which doesn't make them any less true. I'm not sexually sophisticated, no matter what you think. And I'm quite sure that you are, which leaves a big gap between us."

Lenzini regarded her with obvious skepticism. "You're a doctor, Angel. You can't be that naive."

"I'm a country girl, too, as far as that's concerned, but it doesn't make me knowledgeable in a personal way. Cliff, think about it. I'm just enough younger than you that I grew up in a world that knew about AIDS."

"You're not telling me that you're a virgin, are you?" he asked. 'I don't think I could handle that."

"No, I'm not a virgin."

"Then what's this all about? What are you trying to tell me?"

"God only knows," Angel said. She rubbed her temples and shook her head to clear it. "I'm trying to match your vaunted straightforwardness, Cliff. I'm trying to tell you I don't want to get more involved if there are things I don't know about you that would make it a stupid move on my part. Like if you're still involved with someone else."

He reached down for his beer. "I'm not involved with anyone else. Should I ask you the same thing?"

"You could but you don't have to."

"Does that mean you're not."

"That means I'm not."

Satisfied, he took a sip of beer. "So is there anything else I should know? Like that you're phobic to feather pillows or something?"

"I'm phobic to girlie magazines, but they seem to have disappeared."

Cliff grinned. "I only had them there to annoy Jerry. We have kind of a joke going."

"I see." She didn't, really, but she was ready to let the subject drop. "I better check the rice."

"And I should get the birds on."

For several minutes they puttered around the kitchen and the grill. Angel mixed a salad dressing while Cliff put the game hens on to cook. Then he turned his attention to the wild rice, sautéing red pepper and shallots and mushrooms in a skillet before combining all the ingredients. "Pretty fancy, huh?" he asked, looking for praise.

"Absolutely elegant," she agreed, but with a frown. The quiet of the evening had been disturbed now by the screeching and rattling of a vehicle down the mountain road. Speed on such roads was dangerous in the extreme and as the noise approached them, she could feel her heart start to speed up. It seemed entirely possible that an accident was about to happen. And then, as if her prophecy had come true, a truck roared up the driveway onto the grass outside the cottage, where it slammed to a stop.

Cliff was already out the door, and Angel was hard on his heels. The woman who jumped down from the driver's seat was totally distraught. "Thank God you're here! He can't get his breath. You've got to help him."

Already Angel could see a child of about ten in the back of the truck, undoubtedly banged by the rough ride but lying motionless except for the attempt to breath. His face was pale and sweaty and already beginning to swell. She turned to Cliff for consultation, but he was no longer at her side. The screen door slammed behind him, and she could only hope that he would return with the necessary equipment.

There wasn't time for the niceties of removing the boy's plaid flannel shirt, so Angel began to tear if off while she demanded of the mother, "What happened?"

"A bee stung him. God, I don't understand it. The other kids have been stung by bees. And all of a sudden he started to have trouble getting his breath." The woman shuddered and wrung her hands. "I didn't know what to do. John said he'd driven Dr. Lenzini up here earlier, and so I thought I'd come here. It's twenty-five minutes to the hospital. I didn't think Jimmy could last that long. Can you help him?"

"Yes, I'm sure we can help him." Angel heard the screen door slam again. Surely they would have an emergency medical kit here with three doctors sharing the house. But it was easy to get careless about that sort of thing, thinking it would never happen to them.

Jimmy gasped for breath, his hands clawing at his throat. His mother stroked his hair, moaning her helpless frustration. Angel tossed the shirt aside and turned to see what Cliff had brought. With relief she recognized an ancient medical bag, probably from someone's medical school days. He set the bag on the ground, and she automatically flipped it open to assess its contents. Lenzini himself had grabbed a sharp knife from the kitchen.

"He has severe laryngeal edema," Angel informed him. "Do you have epinephrine in the bag?"

"Yeah, but I'm not sure there's time." Lenzini crouched down by the child, running his fingers along his neck. "It would be safest to do a cricothyrotomy." He turned to the child's mother. "I need to bypass the obstruction of his throat and give him a clear airway. That will mean cutting into the cricothyroid membrane. Okay?"

"Anything," the woman breathed. "Just help him."

Angel had already pulled the intravenous supplies from the medical bag. Every movement was made with deliberate speed and efficiency. The supplies for an intravenous line were all there, no doubt Roger's contribution to the collection. Even as Cliff wiped the child's throat with an alcohol swab she was inserting the IV into a vein in the child's right arm. Cliff had the knife ready by the time she had established the line, and she reached for the vial of epinephrine.

"Give me thirty seconds," she asked. "This could work almost instantly, and you wouldn't have to traumatize him by cutting."

"You've got it," he said, watching the child as she administered the treatment. Epinephrine worked on some people with startling speed, and the signs would be obvious to any trained observer. Almost imperceptibly at first and then with growing sureness, the child gulped in breaths of air.

Angel dug in the bag for cortisone, used to prevent redevelopment of the respiratory syndrome. As she administered it, Cliff set the knife aside. It looked as though the crisis would be resolved by medical means. The child's mother shed a few tears of relief as he continued to breathe with more ease. She ran her hands over and over his head, comforting him with encouraging words and endearments. Angel sat back on her heels.

"One of us should go with them to the hospital, just in case he reverses," Cliff suggested. "Why don't I ride in the truck and you follow in the car?"

"I'll make sure the stove's off and follow right behind you."

Angel placed the medical bag in the truck bed. Cliff hopped in and steadied the child while his mother resumed her seat in the cab of the pickup. "There shouldn't be any need to hurry now," Angel said, just to make sure the woman understood. "I'll be right behind you."

The cover was already on the grill, so she simply made sure that the burners were off on the stove, the electric starter was unplugged, and she had her car keys. It was still light out, but dimming, and she wanted to stay within sight of the pickup because of her own unfamiliarity with the narrow, windy roads. If she lost them, she was likely never to find her way to the hospital, and would have the devil of a time even making her way back to the cottage.

She could see the truck's brake lights after a moment and sped up to keep a safe distance behind them. Cliff sat in the back of the truck supporting the IV and watching the child for signs of change. The road was rough, and her Rabbit bumped uneasily along the unpaved surface. With the top down, pebbles and dust kicked up at her in an alarming way, but she pressed on, slowly winding her way down the mountain.

After ten minutes Angel could see by Cliff's intent concentration on the child that something was wrong. He withdrew the epinephrine from the medical bag to repeat the dose. Probably everything would have been fine if he'd had the child's mother stop the truck while he drew the medication.

But he didn't. It probably didn't seem necessary. Angel watched helplessly as the truck hit a rock in the road and slid against the bank with a spine-tingling smack. Even then no one appeared hurt. The mother maintained her position at the wheel, Cliff flattened his body against the child's to prevent its flying out of the open bed of the truck. And the bottle of epinephrine smashed against the steel side of the pickup.

Angel swore. There had only been the one bottle of epinephrine in the medical bag. The cortisone would be of limited use against renewed swelling of the larynx. And they were still fifteen minutes from the hospital.

Cliff's lips tightened but he indicated to the mother that she should drive on. Fortunately she couldn't get a good view of her son with Lenzini's body blocking her line of vision. Angel and Cliff exchanged a knowledgeable glance, but the roar of the truck and the car made it impossible to communicate verbally. He indicated he would keep a close eye on the situation. She could see that the child was struggling again, trying to claw his swollen throat with his hands.

The minutes dragged by as the two vehicles thumped and slid down the dirt road. Daylight was fading from the sky, and Angel put on her headlights. They proceeded through tunnels of trees with shorter open spaces, an occasional cabin to their right or left. But the chances of help at any of them were too small to make stopping a worthwhile proposition. Jimmy's mother must have driven the road a thousand times; she seemed to anticipate every curve and gully. And still they were ten minutes from the hospital.

Angel saw Cliff knock on the truck window, indicating that the woman should stop where they were. Angel couldn't see her face, but she knew the woman must be terrified. Instantly she slammed the brakes on her own car, and jumped down, leaving the lights on to illuminate the scene as much as possible. The truck had stopped a few feet ahead of her, and the woman started to climb down. Cliff shook his head.

"Wait where you are," Angel called to her. "We're going to need you to take off in a matter of minutes, and we don't want to waste time."

Jimmy's mother did not, even in the dim light, look as though she believed Angel. And yet she stayed where she was. Angel climbed over the back of the truck and saw immediately that Jimmy was in desperate straits. There was really no choice but to do the cricothyrotomy. Fortunately, the child was almost unconscious from lack of air and would not be so likely to notice the pain of the incision.

Angel moved into position to hold him in as much light as possible while Cliff readied the knife once again. Almost before she was aware of his intent, he had slid the knife through the space below the bony bulge in the child's neck to make a hole in the cricothyroid membrane. The larynx above was too swollen to admit oxygen, but the trachea would be open. Air could enter there so that oxygen could reach Jimmy's starving lungs, and heart and brain. Especially the brain. Without oxygen for only a few minutes, Jimmy's brain could start to suffer irreversible damage.

"Okay, let's go," Cliff said. "I've got this under control."

Angel jumped down and called to the child's mother, "Everything's going to be okay. We can take off again. A little slower maybe so Dr. Lenzini can keep a good grip on Jimmy."

The woman searched Angel's eyes for only a moment and then nodded. If she drove more slowly,

Angel was unable to appreciate the difference because her own car still seemed to be running over endless rocks and into soft depressions. But Cliff showed no sign of having a problem, so Angel just tried to keep up with the truck. And hoped Jimmy would make it to the hospital under such alarming conditions.

The ten-minute ride seemed to last an hour, the last part of it going through a small mountain town where there was enough traffic to block their way. Jimmy's mother simply laid on the horn and aimed her truck for the hospital. Before she had stopped, Cliff had the child in his arms ready to jump down from the truck. The noise of the horn had drawn the emergency-room staff out in full force (it was not a large group) with a stretcher on which Lenzini laid the child. While Jimmy's mother was sidetracked for admitting information, Angel and Cliff accompanied the child into a treatment room.

Cliff explained what they had done so far, deferring to Angel's description of the child's reaction to the epinephine and cortisone. They stood back while the emergency-room team took over, administering the necessary drugs and attending to the neck wound. When they were satisfied that Jimmy was in good hands and would do very well, they left, encountering Mrs. Thomas as they came past the waiting room.

"They said I can go in in a minute, and that he's going to be all right," she said, a catch in her voice. "I think he wouldn't be, if it weren't for you. I don't know how I'll ever thank you enough."

Angel took the woman's hand and held it for a

moment. "We're lucky we were there, and that it's what we're trained to do. The doctors will teach you how to manage from here on in. Good luck to you and Jimmy."

Out in the parking area, Cliff pulled her against his chest. "Hey, we make some kind of team, huh?"

"I can think of less dramatic ways to be a team."

"I can think of *other* ways," he shot back, "but I'm not sure they'd be less dramatic. Maybe we should find out."

"Maybe."

Angel lifted the lid of the grill to see, even in the darkness, that the two Cornish game hens had been more or less incinerated. Cliff hung over her shoulder and sighed. "So much for impressing you."

"Oh, I'm impressed," she admitted, leaning back against him. "I liked watching you work. You looked as at home on the back of a truck as you do in an operating room. Wretched light, inadequate knife, no anesthesia. You must have nerves of steel."

"Yeah, I was pretty good, wasn't I?" he asked as he kissed the top of her head. "You were pretty impressive yourself, getting that IV started like you did it every day in a truck. You're going to be a great family-practice doc."

Cliff ran his hands through her hair and down along the sides of her body. Her back was pressed against him, and she could feel him become hard. His hands found her breasts, cupping them with an urgency she hadn't felt from him before. In her ear he whispered, "I want you, Angel. Now."

The adrenaline still flowed through her body, heightening her response to his touch. Her nipples hardened and sent delicious sensations surging through her body. Heat rose inside her, warming her groin with a lush need. "Yes, I want you, too."

She turned to face him, unconscious of how grubby they were, only aware of how intense his eyes were and how eager his lips. They pressed their bodies together as though they could melt into one another, bursting into flames in the process. Suddenly he broke away and grabbed her wrist.

"Come on upstairs. I can't wait another minute."

Angel hurried after him, almost alarmed at the strength of her need. Her body pulsed with desire, a desire to be touched, to be filled, to be released. In the bedroom doorway she paused briefly as he dropped her hand and moved to pull back the covers and dig in the bedside table for protection. Her breath caught when he turned to face her.

"Come here, sweetheart," he whispered, his voice gruff. "Let me get those clothes off you."

Angel came to stand in front of him, her heart pounding. He lifted her T-shirt over her head and nudged her bra down with his lips, sucking her nipple into his mouth with an abandon that stunned her. As he drew on her, she could feel her whole body sway toward him, her insides flow with him. Even as he continued to draw on her, his hands moved to push down her shorts and underpants. He pressed himself against her, knocking against her groin with his eager manhood.

And then she was on the bed with him, above

him, his mouth still on her breast, drawing, pulling, swallowing her. It didn't seem possible that she could feel this aroused without bursting apart at the seams, and yet the excitement only continued to grow as he spread her tender lips with his fingers. She touched him in turn, finding him bursting with need, and she found a place for him inside herself. A place where he filled her, and stimulated her, where she could feel that the climax was near.

She rose and fell over him, instinctively drawing him into her and moving against the rigidity that won her over, that rubbed and toyed with her moist vital spot and finally caused the awaited explosion. This was as much as she could bear, rocketing through her body like a Fourth of July display. And in her release she continued to move with him until he gasped with the shock of his own reward, crying out in exquisite agony.

For long minutes they lay there exhausted, spent in their satisfaction of each another. Angel felt almost unreal then, a little lost to time and place, caught up only in the feelings that were her whole reality. "Oriented times one," she murmured.

Lenzini brushed back the hair from her face and asked, "Which one: time or place or person?"

"Just person," she admitted drowsily. "I couldn't swear to time or place."

"That's probably best. If you realized it was after midnight and that you were only a floor above potential nourishment, you'd probably insist on me finding you something to eat."

"Would you?" She opened her eyes and lifted herself from his chest. "Now that you mention it, I'm starving."

"How soon they forget," he sighed. "I'll find you something if you'll come with me."

'Okay, you're on."

Chapter Eleven

Morning sun streamed through the multipaned window, flooding the bedroom with warmth and light. Cliff woke with a sense of well-being that he hadn't experienced in some time. Before he even placed himself in the cottage, he knew he had no pressures on him, that he was languorously happy and that he had something to look forward to that day.

His right arm remained asleep, because there was a body lying on it, a body that pressed against his chest and loins as if it belonged there. Cliff opened his eyes to find Angel's auburn hair strewn on the pillow only inches from his face. He could feel an instant bodily reaction, but he could also tell by her breathing that she was sound asleep. And it seemed unfair to waken her, when she was routinely deprived of sleep.

Even removing his arm from under Angel didn't waken her, so he kissed the nape of her neck and climbed out of bed. He'd let her catch up a little. Not that he would allow her to sleep away the day, but there were tasks he could do to fill the next hour or two. It was early, and he hadn't been to the cottage for over a month. He'd get rid of the poor game hens, and do the repairs he'd planned last time he was up.

Sometimes, when he was alone at the cottage, he loafed the whole day—reading, napping in the hammock, anything where his mind could wander and refresh itself. When scenes from the OR drifted into his mind, or current cases worked their way into his consciousness, he firmly refused to give them space. The whole point of coming to the cottage was to get away from it all.

Last night's interruption of his mini-vacation hadn't bothered him. There was something particularly stimulating about an emergency. If he hadn't become a surgeon, he would surely have specialized in emergency medicine. Nothing challenged him like thinking on his feet, being forced to handle the unexpected. Sometimes even general surgery became routine. He had found himself drifting more and more to the complex cases, the ones other surgeons didn't always want to take. And you could find them at a place like Fielding, where such cases were referred from all over the state. Lenzini felt very fortunate to have landed where he had.

Before taking a shower, he puttered around in the bathroom easing a tight window and adjusting the flow on the shower head. They were relaxing chores for him, and he found an unending source of them at the cottage and in his house in San Francisco. While his own father had shunned such chores, being concerned for his surgeon hands, his mother's brother had felt strongly about the necessity of knowing house repair. Uncle Jack had owned a high-powered construction company and provided summer work for the teenaged Cliff on the understanding that this was necessary knowledge for a man. Though he had never said any such thing directly, Uncle Jack had believed that doctors were somewhat effete, and he wished to make certain that his nephew developed the proper masculine credentials. Uncle Jack himself, to his lasting regret, had had only daughters.

Refreshed by his shower, Cliff poked his head in the bedroom but found Angel still fast asleep. She looked adorable lying there with her arms and legs flung about and her hair in disarray on the pillow. Cliff was tempted to take a picture of her, but the sheet covered only a fraction of her body, and he felt certain Angel would not be pleased at a nude portrayal of herself. So, feeling self-righteous, Cliff abandoned the idea and went down to fix himself some coffee.

He had hung the hammock and stacked firewood, cleaned out the grill, and puttied a window by the time Angel stumbled out the screen door, still half-asleep. "Why didn't you wake me?" she asked.

"You needed your beauty sleep," he said. She was wearing only a green cotton nightshirt, which became her. "It's done wonders for you."

"You're such a flatterer."

She stood on the patio flagstones somewhat awkwardly, as though uncertain what to say next. Cliff, too, felt a little hesitant, wanting to tell her how remarkable the previous evening had been but not wanting to say anything with such potential for clichés and sappiness. He was, in addition, in a precarious position poised on a slanting ladder with the caulking gun in his hand.

"Come and hold this for me, would you?" he finally requested. "I'd hate to crack my head open at this juncture."

"That would be a bit disappointing," Angel agreed.

Cliff squeezed putty from the gun, squinting against the glare of the sun on glass. "They call me Mr. Fix-It around here. But it's a good thing I know how to do this stuff, since Jerry thinks caulking is some kind of psychosomatic behavior and Roger refuses to do anything you can pay someone else to do."

"That's one of my goals in life, too," Angel confessed. "Paying someone to do stuff for me, like clean the house and wax the car. I want to spend my time doing something more interesting."

He grunted. "And more lucrative, I hope."

"The money isn't as important as the interest, or the work being something worthwhile."

"Spoken like a woman," he decreed. From his perch on the ladder, he frowned down at Angel. "No wonder women don't earn as much as men. They're more interested in charity than in business."

She released her hold on the ladder. "I'm going to get my breakfast now and try to forget you said that."

"Well, it's true," he called after her retreating form. "If they insisted on being paid for what they did . . ."

"The world would fall apart!" she finished as the screen door slammed behind her.

Lenzini growled.

Angel had finished eating her cereal and banana before Cliff finished his work on the window. She was trying not to be irritated with him, knowing that he loved to bait her. But he kept stepping on her toes in a way that made her question whether she should be here with him at all, and that made her edgy. When he arrived at the kitchen, he stuck a handful of fuchsia blossoms in before himself, calling, "Truce!" before sticking his head questioningly around the door.

"You're going to have to do better than that," she insisted as she wiped her hands on a dish towel. "You're going to have to push me in the hammock. I haven't been in a hammock in years."

"This one's about ten years old. You'll love its fresh mildew scent."

"You're just trying to talk me out of it."

By now he was all the way in the room, tucking the blossoms in the first container he found, an empty beer bottle. He ran water into it and placed it on the window sill above the sink. "I have about ten different kinds of fuchsias around my house in the city. Do you realize you've never even seen my house?"

"Yes, and I'm not sure I ever will if you don't agree to push me in the hammock."

"Pushy, pushy," he complained, moving to put his arms around her waist and pull her against him. "Wouldn't it be more fun if we laid down in the hammock together?"

"I'd have to see how strong it is. And you'd have to push me for a while first."

Lenzini shook his head unbelievingly. "A woman

with a one-track mind. Here I'm offering you the comfort and excitement of my very own gigantic body, and you'd rather be pushed in a hammock."

"Right." She stood on tiptoe and gave him a peck on the cheek. "Mind you, I'm getting very fond of your gigantic body, but we had a game when I was little. The first one to call for it got pushed in the hammock. You're as bad about trying to avoid it as my brothers were."

"I don't feel at all like one of your brothers," he grumbled. "Come on. I'll push you—for a while."

And thus began an idyllic day. Angel could not remember when she had last felt so luxuriously happy. The sun shone, the birds sang, the air smelled sweet, the stream tumbled merrily down the mountain. And Cliff. Obviously he had decided to behave himself because he was a pure delight. Every word he spoke was endearing, every deed he did was thoughtful. Angel decided to let her suspicions go, to accept him as he was presenting himself. Tomorrow he might very well revert to type, but today he was a paragon of loverlike virtue. If it hadn't been so delightful, it would have made her laugh.

They walked along a forest path crushing pine needles underfoot, their arms around each other's waists. And stopped to kiss in the shade of a granite boulder. They talked of their childhoods and of their special attraction to medicine. They talked about friends and colleagues. He talked about his wish to have a dog; she talked about the neighbor's cat that had semi-adopted her at the flat.

In mid-afternoon they took a brief swim and then returned to the cottage for a leisurely stretch of love-making, after which they both fell sleep. Angel awoke feeling languidly voluptuous. She turned on her side to observe Cliff as he slept, his body sprawled over two-thirds of the bed. Even asleep he looked imposing, with the straight nose and solid chin, the wide brow and vigorous hair. Only his lips seemed vulnerable, as though they concealed something mysterious and perhaps unknown even to him. Angel bent to kiss his lips just as the phone rang downstairs.

"Oh, hell," he muttered. "Did we leave the machine on?"

"I don't think so. Do you want me to get it?"

"No, that's all right." He jumped up naked from the bed and strode out of the room.

The phone had rung five or six times before he reached it, but apparently the caller had not given up, since Cliff also talked for some time. Angel could only hear the cadences of his voice, low and strong, but she knew it was a medical call. Someone had gone to the effort of tracking him down even when he wasn't on call and should have been in Los Angeles. It would probably mean they should head back, so she reluctantly deserted the bed and began to pack her small bag.

"Hey, I wanted to find you in bed," he said when he appeared in the doorway. "With your clothes off."

"To match you."

"Well, and for other reasons."

"I've got to get back, and I imagine you do, too. We can look in on Jimmy on the way down to see how he's doing." Angel had taken the call from Mrs. Thomas that morning again thanking them. She hadn't told Cliff that Mrs. Thomas had been so grateful that there were "a doctor and a nurse available." That kind of thing happened all the time, and she wasn't going to let it spoil her day.

"We probably have time to play around a little," he coaxed.

"You're just showing off. Everyone knows men pass their prime after eighteen."

"Oh, yeah?" He captured her and held her against his solid torso. "And I suppose you're approaching yours. That's a lot of hogwash."

"It's a scientific fact, Doctor." Angel kissed him temptingly and drew back. "Nope. I think we'd better hit the road. What was the call about?"

There was nothing like distracting medical people with a case. Almost unconsciously he began to pull on his clothes as he replied. "A postop patient who's having trouble. The resident wondered what I wanted to do since he didn't like the advice the doc on call gave him. These guys!"

But Angel knew it was more than that. No resident would have tracked Lenzini down to his cottage in the woods unless he really wanted *Lenzini's* advice on his own patient. Angel zipped her bag closed. "So you need to get back, too. Is there time to stop to see Jimmy?"

"Oh, sure. Probably a good idea, too, since we don't want to get sued if anything goes wrong."

"That's not why we're stopping."

"Well, it's part of the reason," he insisted. "Come on, Angel. It's in the back of every doctor's mind all the time. You wish it wasn't, I wish it wasn't. But it is." He cocked his head at her. "You're not going to deny that, are you?"

Angel sighed. "No, but I did want to see how he's doing. After all, he's our patient."

"Yeah, and it would be interesting to see what he looked like when he's not cyanotic."

Angel threw a pillow at him.

There was a special intimacy about the car ride back to San Francisco. After visiting Jimmy at the hospital, they put the top up on her car against the cooler night air. It felt almost like lying in bed after making love, with a spate of conversation followed by cozy silence. Cliff drove down the mountain roads, and Angel took over on flatter ground.

"Do you think," she asked when she'd been driving for a while, "that it's possible to go through all this school and training and not become cynical?"

"I'm not cynical."

"No, I don't mean you particularly. And maybe the word isn't cynical. Maybe it's cautious or skeptical or something like that." Angel waved a hand in frustration. "You know. Like what you said about being sued. And how everyone talks about patients, as though patients were responsible for being sick."

"Sometimes they are."

"But lots of times they're not." Angel checked the rearview mirror and passed a slow car she'd been following for a while. "When I started medical school in Madison, my whole class seemed to be full of idealistic men and women who were going into medicine to help people."

"That's how we all started," he said, making it sound like a long time ago.

"But does it have to change this way? I talk with some of them now, and it's like patients are the enemy, like they barely deserve the help we can offer."

Cliff shrugged. "It's the system, Angel. You work someone twenty-four hours a day, they're bound to get a bit edgy. And then there are all the drug addicts and alcoholics and crazies who just go back out after you've worked your hardest to help them and start up the old habits that are going to kill them. It's frustrating and disheartening."

"But they're human, and we don't always treat them like they are."

He regarded her curiously. "Are you getting burned out, Angel? Is it all getting to you?"

"Sometimes I think so." She sighed. "I hate having my picture of medicine change. I've started to feel naive for being idealistic because of the way other doctors treat me. Medicine has become a series of problems to be solved, too much to fit into a day, and a lot of one-upmanship. Some of the attendings are more interested in making money and living the good life than they are in their patients."

"You think doctors should devote their lives to their patients."

Angel could tell from the tone of his voice that he was mocking her. "I don't know. I think they should care about their patients. I think they should work hard and play hard, if they want, but they should care about their patients."

"So how many patients do you think these docs see in a day?" he asked. "Some of them thirty or forty, right? How much can they care about each of those patients? I don't mean that they won't do their best to treat them appropriately, to make some human contact, but just how deeply involved can they get in their lives?"

"Well, maybe that's one of the things that are wrong with the system: they see too many patients. And why do they do that? To make more money, or because it's expected of them, or because they think they're the only ones good enough to handle something. I want to see fewer patients when I'm in private practice."

Cliff's expression was skeptical. "That's what lots of doctors say, at first. You get caught up in the game, Angel. There's the money and the prestige and the expectations. You can't get too far out of step with everyone else or you feel the censure."

"You don't think having more women in the profession will help soften things a bit?"

"From what I see, we're just hardening the women up."

Angel responded with a flash of temper. "This macho training is so stupid! As though you had to be Superman to be a doctor. As though you had to stay awake, working, for thirty-six hours to prove yourself. Endangering patients, ruining your health, making a permanent impression on young doctors that however much money they earn later on, they deserve more because they've been put through hell. Well, I'll tell you something, Cliff. If I ran the game, it wouldn't be played this way."

"Why do you think we're keeping women from the top spots in medicine?" he teased.

"That's not funny! You *are* keeping women from top spots in medicine, and you always have."

"Hey, Angel. Not me personally."

"Oh, I imagine you personally have done your bit, Cliff. Didn't you just tell me you'd given a woman an exceptional rating for the first time the other day? Obviously you're judging women harder than men, because I assure you there have been plenty of exceptional women through your department."

"Maybe. It's harder on women, surgery."

"You surgeons just want to believe that because you're such a macho group. And you *make* it harder on women. There's nothing inherent in the female makeup that would make it more difficult for her to stand on her feet for hours, or make rapid decisions, or use her hands with skill in cutting and sewing. Women are *known* for their endurance and manual dexterity. They just don't see the necessity of some of the hoops you've set yourselves to jump through."

"Maybe being a surgeon means you like to jump through hoops," he suggested, not attempting to put a lid on the escalating argument. "Maybe that's the kind of personality it takes."

Angel gave a tsk of annoyance. "Don't you see that's what you've allowed yourselves to believe? Sure it takes nerve to be a surgeon. It takes liking a challenge and being sure of yourself. There are plenty of women who fit that profile, and there would be more if you didn't discourage them."

"Now that's a contradiction. If they fit that profile, they wouldn't get discouraged."

"That *sounds* right, but it's not. Medical training is hard enough without extra burdens being placed on women. You know, that day I met you in the operating room, I bet you wouldn't have refused me the chance to remove the ovary if I'd been a *man* in the family-practice program."

"Hmmm." Cliff seemed to be thinking back to that fateful day in the OR. "I'm not sure. I think it had more to do with Williams. If he'd stood up for you. Probably he would have for a man."

"Right. Men think with their dicks."

"It's not that simple, Angel. It's got a lot to do with tradition and a respect for the profession and wanting to see its best preserved. Not wanting to lower our standards."

"Since when did anybody have to lower their standards for women? It's more likely the other way around."

"Well, academically maybe. But we're talking about clinical practice. At least I think we are."

"We can talk about any facet you like," Angel assured him. "So what's your criteria for a good clinician? One who's right all the time? One who gives the patient a feeling of confidence? One who spends time with patients? One who keeps up with the work load? One who keeps up with the literature?" Angel made an expansive gesture with one hand. "I'll bet patients have a different definition of who's a good doctor than doctors do."

"Yeah, but we're right."

"Are we?" Angel glanced over at him in the gathering darkness. "There are a whole lot more of them than there are of us."

"But we've got the knowledge and the skills. We know how to judge our own performance. Sometimes a patient thinks a doc is great because the doc has a good bedside manner, when he's actually provided shoddy care. Only another doctor would know."

"I suppose." Angel snuck a glance at him. "But when another doctor testifies for someone in a malpractice suit, other doctors are outraged."

"They're hired guns," Cliff retorted, disgusted.

"So what's a patient supposed to do? Put up with shoddy care because doctors don't want to testify against each other?"

"Everybody makes mistakes sometimes, Angel."

"Absolutely. And why shouldn't a patient be recompensed for our mistakes if they're big, bad, incompetent ones?"

Cliff reached into the backseat for a soft drink from the cooler. "Want one?"

"Sure. But don't change the subject."

"I'm not. I'm thinking." He snapped open a soda and handed it to her. "Everything gets out of proportion in a court. The patient is made to look helpless and vilely mistreated. The doctor is made to seem incompetent and careless, if not downright criminally negligent."

"Sometimes they are."

"Well, not as often as lawyers make them out to be." He snapped open his own can and took a long draw. "Lawyers are such sleazebags, acting like they're interested in justice when all they care about is money."

"They could say pretty much the same thing about us, except that instead of justice we're pretending we're interested in a patient's well-being."

"You know, Angel, you're entirely too open-minded on this subject. Any self-respecting doctor should hate lawyers and be extremely skeptical of patients."

"So I've noticed," she said ironically. Angel watched as an eighteen-wheeler roared past her doing more than seventy. They were getting into heavier traffic now as they approached the Bay Area. "You know, when I was an intern, I assisted at a delivery where everything seemed to be going okay until after the head presented. I was going to deliver the front-facing shoulder but that didn't work. Then I tried the posterior shoulder, but it wouldn't budge. My resident took over then, since I'd never been faced with shoulder dystocia before."

"Too late for a C-section. Hell of a problem."

"You said it. Paul tried the McRoberts maneuver and the Woods maneuver. Usually the corkscrew method works, I guess, but not this time. If we didn't get the kid out, it was going to die or be brain damaged. We tried pressure on the mother's abdomen; didn't work. Paul considered breaking the clavicle, but he'd never done it and hadn't ever seen it done, and he was afraid of severing an important blood vessel. We were about to get drastic and do a Zavanelli—push the baby back and do a C-section. But we applied a little more suprapubic pressure and finally the baby popped out."

"Baby okay?"

"Not completely. At five minutes his Apgar evaluation was 9, but one arm didn't look so good, and we learned later that the nerve injury would be permanent. He wouldn't be able to use the arm for much.

But hell, he was alive. Pretty good under the circumstances."

"Everybody was sued," Lenzini guessed.

"Yeah. It hangs over you, a malpractice suit. The mom was from my continuity clinic. Her pelvis was a good size, the baby didn't seem to be particularly big, and, in fact, didn't weigh all that much. He just had wide shoulders. The mother wouldn't come back to me after she filed the suit. Maybe that's best. Maybe you can't treat someone who's suing you."

"I don't think even *you* are that objective, Angel," he said. "People come to expect perfect outcomes—from pregnancy, from surgery, from medical treatment in general. Hell, these people would probably have sued you if you *had* broken the clavicle, too. You can't win in some cases. Unfortunately, they're usually the most difficult ones where you've actually performed rather heroically."

"Paul says the hospital will settle to get it all behind us, but that doesn't seem fair either, when we didn't do anything wrong."

"Hey, what did I tell you? Lawyers are money-grubbing sleazebags."

"I don't suppose we can blame them for taking cases like that."

"Sure we can. You and I know the case has no merit. A child suffered, but it wasn't the doctor's fault."

"People think someone should pay when they get an imperfect child. Why is that? There have been imperfect children from the beginning of time. It doesn't mean a doctor is at fault."

"Well, we've got them thinking we're God. That's

probably part of the problem. It's the same thing with surgery, Angel. You can tell them over and over that you can't guarantee the results, that twenty percent of the time something goes wrong, but if it goes wrong with *them*—pow! Lawsuit."

"I wonder if surgeons get sued more than medical doctors. You know, the irritation factor of arrogance." Her eyes sparkled with mischief.

"Surgeons are only marginally more arrogant than other doctors. Patients, for instance, don't notice our arrogance as much as medical doctors do."

"But they must notice that surgeons are the only ones who consider an operation a success when the patient dies."

"I've never considered an operation successful if the patient died," Lenzini protested, though he nodded thoughtfully as he added, "Sometimes technically an operation really did go very well, though, before the patient expired."

"You're incorrigible."

"Probably." He reached over to rub her hand on the steering wheel. "Don't you think maybe that's something you like in me?"

"God, I hope not."

Chapter Twelve

Angel had been looking forward to her obstetrical rotation. Despite the problem she'd told Cliff about during the first year in the family-practice residency, for the most part the obstetrics floor was the happiest one in any hospital, and it was exhilarating to work there. Babies came at any hour of the day or night, but it always seemed to doctors that they predominantly chose the late night to show.

The obstetrical floor at Fielding had had changes over the last decade to bring it in line with the contemporary attempt to make delivery seem more natural and homelike. There were three birthing rooms that were some interior decorator's idea of a woman's bedroom at home, though Angel might have done them a bit less cutesy. Lacy lamp shades and frilly curtains were not necessarily her idea of homey.

Still, it was a great improvement for the mother from the blinding white and hard metal of the usual delivery room. And for the majority of deliveries, there was no need for all that high-tech equipment. The medical staff were always intent on safe deliveries, so they stepped in to intervene when things got a bit rough, but for the most part they allowed nature to take its course.

Angel, of course, as a third-year resident, was dealing more with high-risk pregnancies. The management of complicated deliveries and first assisting at cesarean sections had become her chief role during this period. As with all other procedures involving surgery, she pushed to learn what she could and to perform as much by herself, under supervision, as she could. C-sections were not, in themselves, particularly difficult. Often they were performed, however, under the most demanding, time-restricted circumstances to provide the best possible outcome—a healthy mother and baby.

The on-call schedule was every third night, and though there were nights when Angel was able to sleep for a few hours, most nights seemed to brim with urgent situations. Patients from her continuity clinic of the first and second years were more frequently showing up pregnant and eventually delivering, often during her nights on call. She was particularly challenged by the care of a diabetic young woman who probably never should have become pregnant in the first place because of existing problems. Serious complications had threatened both the mother and the fetus throughout the eight months so far.

When Sharon presented in labor a month early, Angel was actually pleased to be on duty. After all, she'd followed this patient for months, knew her history inside out, and felt prepared for whatever emergencies might arise. Sharon, a thin, anxious Hispanic woman, grinned at Angel. "Just my luck.

This baby has been nothing but trouble for you all along, and now you get to present him to the world."

A previous ultrasound had determined that she was carrying a boy, about which she and her husband were very pleased. Angel tucked her hair into her surgical cap and cautioned, "You'll have to have him within the next twelve hours, Sharon, or I'm out of here."

"*No problemao*. The nurse said I was already practically fully dilated."

"Really? Always in a hurry." Angel checked the fetal monitoring strip, which was almost normal. "Things look okay."

"Ohhh," Sharon moaned as she suffered through a contraction. "You'd think there'd be an easier way to get kids, huh?"

"Yep. This seems pretty old-fashioned and low-tech." Angel rested her hand for a moment on the patient's abdomen. She was still enamored of the fact that one minute there was just this round protrusion on a woman and the next a living, breathing child.

But the monitoring strip now showed deep decelerations. There was a chance the baby wasn't getting enough oxygen. A definite indication for an emergency cesarean section. But the heart rate could stabilize. Too many C-sections were done prematurely, at the first hint of trouble. Angel would have to sit tight and see what developed. Everything depended on how quickly Sharon became ready to deliver.

"Does Luis want to be with you for the birth?"

"Nah. He says it's woman's work." Sharon's eyes misted momentarily. "I tried, you know. I said he should come with me to the classes, but he wouldn't. These guys, they think it's not macho. Some of them anyway. Like Luis."

"Well, we'll manage just fine by ourselves. Trudy here thinks men get in the way."

Trudy—white of hair and starched of uniform— had been a nurse for forty years. "Especially the Hispanic men," Trudy said, playing along. "They faint at the sight of blood, macho scoundrels that they are."

Sharon laughed briefly before another contraction caught her. Trudy held her hand, and Angel leaned down to study the monitoring strip. "They're coming pretty close together," Angel said. "Won't be long now."

"I feel like I have to push," Sharon gasped.

"That's great." Angel took another look at the strip. Better but still showing a slowed heartbeat. Usually the heartbeat was one-twenty, one-fifty when they were about to be born. But Sharon was ready to push. That made a big difference. Angel and Trudy went into action. Sharon was dilated to ten centimeters, and Angel drew a stool up close to the bottom of the delivery bed. "When you have to push, bear down as hard as you can. This baby is ready to be born."

Sharon's brow drew down and broke out in sweat as she attempted to push with all her strength. Trudy wiped her forehead, and Angel said, "That's great. Ready? Push now. Push, push, push, push. Great! That's great. Breathe, breathe, breathe. You're doing a good job. Keep it up."

"Wow!" Sharon panted. "This is hard work."

"You said it. Okay, time to push again. Push, push,

push. That's it. Let's get this baby out. Take a break now. Breathe, breathe. You're doing super."

The monitoring strip had gotten no worse. Angel knew they were pretty well locked into a vaginal birth now, and she found herself almost holding her breath. "Here we go again. Okay, push, push, push. Great. Push, keep pushing. I can see his head now. Lots of dark hair. Just a little more. Okay, relax."

Trudy cast a worried look at Angel. Clearly Sharon was tiring, and the decelerations hadn't improved significantly. They needed to get that baby out of there. Angel asked Trudy for the Mityvac, a suction instrument. "We're going to put this on his head to help draw the baby out, Sharon. It will just be that extra bit of help we need."

Sharon bit her lip and nodded. "Anything you say, Dr. Crawford."

With the next contraction, Angel used the Mityvac to draw the baby down. She could see the infant's head and called, "Great, Sharon! You're just about there. Push real hard, then we'll have him out."

Angel cupped the baby's head as it burst out with the next contraction. The umbilical cord was wound twice around his neck, cutting off oxygen to the child before he could breathe on his own outside his mother's body. His face turned down, and he automatically rotated forty-five degrees. Another push brought the first shoulder out, and he slipped into Angel's waiting arms.

Quickly slipping her fingers under the cord, Angel maneuvered it off over his head. Almost immediately he took a deep breath and howled, pinking up very nicely. "Look!" she said, laughing. "He's here and he's loud and he's gorgeous."

"Is he okay?" Sharon asked. "Can I hold him?"

"Sure. He looks fine. We'll have the pediatrician check him out to make sure, but he seems to have all the necessary equipment."

And then something odd happened to Angel. For the first time in all the long years of studying and training to be a doctor, she found herself feeling just like an ordinary untrained woman, totally astonished by the miracle and with an almost physical longing to experience this amazing process herself. It was with reluctance that she handed the newborn child to Trudy to place in Sharon's arms. She wanted, at the moment, just to hold him for a few more minutes, to experience the newness of him, the tiny weight, and the excitement of new life.

How very strange of me, she thought, trying to shrug off the experience. She had delivered more than a hundred babies. She had shared the excitement of the moment and been charmed by the wonder, but she had not felt this visceral response before. For a moment she could imagine what it must feel like, having this new life growing in her womb, erupting into life outside of her. Angel had always wanted to have children—someday. Briefly, she felt regret that it was not she lying there on the delivery table with a child in her arms.

And then she shrugged and turned her attention to finishing off the delivery. Angel was used to submerging her own feelings to the demands of her profession. Her focus moved naturally to the afterbirth and checking it for any indication of problems.

Within a short while, others were taking the baby to the nursery and Sharon to her room. Angel snapped off her gloves and tossed them into the trash. Her time would come.

Cliff was astonished to find his sister sitting in her car outside his house on Twin Peaks. He pulled into his driveway and hopped out of his car to give her a big hug. Catherine was five-ten in her stocking feet, on the thin side, with long straight brown hair. She burst into tears when he exclaimed, "Hey, I didn't expect you! Did you call?"

Awkwardly he patted her shoulder, mumbling, "Everything's going to be all right, sweetie. It's not Mark or the folks, is it? Nobody's died, have they?"

"No," she hiccuped. "No one's died." But her tears didn't stop, and they stood that way for some time.

"We could go inside," Cliff suggested, nervously glancing around him. "They're going to think you're some girl I've gotten pregnant."

With a shuddering breath, she stepped back from him. "Yeah, I'd forgotten how much tears bother you. You and Dad."

"Tears don't bother me," he insisted, shepherding her into the house by the front door, which he very seldom used. He left his car straddling the sidewalk; he could move it into the garage later when things had settled down.

Catherine Lenzini Ferguson was twenty-six years of age. She had been married for two years and five months. Cliff distinctly remembered her wedding, a formal, extravagant affair that their parents had insisted upon, even though Catherine had wanted something much simpler. Cliff felt moderately comfortable with his brother-in-law, owner of a computer company in San Mateo. Lenzini pushed Catherine in the direction of the bathroom, saying, "I'll mix you a martini while you wash your face."

"Make it white wine," she sighed as she disappeared.

Before he even opened the bottle of wine, Cliff dialed Angel's apartment number, but there was no answer. He left a message on the machine for her to call him. She was supposed to show up at his house, for the first time, at any minute, depending on when she left the hospital. He considered paging her, but decided against it when he heard the bathroom door open.

Though Cliff considered himself something of a wine connoisseur, his sister was even more knowledgeable, and he held up two bottles for her inspection. "Which will it be?" he asked.

"The Chardonnay," she said indifferently. "God, I'm tired of Chardonnay. I hope the pundits move on to something else soon."

"I've got sherry or a white Zin or a good Riesling."

"How about the sherry? That would be a nice change." Catherine slid onto a tall stool that most guests fumbled over. "I see you still have the same cleaning woman."

He regarded her quizzically, and she said, "The trivet on the wall. She always hangs it upside down. It's supposed to be a Picasso takeoff."

Cliff, chagrined, restored the trivet to its proper position. "I hadn't noticed."

"No, you wouldn't. That's all right." Catherine

shrugged her narrow shoulders. "You have good taste naturally, Cliff. And then, I think, Sally was a good influence on you when you were decorating." She turned to regard him closely. "Do you ever hear from her?"

"No. That was all over a long time ago."

Catherine rolled her eyes. "February. A long time ago."

"I'm seeing someone else now."

Catherine blinked at him. "Really? I'm surprised."

Cliff grunted as he poured them each a glass of sherry. "Why would you be surprised? I'm a red-blooded man."

"It's not that. It's just that you were so fond of Sally. You took it hard when she left."

"It just seemed that way. I'd sort of expected that we'd stay together. Her decision was out of the blue, as far as I was concerned." He shrugged and raised his glass to her in a silent toast. "I'm good at getting on with my life."

Though she stared at him doubtfully for a full minute, Cliff did not back down from the patently false statement. He had, it was true, continued work; in fact, he attacked his medical life with a vigor that was little short of obsessive. The hours he'd worked would have done credit to an intern, and he'd driven several secretaries to distraction with his volume of dictation on patients. Getting on with his life had meant leaving no time for anything but work and sleep, and a few scattered, on-the-run meals.

Catherine followed her brother into the living room, which had a view over downtown San

Francisco. It was a clear evening, and the sky was beginning to streak with shades of pink and orange and purple. "Gorgeous," Catherine said. "You really have the most spectacular view. It's a shame you're never here to see it."

"I *am* here," he insisted. "You see me right in front of you, and it's not even seven o'clock."

"So you're better."

"Cath, it's not that I'm better. I'm fine. I've been fine. It was everyone else who thought I took Sally's leaving so hard."

"Horse manure. You were a wreck. Though I must admit, it might have been more the shock of someone rejecting you, Dr. Clifford Lenzini, the magnificent surgeon, rather than your own emotional state." She caught her lip between her teeth for a moment. "But I don't think so."

"Emotional state!" he snorted. "Hell, everyone wants to make out like I was a basket case. You'd think I'd ended up on the psych ward."

"Well, I'm grateful for your friend Jerry. You don't appreciate him enough."

"I appreciate him! I own a cottage with him and bring my problems to him. I *share*, for God's sake."

Catherine giggled. "You're too much. Someday someone's actually going to make you face what's going on inside you, Cliff. I hope I'm not there when it happens."

"Why? Do you think I'm going to crumble like a cracker? I'm made of sterner stuff, my dear sister."

"We both are, aren't we?" she asked, leaning back against the sofa and briefly closing her eyes. "That's the way we were brought up."

"There was nothing wrong with the way we were brought up."

"Oh, grow up," she snapped. "There were lots of things wrong with the way we were brought up, just like there are with everyone else. You do better if you acknowledge them and accept them, rather than pretending they don't exist."

"Hey, you're beginning to sound like that Bradshaw fellow," he protested. "None of this damaged inner-child stuff, Cath. We had a very ordinary childhood. No one abused us. There was nothing dysfunctional, or whatever they call it, about our family."

"Wasn't there? I suppose not. They're both good people, Mom and Dad. I'm not saying they aren't."

"What are you saying?"

"That we weren't necessarily equipped for the real world, you and I. All that privilege, that attitude of superiority. The country-club life. I guess it worked okay for you, in some ways, different ways than it did for me."

"So what's the problem?" Cliff asked, knowing he'd put off asking as long as he could. "I take it this has something to do with the tears on my arrival."

"God, you're so astute," she grumbled. "I can't imagine why I thought it would help to talk to you."

"Because I'm reasonable, available, and incredibly clever," he suggested.

Catherine let out a puff of disgust. "Exactly. And not at all self-satisfied. Look, Cliff, I have a problem with Mark."

"Well, it better not be a sexual problem because I

am not going to discuss sexual problems with my sister."

"No, it's nothing like that." Catherine took a sip of the sherry and absently replaced the glass on the glass coffee table. "He wants me to get a job."

"I beg your pardon?"

"The economy's bad, his computer company is hurting these days, and he wants me to help support us."

"You must be kidding. *He* must be kidding. What the hell could you do that would make enough money to be the least help?"

Rather than being hurt, Catherine said, "Exactly. I don't think I'm cut out to be a waitress, and I don't think they make much money anyway. Besides, Cliff, I do work. I mean, I have my painting. It's my vocation. He says if it doesn't make money, it's not a job."

"Crass commercialism," Cliff teased, but he didn't really find Mark's attitude amusing. "He used to be proud of your painting. Isn't he anymore?"

Moisture glistened suddenly in his sister's eyes, but she merely shrugged. "He says it's a hobby and one I'm good at, but that I should look around me and see what all the other wives are doing. They're all out there being doctors and lawyers and executives in *Fortune* 500 corporations. He says I could do that if I set my mind to it."

"And what about your painting?"

She looked down at her hands folded in her lap. "I guess he thinks I could do that in my spare time." She smiled wanly. "There are no more wall spaces for my paintings, Cliff. I've filled the house, so . . ."

"Hell!"

Twice she started to say something, and stopped. Finally she managed, "That's what I meant about the privilege, Cliff. All the other women of my generation were sort of prepared to have a career with financial rewards. I paint. I don't know how to do anything else. I've never wanted to do anything else. I thought I'd always be able to do it, you know? I mean, Mom didn't go out to work."

"You know I could help you financially if that would solve the problem."

Catherine wrinkled her nose. "Thanks, but I don't think so. I feel like such a jerk, you know, whining about having to go out and do what everyone else does."

"Everyone else isn't a painter."

"Well, art is a luxury. Especially if you're not good enough to sell your work."

"You know very well you could sell your work if you compromised. It doesn't sound like even Mark is suggesting that you compromise."

"No." Restless, Catherine rose from the sofa and walked to the huge windows overlooking the city. She looked young and elegant outlined against the dramatic backdrop. "I thought we'd have a family, and I'd stay home like Mom did and all the while I'd paint, because I'd have household help, like Mom did, and now everything is screwed up. I resent him for not earning enough money, and I feel terribly guilty because I resent him, and spoiled and very un-American. I . . ."

The doorbell rang, and Cliff, surprised, bolted from his chair. "Oh, my God. I forgot about Angel."

"Your girlfriend?"

"Um, yeah. She hasn't ever been here before, Cath. Um, do you think we could talk more about this later?"

"Your girlfriend hasn't ever been here before?" she said, amused. "And her name is Angel? This doesn't sound at all like you, Cliff."

He was on his way to the door and merely glanced at her. The bag of groceries he'd purchased for their dinner was still in the car and of course he hadn't done a thing about it. When he opened the door, he blocked the living room from Angel's view.

"My sister's here," he informed her before he even said hello. "She dropped in unexpectedly. I haven't done anything about dinner."

"So would you rather we put this off till another night?" Angel asked.

Cliff frowned and scratched his head. "Hell, if we try to do that, it will be another week."

"I don't mind."

"Well, I do." He hesitated a moment, and then pushed the door open behind himself. "Come on in. Let me get the groceries, though."

If he thought she'd wait for him, he was mistaken. By the time he had moved the car into the garage and brought the groceries through to the kitchen, he found Angel and Catherine already talking in front of the windows.

"I don't *think* he's ever mentioned you," Angel said with a grin. "He thinks anything that went on in his life before I met him is none of my business. I suppose he'd have gotten around to mentioning you sooner or later, though, because you live so close by."

"I never said that," Lenzini protested. "And I'm sure I've mentioned Catherine. She paints."

"No, you've never mentioned her," Angel assured him. "I would have remembered. You've never mentioned your parents except in terms of what your father does and where they live. And that you made Cornish game hens for them for their anniversary once."

"Well," Catherine said, "I taught him how to make the game hens. He really should have mentioned that to you."

"No, he led me to believe that their preparation was a discovery of his very own. Of course, the time he attempted to make them for me, he cremated them."

"I did not! We had to leave them on the grill when we went with that kid to the hospital. There was nothing I could do about them."

"He always lets medicine get in the way of his other talents," Catherine confided. "My dad had planned for him to be a neurosurgeon, but Cliff refused to be railroaded. *His* kind of medicine turned out to be general surgery, and nothing Dad did could convince him to change his mind."

"I hated neurosurgery," Cliff muttered. "You have to work on people's brains."

"No kidding," Angel said, laughing at him. "So what's wrong with working on people's brains?"

"It seems so intimate," he admitted. "And so unfathomable, really. You know, cut a zillionth of an inch too far, and they can't walk anymore. I like a little room for error."

"Not that he ever takes any, or gives any," Catherine said. She gestured toward the kitchen. "Want us to watch you cook dinner?"

"Actually I bought everything. And I'm not sure there's enough for three of us. Let's eat out."

Catherine looked at Angel, who shook her head. "We'll make do," Catherine decided, undeterred by her brother's look of disgruntlement. "It's quieter here, and I'd like to have a chance to talk in peace. Angel won't mind, will you?"

"Nope." Angel turned to Cliff. "Catherine and I can set the table while you get the food ready."

Lenzini growled and headed for the kitchen.

Chapter Thirteen

Angel wasn't at all sure she should have stayed. Not that she wanted to miss an evening with Cliff any more than he did. But there was Catherine, whose eyes were slightly red-rimmed, hinting of some tears earlier. It seemed entirely possible that Catherine was here to have a heart-to-heart discussion with her brother and Angel would only be in the way.

When Cliff had disappeared through the kitchen door and she and Catherine had moved into the dining area, Angel made a quick decision. "I think I'll go," she said, picking up the sweater she'd worn over her blouse. "Cliff and I can see each other any time. You probably don't have a chance to meet with him very often."

Catherine cocked her head at Angel in a way very similar to Cliff's. "Don't go. I've already told him what my problem is, and I can't imagine why I thought it would make any difference. I guess I just needed someone to hear it who's come from the same place I have. And he understands. There's just nothing he can do about it."

"You never know. Surgeons just hate not being

able to act. He'll probably figure out some impossibly obscure way that he can help you—like sending you a personalized license plate, or getting you a dog." Angel still hesitated, her sweater in her arms. "He means well, I can tell. He just doesn't always have the picture on the right channel."

Catherine grinned. "Yeah, I've noticed that about him. But it's not just him, either. My husband's the same way. They're not seeing quite the same picture as I am." She moved over to where Angel was standing and took the sweater from her arms. "Stay. It was nothing earth-shattering, I promise. My husband wants me to get a job."

"What kind of job?"

"Oh, anything that will make lots of money. Very unrealistic of him. I don't even know how to type, let alone use a computer. I think he imagines me as some kind of junior executive in a tailored gray suit that matches one of his."

Under the teasing, Angel could hear a real distress. "I thought Cliff said you were a painter."

"Yes, well, that's only good as long as you have the time for it." Catherine sighed and put Angel's sweater on the arm of the sofa. "Cliff has a couple of my things. I'll show them to you after dinner."

"Great. I haven't been here before, but I've been to Cliff's cottage. There were some watercolors of yours there."

Catherine shook her head. "Those are Cliff's. He didn't tell you, did he? He thinks it's not macho to do them. I told him Prince Charles does watercolors, but he said Prince Charles was a wimp."

"They seemed rather good to me," Angel suggested, hesitant.

"Yeah, he's got talent. But he'd never spend the time to develop it with artistic things. Maybe he'd learn how to skin deer or something."

Angel grimaced. "I hope not. Anyhow, I was just so sure they couldn't be his that I didn't ask. Guess I made a few assumptions of my own."

"Exactly the ones he'd want you to make," Catherine assured her. She pulled open a drawer in the sideboard and started taking out flatwear. "Were you serious that he doesn't tell you anything about his life before you?"

Angel shrugged. "Pretty much. He doesn't seem to be interested in what I did before we met, and he expects me to restrain my curiosity about him. But my roommate told me he'd been living with someone for a long time." Angel glanced questioningly at Catherine, but didn't wait for her to say something. "It makes a difference to me. Someone like Cliff wouldn't live with a woman for a long time if he weren't really fond of her. At least I don't think he would."

"No." Catherine made a moue of annoyance. "We were discussing her just before you came. Well, I was, at any rate. Cliff would have been perfectly content to drop the subject. But really, he's going to have to be the one to talk with you."

"Of course." Angel placed green-plaid napkins at three places around the oak table where Catherine was distributing flatwear. "Except that he won't."

"Men are just incredibly good at that kind of thing, aren't they? If they don't want to talk about a subject, or if they don't want to take care of something, they simply manage not to do it." Catherine shook her head wonderingly. "Do you suppose it's a gene they have?"

"I call it the stonewalling gene," Angel confessed. "My dad and my brothers all have it. Mom and I don't. Women can learn it, of course, but it takes time. Doctors are supposed to learn it, if they don't already have it. I'm a doctor, by the way. I don't think Cliff mentioned that. A third-year family-practice resident."

"Family practice," Catherine mused. "Does that mean you want to practice in the wilds?"

"Something like that."

"Oh, boy. You and Cliff really were made for each other, weren't you?"

Angel laughed, and sighed. "Right. So maybe it doesn't matter after all if I know about this woman he was with."

"It may matter a lot why he isn't with her any more." Catherine lit a candle she'd placed in the center of the round table. "It drives him crazy when I make things all chichi. But I like getting his goat. It makes him feel more human to me. Like Dad, he can sometimes be intimidating and distant."

"Who can?" Cliff asked as he pushed through the swinging door from the kitchen.

"You, of course. Who else would we be talking about?" Catherine took two plates from him and set them at places on the table. "This looks great. Find a new caterer?"

"I'm not intimidating," he protested. "And I'm certainly not distant. You think if someone doesn't spill their guts to you, there's something wrong with them. When will women stop expecting men to spill their guts?"

"Never," Catherine and Angel said together. "But we know they won't because of their stonewalling gene," Catherine added.

"I'm not even going to ask," he insisted, heading back to the kitchen. "It's dangerous to leave two women alone together these days."

"You don't know the half of it," Catherine muttered. When Cliff gave her a real look of concern, she merely smiled. "The food," she reminded him.

Angel was a little nervous about the way things were going, but she realized Catherine meant to help her, and she could use the help. It would be foolish to become more involved with Cliff if . . . what? If he'd just been in love with someone else? Certainly if he still was. Was his not discussing Sally simply a matter of privacy, or concealment? Angel accepted the spot between Cliff and Catherine that they both indicated, as if it had been used by others in her position before.

"So do you cook?" Catherine asked Angel as she passed on a plate of stuffed grape leaves.

"Not much. I know how, I guess, because my mom taught me, but I haven't much interest, or much time."

"Sally cooked," Catherine mused. "Only gourmet things, though. I don't suppose she'd have made a chicken-salad sandwich, would she, Cliff?"

Angel was awestruck by her boldness. This young woman was having trouble getting her way?

Cliff scowled at his sister and said nothing.

"She made moussaka," Catherine remembered as she passed the self-same Greek dish on to Angel. "Always with lamb, which is best, and she had the nerve to serve it with retsina. Have you ever had retsina?"

"Ugh!" Angel made a face and helped herself to the casserole. "You must have to develop a special taste for it. Who would want to ruin wine with resin?"

Cliff seemed to think he had something to offer to the conversation at this point, so he said, "Actually it was originally the Germans trying to ruin the Greek wine supply. The Greeks outsmarted them by drinking it anyway—and not even dying."

"When Mark and I were in Greece on our honeymoon, we sat at a little café on the beach and ate Greek salads with this incredible bread to dip in olive oil. The sun was beating down and the water was this intense shade of blue and the sand was so hot it glared. And we drank retsina, a whole bottle. And by the time we were finished, we were a bit tipsy, but we'd developed a taste for it." Catherine smiled reminiscently. "You and Sally went to Greece once, didn't you, Cliff? Did you try retsina there?"

"I did not go to Greece with Sally," he growled.

"Oh, that's right. It was Italy, part of your European swing last summer. Well, you wouldn't have had retsina in Italy."

"Why are you doing this?" he demanded. "I thought you were here for my help."

"I've decided to help you, instead," she retorted, virtuous. "Angel doesn't seem to know anything about Sally."

Angel considered putting in a protest here, but held her tongue. If Catherine was willing to do battle for her, she was willing to be patient.

"Angel doesn't need to know anything about Sally." Cliff turned to Angel to ask, "You don't even know who Sally is, do you?"

"I gather she's the woman you lived with for so long. And took trips with and had dinner parties with. I think she's probably someone I should know about."

"Nonsense. She's gone. She doesn't even live in San Francisco anymore. She's in Boston or somewhere. Catherine is making a mountain out of a molehill."

Catherine considered this possibility. "If you'd been married before, you would naturally tell someone about your former wife. What's the difference? You lived with Sally for five years."

Angel felt her breath catch in her chest. "Five years? That's longer than half the medical marriages we run into at the hospital."

"Well, what was I supposed to tell you?" Cliff demanded. "I *wasn't* married to this woman. I haven't had any contact with her since she left. She has nothing to do with my life now."

"That's only partially true," Catherine said. "She chose these napkins, for instance."

"Who cares about the damned napkins?" Lenzini roared. "I could throw them away. They don't mean anything. I don't keep them because she got them; I keep them because they're in the drawer!"

Angel considered the green-plaid napkins. "Well, I don't know. They don't really seem like you, Cliff.

You probably should have black ones with your initials on them in gold thread."

Catherine giggled. "Yes, and matching place mats in raw silk."

"*If* I cared about place mats and napkins in the first place, I'd probably go to Crate and Barrel and tell them to put something together for me that matched," he grumbled. "I'm not likely to have something that looks like church vestments."

"I remember your bringing Sally to my wedding," Catherine said as she helped herself to the Greek salad, making sure she had her share of the black olives. "She wore that smashing linen suit, remember? And you guys stayed at the Del Coronado. I've always wanted to stay there, but Mom and Dad insist on our staying with them when we're down."

"They have plenty of room."

"Yes, but it's hardly a vacation that way."

Of course he would have taken Sally to his sister's wedding, Angel realized, if he was living with her at the time. There suddenly seemed to be a lot about Cliff that she didn't know, and in addition to what she did, she felt a sinking in her stomach. He wasn't being open with her, at the very least. He could attempt to justify that by saying he was preserving his privacy, and hers, but right now his reasons looked a lot more complicated—and a lot more worrisome. And just what had Catherine meant that it might matter a lot why he wasn't with Sally anymore?

The brother and sister continued to banter, but Cliff threw glances her way when she remained silent. Finally he turned to her and asked, "Don't you like it, the Greek food? I've got other stuff in the fridge if you'd prefer."

"Actually, it's great. I'm just thinking, about you and Sally and your not telling me about her. Catherine's right, you know. She was a real part of your life, even if she isn't now." Angel frowned, trying to explain what she meant. "If it had been me, I'm not sure I'd like your just shutting me out."

"She left *me*, Angel. Not the other way around."

"Even so." Angel lifted her shoulders in a helpless gesture. "Five years, Cliff. And now it's like she never existed for you."

"That's not true. I just don't talk about it." Cliff turned to his sister and said, "See what you've started?"

"No," Angel said, "we started this discussion in the mountains. I was willing to let it go then, but it would have come up, and soon. Catherine was only trying to speed things up."

"Well, I don't want them speeded up."

"I know."

Catherine helped herself to more salad. "See, there was plenty of food. Cliff, everything can't always go your way. Sometimes you have to compromise. Sometimes you have to realize that the other person has different needs than you, and ones that have to be honored."

"Oh, for God's sake!" Cliff's eyes flashed with frustration. "You sound like some kind of marriage counselor. And why are you here, Catherine? Because you and your husband don't agree about something, where you're having trouble adapting to his *needs*."

"The reason I'm here," she retorted quite calmly, "is because I'm trying to accommodate to his needs. If I weren't, I'd just ignore them, like you do."

"I don't ignore people's needs!"

"Sure you do," Catherine said. "You don't even know you're doing it because you assume everybody wants what you want. And, surprise, they don't!"

Angel shook her head in wonder. "See how helpful it is to have someone around who knows you so well? I could have knocked my head against a wall for a week trying to get across the same thing Catherine's just said."

Cliff regarded the two of them with astonishment. "That's simply untrue. Women have a tendency to do that, you know. Gang up on a man and tell him what's wrong with him. But it doesn't make what they say any more true. I'm not some kind of heel. I don't ride roughshod over other people."

"No one is saying you're a heel," Catherine assured him. "You're a terrific guy. But like most men, you have an incredible blind spot. Now, you can argue that I have blind spots, too, and I wouldn't deny it, but we're not actually concerned with me right now."

"Even though she came here for your help," Angel pointed out. "Here's your poor, selfless sister trying to help you when she herself is in need. Truly, you're a lucky man."

"I don't want your help! I don't want anyone's help! I don't need help."

Catherine shrugged. "Okay, then, let's work on my problem after all. What am I going to do about it?"

Patently relieved, Cliff explained to Angel, "Her

husband wants her to get a job, which is not a good idea because one, Catherine has never worked and has no office skills, two, she's an artist, and three, anything she could do would earn so little it's hardly worth the effort."

"So why does he want her to get a job?" Angel asked, confused.

"Because his business isn't going well," Catherine said. She pushed the olive pits to the side of her plate and helped herself to more moussaka. "I'd like to help out if there were any way I could do it logically. But I wasn't really trained to work, you know? Which sounds pretty wimpy, I suppose, to a family-practice resident."

Angel frowned. "I chose to be a doctor. You chose to be an artist. There was an understanding that you'd do that when you married, right?"

"Sure, but times change." Catherine sighed. "Lots of women who never expected to have had to go out to work. Why should I be any different than they are?"

"Why, indeed?" Cliff interposed rhetorically. "Because you'd be useless being a waitress or a cashier. And I doubt if you'd stand for being a receptionist. Plus you'd make next to nothing at any of those jobs. Mark can't have thought this through very well."

His sister shook her head hopelessly. "But I've pointed all that out to him. He thinks I can become some kind of junior executive overnight. He sees the wives of all his friends doing it."

"They didn't do it overnight, in the first place," Cliff said knowledgeably. "They work their way up just like everyone else."

Had Sally been a business executive? Angel wondered. She turned to Catherine to ask, "Is your husband suggesting that you get training in something?"

"Not really. He looks at ads in the paper for management people, says I could do that and look at how much they make." There was a touch of asperity to her words, but Catherine remained dispirited. "I tell him no one would hire me for something like that, without any experience."

"Certainly his own firm wouldn't hire you. Have you pointed that out to him?" Cliff asked.

"He says I could exaggerate about my experience."

"He can't be serious." Cliff frowned across at his sister. "He's just blowing off steam. He's frustrated with his own problems, and he's taking them out on you. You look like you've got it good: you can do whatever you want, stay at home all day and eat bonbons, dabble at your painting, meet your friends for lunch. He resents you."

"Mark's not like that," Catherine protested. "Besides, he knew what I was like when he married me."

"But he was riding high then," Cliff reminded her. "And now he's not. Which probably makes him miserable, and so he's going to make you miserable, too."

Catherine stared at him in astonishment. "He wouldn't do that."

"Not if he realized what he was doing," Cliff agreed. "But he probably doesn't. It's natural enough to want to spread around the responsibility when things aren't going well."

"Yeah, we blame a lot of stuff on patients," Angel

said, grinning. "We accuse them of deliberately having their organs in the wrong place or spiking a fever. Hey, it's not *our* fault."

"What you have to do is ignore him," Cliff advised. "He'll get over it. Tell him you want to start your family."

It gave Angel a jolt to hear him speak so offhandedly about a subject so important to her. Apparently Catherine was put off, too, because her brows lowered thunderously and she snapped, "I don't lie to my husband, Cliff. And I don't try to manipulate him, either. You have an awfully distorted idea of how women behave with men."

He threw his hands up to ward off her criticism. "I didn't mean anything by it, Cath. You'll probably start to have kids soon. It was just a thought."

The two women exchanged a look of sad understanding. Angel knew precisely what Catherine was saying: Cliff automatically thought of women as self-serving and manipulative, even deceitful. Suddenly Angel was assailed by all the doubts that had ever occurred to her about him. He seemed, even in this most delightful of surroundings, a dangerous man for her to be falling in love with. A man who wouldn't ever really regard her as an equal, simply because she was female.

Before she realized what she was about to do, she'd risen to her feet. "I'm sorry. I just have to leave. It was a pleasure meeting you, Catherine. I hope everything works out okay for you."

Catherine bit her lip and nodded. Cliff pushed back his chair with an excess of energy and followed Angel as she hurried over to grab her sweater from the sofa. He didn't say anything until he'd followed her out the front door.

"What the hell is going on? Are you sick?"

"No. Yes. I don't know. I couldn't breathe." Angel rubbed her forehead and leaned against her car. "This isn't working, Cliff. I'm sorry. It's my own fault. I should never have let it go this far. I'm sorry."

"Quit saying that. *I'm* not sorry. Don't pay any attention to Catherine. She just likes to bait me."

"Don't pay any attention to Catherine," Angel repeated, unnerved. "You see, that's what you do. I'm sorry. I just . . . I'm sorry." She reached into her purse for her keys, but Cliff locked his hand over hers.

"Don't do that. I don't understand what's going on. Stay, and we'll talk. Catherine will leave. She'll understand."

Angel shook his hand off hers, feeling tears now very close, stinging behind her eyes. She would not let them fall. "I have to go. I can't breathe here." Her throat felt choked. She stabbed the key at the lock unsuccessfully. After a moment's hesitation, Cliff guided her hand so that the key fit and turned. The car door swung out.

"Promise me you'll explain this tomorrow," he insisted. "Promise me, Angel."

"I don't know if I can."

"I'll call you. We'll talk."

Angel said nothing. She slid the key in the ignition and turned the motor on.

"Promise me, Angel."

"If I can, Cliff."

"Of course you can," he said, but she was already driving away and she didn't try to answer. By the corner of his street, the tears had begun to pour down her cheeks, but she drove around the block, out of sight, before she pulled over to the curb to wait out the storm.

Cliff stood on the sidewalk for a long time looking after Angel's car. A sensation of dread had gripped him as she drove off. No specific cause seemed apparent to him. He wasn't afraid that she would have an accident, or that he wouldn't be able to straighten out this mess, whatever it was. There was just a feeling of apprehension that enveloped him, quite unreasonably.

Because Cliff didn't believe in anxiety attacks, at least as far as he himself was concerned, he chose to ignore the feeling. What if he gave in to something like this and it happened when he was operating, for God's sake? Obviously it was just a physical reaction to the unaccustomed stress of his sister's psychological problems and Angel's psychological problems, and had nothing to do with his own mental state. Or it might even be a reaction to the Greek food. They might use some exotic spice that he was allergic to, for all he knew.

Though Cliff eventually returned to the house, and found his sister removing the food from the table, he shrugged off her attempts to discuss the situation with him. To his mind, she was responsible for what had happened, but he was not going to blame her because she had enough problems of her own right then. So he responded only to subjects that had nothing to do with what had passed during the last two hours, and they found themselves discussing their favorites of the current crop of movies.

Chapter Fourteen

It had taken all of Angel's resolve to answer the
phone at the nurses' station when she was informed that it was Dr. Lenzini. She had a patient in
labor who was progressing very slowly, and she was
able to take time away from her, but she most certainly didn't know what to say to Cliff.

"Dr. Crawford," she said automatically into the
phone.

"It's me," he said. "We have to talk, Angel. I could
come up there now."

"I have someone in labor."

"You don't have to be with her all the time. Is she
in any danger? Or about to deliver soon?"

"No. Cliff, I don't know if it will do any good for
us to talk."

"Of course it will. I'll be right up."

Angel checked on Mrs. Chu once more before
taking up a position in the conference room where
she could see Cliff as he came off the elevators. She
was on call that night and feeling more than a little
exhausted already. Fortunately there would probably
be time to catch a nap off and on as the floor wasn't
busy. Angel noticed that her arms were folded tightly

across her chest, and she forced herself to relax. This too shall pass, she reminded herself, as she'd done all her life about unpleasant things.

He saw her through the open door almost immediately when he stepped out of the elevator. His hair was smoothed down, as if he'd made a special effort to bring it under control. Angel felt her throat constrict at the small symbol of his caring. She motioned him into the room and watched as he closed the door behind him. And remembered the first time she's visited his office when he had locked the door. He moved toward her, but she motioned to a chair opposite her across the rectangular table. His eyebrows rose with skepticism but he took the appointed chair.

"I feel like we're a mile apart," he remarked with mild disapproval.

"Yes." Angel felt they were, too, but not in the way he meant. "I don't know where to start."

"Try telling me why you left last night."

Angel could feel again the breathlessness she'd experienced at his dining table, listening to him. "I suddenly realized that you don't really respect women. No, please, let me try to say what I mean. Your comments about how Catherine could manipulate her husband, they made me very uncomfortable. Like that's what you expect of women. Even though it was obvious that's not how your sister behaves. Or maybe you don't even see that. She was there because she was trying to respect her husband's wishes, even if they made no sense and they were entirely opposed to her own."

"I could see that. I don't know what you mean about my not respecting women." He bent toward her, his eyes intense. "What did I say that made you think that?"

"Oh, Cliff." Angel felt almost impatient with him. "What haven't you said?" Then she shrugged off her irritation and said, "No, I'll try to explain. It's just so difficult, because you don't see it."

"What don't I see?"

"That every time you say something like, 'Tell him you want to start your family,' you're saying you think women naturally lie and manipulate men. You can't dismiss it by saying you didn't mean it. You said it because it's the first thing that comes to your mind."

"I said it as a joke, Angel."

"But, Cliff, it isn't funny. It *isn't* a joke. It would only be funny to another man who had a bad opinion of women. You have to think before you speak. If for no other reason than that you hurt people like Catherine and me when you say things like that."

"I didn't intend to hurt you."

"No, I don't think you did. But unless you stop saying things like that, you'll continue to hurt me, and Catherine, and all the other women who hear you. And until you understand why you shouldn't say things like that, you're not going to be able to resist saying them. You think they're amusing, but they show other people that you hold women in contempt."

His anger flared. "That's simply untrue. I do not hold women in contempt."

"Maybe contempt isn't the word. I said a lack of respect a minute ago. That's more what I meant. You don't credit them with the same standing you'd credit men—that they're honorable, trustworthy, sincere, admirable people, just like men. You think they're less, Cliff. That they aren't only different, but that they're . . . not as good as men."

She could see that he was about to make a joke and thought better of it. "Exactly," she said. "Except for sex, and serving men and being some kind of unequal sidekick, women don't have much place in your opinion. And you aren't even aware of it. You think it's okay to joke about them, that it doesn't mean anything. Or that you can simply say, 'Hey, I didn't mean anything by it, 'like you did with Catherine last night. But you do mean something by it, Cliff. You mean that you don't consider women your equal."

Though he was obviously upset by her summation, Lenzini sprawled back in his chair and shook his head in only mild chagrin. "You're mixing oranges and apples, Angel. Doctors in some ways don't consider anyone their equal. Because of all the things we've talked about—the involvement with life and death, the grueling training, the specialized knowledge. It doesn't have anything to do with whether they're men or women."

Angel tapped the table with impatient fingers. "We're talking about *you*, Cliff. Being a physician is your job. And I don't doubt that it's a real part of your image of yourself. But you wouldn't regard a woman physician any more equally than you would your own sister. I'm talking about at the very bottom, Cliff. At the place where you're just a man like every other man."

"I'm not like every other man."

"Look, I'm not saying that you aren't special. I wouldn't have spent so much time with you if I hadn't thought you were special." Angel felt the stricture in her throat again. She had to force herself to meet his gaze, which seemed more satisfied after what she'd just said. "Ever since the beginning, I've had to fight off this feeling that you weren't the right man for me to be with. I was attracted to you, and I let myself see you against my better judgment, because from the very first I knew you were a sexist. Not playing at it, not just teasing about it, but a real, live, down-to-the-core sexist."

"But I'm not. I'm no more sexist than any other man, and that's just saying that we're different from women."

Angel shrugged. "I think you believe that, Cliff, but you're wrong. What I'm trying to do is explain why I left last night and why I couldn't possibly see you anymore."

"I said something careless last night. I didn't really mean Catherine should or would try to manipulate her husband. Hell, the two of you were ganging up on me. I was just getting back at her. We're brother and sister. We do that kind of thing." He shoved back the chair and paced over to the windows, where he turned to face her, his eyes earnest. "Listen. This has something to do with your being a resident and my being an attending. You may not realize that, but until you've finished your residency, you'll continually feel like other people are abusing you. I felt it, everyone I know felt it. That's just the way life is during residency. It has nothing to do with sexism, or even with the hierarchy, really. It's just a phenomenon of sleep deprivation and over-work, and continually facing hard medical and ethical decisions."

"Residency is hell. But it's more than that," Angel said, her voice catching. In the time it took to rise and push in her chair, she brought her sorrow under firmer control. "I'm not going to see you anymore, Cliff. That's the bottom line. You don't have to listen to what I'm telling you, but you asked me to explain something to you, and I've done my best. I don't really have anything else to say."

"But we were starting to love each other!" he insisted. "That isn't something you let go, when you find someone special. You said I was special to you. You're special to me, too, Angel. You don't just throw that away."

"I'm not just throwing it away, Cliff." Her voice had fallen to a whisper. "This is *important* to me. I can handle sexism when I find it on my job, or just about anywhere else in my life. But I can't have it in my most intimate relationship. And I'm not saying that your sexism wasn't in some way attractive to me. It must have been or I wouldn't have been so drawn to you. But I can't *live* that way. I couldn't have the most important person in my life feel that way about me just because I'm a woman."

"I don't feel that way about you."

"You need to find someone who fits into your way of seeing things. I'm not that person. I'm not doing this just for me; I'm doing it for you, too. I'm not the right person for you, and I don't want to get more and more involved, only to have it end eventually because of that. It would have to end eventually."

"Not necessarily. I mean, I know we have different ideas about things, and you want to live in the country and all, but we could have compromised about that. We could have been grown-ups and found some way to work it out."

"I don't think so." Angel gnawed on her lip before drawing a shaky breath. "Thanks for everything, Cliff. I'm not sorry we met, just that it didn't work out better."

Angel moved toward the door of the conference room. She just had to walk through the door, and leave him there behind her.

"Don't do this, Angel." His voice was rough, with an edge of pleading to it. "I like having you in my life. We're . . . we're good together."

"I'm sorry, Cliff. Really, truly I am."

"If you go now, I won't call you again."

She nodded. "Good. That's what I want. It's better ended like that."

His huge figure was haloed against the sunny windows. She couldn't really see his face because of the glare. The glitter of light from his eyes could not possibly have been tears. He wasn't that kind of man. Even if it hurt him for her to leave, he wouldn't be able to express it that way, he wouldn't want to express it that way.

"Good-bye, Cliff," she said, and slipped out the door.

Cliff was angry with her: angry because she'd so misread his character, and because she hadn't given him a chance to really respond to her charges, and because she'd ended their relationship just at the point where it had been the most exciting. He didn't call her, or try to see her, or even write a letter explaining how wrong she was. If she didn't want him in her life, then he certainly wasn't going to make a nuisance of himself.

This was really a busy period for him, with his research and his surgery and his teaching responsibilities with the surgical residents. He had neglected the residents while he was caught up with Angel, and he made up for his neglect with a vengeance. One of them even told him there were only twenty-four hours in a day, and he could not possibly read up on five different procedures. Wimps! Cliff felt sure he had himself spent more than twenty-four hours a day working on surgery when he was a resident.

When there was a knock at his office door one day a week later, late in the evening, he suspected for a moment that it was Angel. That she had changed her mind and decided to give him the benefit of the doubt. And of course he would be generous and agree that they should try again because she really was very special.

"Come in."

Jerry Stoner stuck his head around the door. "Have a moment to see me?" he asked.

Cliff was unaware of the disappointment his face registered. With an expansive gesture, he waved his psychiatrist friend into the office. "What's dragged you out of your hole?"

"Oh, a few standard complaints about how you've

started driving your residents again. No names!" he insisted, laughing. "I think every one of them has happened to stop me in a corridor or pass by my open office door in the last week. What is it this time, Cliff?" He plopped down on the chair across from Lenzini's desk.

"I'd been too slack with them. I was just trying to catch up. They don't make residents the way they used to."

Jerry shook his head with wry amusement. "They're only human, Cliff. Unlike you, of course."

"When I was a resident, I wouldn't have thought of complaining."

"The hell you wouldn't. I very distinctly remember your coming to me several times."

"Well, we were friends."

"We got to become friends because you came to me several times."

Cliff shrugged. "All right. I'll ease up on them. Maybe I'll write a book instead."

"Now there's a good idea. What on?"

"Oh, I don't know. The fickleness of women, probably."

"I see." Jerry leaned back in his chair and considered Cliff with shrewd eyes. "You're having trouble with Angel Crawford."

"Having trouble? No, I'm just not seeing her anymore."

"And it was her decision?"

Cliff hesitated. "Yeah."

"Did it have anything to do with the same reason Sally left you?"

"They're both independent women. They don't need a man in their lives."

"Is that what either of them said?"

Cliff's eyes narrowed. "Look, Jerry, it's really none of your business."

"Marginally my business," his friend stated. "Because every time something like this happens, you start to drive yourself *and* your residents something crazy, and I'm here to protect your mental health. Cliff, I think I mentioned when you started seeing Angel that you should think about why Sally left."

"Is this 'I told you so'? That doesn't sound very professional."

Jerry ignored him. "Sally left you because you didn't treat her like an equal, right? You told me that yourself, Cliff."

"Hey, that's the way doctors are. You know it, I know it. They don't think other people are quite on the same level they are." Cliff felt like he was repeating himself, but he drove a hand through his unruly hair and continued. "Doctors think they're special people. They dedicate themselves to their profession. They think that entitles them to some kind of special consideration. And in some ways it does."

"Angel's a doctor, too, Cliff. You could get away with that garbage trying to explain away Sally's objections, but not Angel's."

"Angel is a resident. I told her it has a lot to do with the stresses of residency. She's bound to feel a little intimidated by me as an attending."

"I'm sure Angel didn't buy that."

"Angel didn't really listen to me."

"Like you didn't really listen to her, or Sally."

"What am I supposed to listen to?" Cliff demanded. "They think I don't like women. That's ridiculous. I like women. I love women. I think women are great."

"You just wouldn't want to be one."

"Be a woman?" Cliff's voice sounded horrified. "What the hell are you talking about? I'm not having some kind of sexual identity crisis, Jerry. Of course I wouldn't want to be a woman. I like being a man. But it wouldn't be so bad being a woman. They get taken care of. My sister Catherine . . ."

But Jerry didn't allow him to finish his sentence. "Let's stay with that idea, Cliff. You think woman are taken care of—by men, presumably."

"Sure."

"In what way are they taken care of?"

"Financially, of course. Their husbands bring in the major income, almost always."

"So you felt like you were supporting Sally when you lived with her?"

"No, of course not. She made a good salary. Not as much as I did."

Jerry frowned. "So you weren't supporting her, but because you made more money, you thought you were somehow superior to her."

"I didn't say that, and it's not what I meant. It may have irritated her, though. She was the one who left."

"You think she left because you made more money than she did."

"You're purposely trying to distort this," Cliff accused.

"No, Cliff, I'm trying to help you get it sorted out in your mind. Here was a bright, attractive, accomplished, assertive, motivated woman, who apparently loved you, who left because you didn't respect her."

"I did respect her. She just didn't think I did."

"Where would she have gotten that idea?"

"The hell if I know! Women get ideas like that! Look at Angel."

"Okay, let's look at Angel. You weren't living with her, so I assume you don't feel that you were supporting her, though you probably spent a little money wooing her."

"Wooing her!"

"Whatever you want to call it. She's a resident, makes a living wage, has wretched hours, and possesses all the great qualities Sally did—looks, intelligence, skill, potential. So why did she think you didn't respect her?"

"I didn't say that's what she thought."

"Yeah, well, I'd be willing to place a pretty heavy bet on it, Cliff."

"She thinks I'm a sexist. She's remembering how I teased her in the operating room when we met. Everyone talks like that in the OR. It didn't mean anything."

"This may surprise you, Cliff, but it does mean something to some people. It sounds very degrading to them. They often go along with it because everyone else does, or because not going along might cause them trouble, but they don't like it and they feel demeaned even by having to keep their mouths shut."

"Angel didn't keep hers shut that day. And I tried

to help her afterward. It's about power, not about women at all."

Jerry lifted one shoulder in a helpless gesture. "Usually it's about women. And what the men are doing is showing the power they have over women. And the women recognize that. Cliff, the record is pretty clear here. We men in the medical profession have not treated women as equals. We haven't done the same research on them, we haven't given them equal treatment. How do we explain that? They're half the human population."

"I didn't have anything to do with that situation. That's not what we're talking about."

"In a way it is, Cliff. You see, that's what men say: It wasn't my fault. But it is your fault, and it is mine. Everything we've done, everything we've said that belittles women, whether we said it as a joke, or because we accepted the inaccurate truisms of the medical profession, is wrong. You've had women patients you didn't think were physically sick. You've said to yourself, 'It's all in her head because she's a woman.' And you've found out that it wasn't in her head, but you didn't make the connection that as a man, as a doctor, you were judging women in an inappropriate way."

Cliff frowned. "I've done it, sure. All of us have done it."

"That's not good enough, saying we've all done it. We have to stop doing it. But as important, we have to realize why we've done it, and it's because we don't have the same esteem for women as we do for men. And, Cliff, you've been told now by two women, women who were attached to you, that you're worse about it than most men."

"I don't see how that's possible, Jerry. I'm just like everyone else."

"No, actually you aren't. And you have to think about why that is. You've been influenced by the masculine setup in medicine, but that's only part of it. Mostly this sort of thing starts when we're growing up, in our families."

"I have a great family."

Rolling his eyes, Jerry said, "Right. One macho surgeon father, one feminine stay-at-home mother. It's not exactly a prescription for coming out as the most liberated man on Earth, Cliff."

"I don't want to be the most liberated man on Earth."

Jerry stood up. "Well, there's your problem. Next time, Cliff, choose an unliberated woman. See, it works better that way. There are plenty of them around. You won't have trouble finding one."

"I don't like unliberated women. They don't have any fire. Angel has fire. I really . . . adored her, Jerry. Somehow that seems like it should be enough."

"Well, it's not. You have to respect her as much as you would a man. You can have fire or you can have control. You can't have both. You're going to have to make up your mind what's important to you."

"Oh, go to hell."

Jerry sighed as he opened the door. "I probably will."

Angel had agreed to go to dinner with Roger, even though she was so tired she thought she might fall asleep in her pasta. She had agreed to meet him in the parking lot at six-thirty, and found herself there alone when she arrived several minutes ahead of time. Because she knew his car, she leaned against the passenger door, lost in thought, or, more precisely, half-asleep.

"Are you all right?" a familiar voice boomed, startling her out of her fog.

Her heart pounded ridiculously in her throat for a moment. She straightened and blinked at Lenzini, standing close to her with a concerned frown knitting his brow. "Yes, sure," she said. "I just sort of fell asleep, I guess."

"You can wait in my car."

"No, that's okay. Roger should be here any minute." She glanced at her watch. It was already six-forty. Roger wasn't always on time, but one forgave him because he was invariably so sincerely apologetic. Angel swept her gaze over the approaches to the parking lot, but saw no sign of Roger.

"Maybe he's been held up. I could call and check for you," Lenzini offered.

"No, really. It doesn't matter. I'll find a bench and wait for him. He's had to wait for me."

"But it's cold and foggy, Angel. You don't even have a jacket."

"Well, if I catch a cold, maybe I can stay home sick for a day," she said with forced cheerfulness. "Really, Cliff, I'm fine. You go ahead."

"How's Roger doing?"

"He seems to be managing. Don't you talk to him?"

"Sure, but not much about Kerri."

"Really, you should . . ." Angel clamped her lips shut. "Never mind."

They heard feet pounding toward them, and there was Roger, still in scrubs with a bright-patterned scrub cap covering his hair. "I'm sorry, I'm sorry, I'm sorry. The guy just wouldn't wake up. Thought we'd lost him there for a minute. But he finally came around. Hi, Cliff. Want to join us for dinner?"

Angel stared at Roger, who should have known better. It was obvious that Lenzini was on the point of accepting when he thought better of it. "No, thanks. I have plans. See you." And he lumbered off toward his car across the lot.

If it would have done any good, Angel would have scolded Roger for not remembering that she and Cliff were not actually speaking—more or less— these days. Instead she climbed into his car to get out of the cold and fog, huddling against the seat while he climbed in.

"It would have been all right," he assured her. "You and Cliff are going to see each other around the medical center. You should get used to being friendly, you know, no hard feelings and all that. He's into one of his rampages," he added absently as he turned on the car.

"Rampages?"

"Oh, he got crazy like this in the spring, too, when Sally left. Not that I'm comparing you with Sally, Angel. You're really not at all like her. She wasn't right for him. Too stiff and distant."

Angel would have liked to have had the personal integrity not to have asked, but she found she couldn't resist. "How do you mean, stiff and distant?"

Roger eased the car out of his slot while the warm air began to thaw his passenger. "She was bright, you know? And very clever. But you always had the feeling she wasn't opening up to you. Even when she sort of seemed to be. You know what I mean?"

"Not really."

"Hmmm. Well, like Kerri said, she was a public person. She always acted like she was in public, said things that could be quoted, never talked about her personal life, just business stuff. Apparently she was real good at that—the business stuff. A company hired her away from San Francisco to be a vice-president in charge of marketing or something in Boston. I don't think it ever occurred to her not to take the job."

"And Cliff went on one of his rampages when she left," Angel reminded him, annoyed with her interest and persistence.

"Hell, yes. You'd have thought he was single-handedly going to operate on every surgical problem at Fielding. Geez! I don't think he ever left the hospital before ten at night. And he drove the poor residents to distraction. Which is exactly what he's doing now, apparently."

Secretly this pleased Angel no end. Not because of the poor residents, with whom she could sympathize, but because Cliff had at least cared enough about her to need the diversion of hard work and long hours. She was herself provided with that kind of diversion without having to seek it out. Not that all the hard work and long hours had kept her from experiencing the loss of Cliff from her life. There seemed to be a constant ache in her throat, a surprise tingling at her eyes when she least expected it. But it had been her choice, and here was Roger who had not had any choice at all.

"He'll settle down in a few days," she predicted.

Roger threw a sharp look at her. "How are you doing?"

"I'm . . . okay. You know what residency is like. You're almost too busy to think. And I especially like obstetrics." She made a dismissive gesture. "Besides, it's nothing like what's happened to you. I've only known Cliff for a couple of months."

"That doesn't really matter, you know. What bothers me is that you two really are right for each other, in so many ways. He's really a good guy, Angel, even if he is a macho jerk sometimes."

Angel felt that lump in her throat again, threatening to choke her up. "I know, Roger. But if you're smart, you don't count on changing people: he wouldn't change me and I wouldn't change him, but that's what we'd be trying to do. It's better this way."

"I suppose so," Roger said doubtfully.

Chapter Fifteen

Y our sister on line two," his secretary said over the
intercom.

Cliff picked up the phone reluctantly. He wasn't
sure he was in the mood for a conversation with
Catherine, who seemed truly irate with him about
his handling of the Angel affair. "Hi, Cath. What's
happening?"

"Next week is Labor Day," she announced.

"No kidding."

"Mark and I are having a barbecue."

"That's nice."

"We want you to come."

"Sorry. I'm far too busy for that."

"Mom and Dad are coming."

"Why, for God's sake?"

"Because Dad has a scheme to improve Mark's
business."

Cliff rolled his eyes. "Since when have any of
Dad's schemes been of the least use? Doctors don't
know diddlysquat about business."

"Still, they're coming up for the weekend, and you
should at least put in an appearance on Labor Day.
It's a holiday, Cliff. You won't be operating."

True, Cliff was not scheduled to be anywhere near the hospital. Not that he couldn't change with someone. "I'm not feeling very sociable these days, Cath. You're probably having half the world over."

"Only two other couples."

"Well, I don't know. I wouldn't have anyone to bring. And I *don't* want you to fix me up with someone."

"I wasn't planning to. We'll have a lot of fatty red meats grilled to carcinogenic perfection. What more could you ask for?"

Cliff knew that if his parents were in the Bay Area he wasn't going to escape seeing them. Maybe the barbecue was the simplest way of handling the situation after all. "Okay, but, Catherine, remind me. Leave a message on my machine if I'm not home. And call that morning. I've been forgetting all sorts of things lately, and I don't want you furious with me when I don't show up."

"Okay." Her voice became less persuasive and more empathetic. "How are you doing?"

"Oh, I'm fine. I've been busy trying to finish up the research because the grant money's running out. The medical center has been no help at all in allocating space or resources. Hell, you'd think I was a neophyte. There's never enough money." He sighed. "But you don't want to hear about that. How are things with you and Mark?"

"Well, I told him I'd rather retrench than get a lousy job. He didn't like the idea, but with the folks coming we've sort of put the discussion on hold."

Cliff grimaced. "Great. Dad will help him make a

bundle, and then you won't have to worry about it anymore."

"Do you talk with Angel at all?"

He stiffened. "No, Cath. When it was over, it was over. I run into her every once in a while. And Roger sees her a lot. You remember Roger, who married the young woman just before she died. Kerri and Angel had gotten close during her last illness, so she and Roger sort of comfort each other, I guess. Maybe it's more than that. I don't know."

"Of course it's not more than that," Catherine said. "He's just had someone he loves die, for heaven's sake."

"It doesn't matter, in any case."

"Oh, sure." But Catherine let the subject drop. "We'll see you Monday, then. About one. Okay?"

"See you then."

Catherine left two messages on his machine and actually caught him at home on Monday morning. So, even if he'd wanted to, he had no excuse for missing her barbecue. Though it was cool in San Francisco, Cliff knew that San Mateo was likely to be warm and sunny, so he put on a pair of seldom-worn shorts and a suitably sporty shirt that his sister had given him for Christmas the preceding year.

It bothered him that he didn't have a date to take with him. Maybe he should have asked one of the nurses, or that transcriptionist who had the most eclectic taste in clothing. But it was too late now, he admitted as he climbed into his car. Still, he had a moment's vision of himself arriving there with a beautiful woman, who smiled up at him adoringly. Angel had never done that.

Sally hadn't either, for that matter. But she had had a profound respect for his position in society. She had, he thought, considered them very well suited in that way. Her own family was socially prominent in the East, her father a lawyer whose name hit the headlines now and again. Though Sally had a law degree, she had parlayed her talents into success in the business world. She was an elegant woman, who did everything with flair. He had admired her for that, and for her intelligence.

Cliff headed toward 280, wanting to drive down the back way to the peninsula. He was in no hurry. He could use a little time thinking about what was going wrong with his life, and what had been happening for the past year.

His admiration for Sally, for instance, must not have been obvious to her. If it had been, surely she wouldn't have accused him of having so little respect for women. He was impressed by her elegance, her beauty, and her accomplishments. He thought he had let her know that. She told him he treated her like a trophy.

A trophy! Women were totally incomprehensible. What was the point of her being so perfect if he didn't appreciate her perfection? *She* said she wanted him to love her for herself. Now what was that supposed to mean? He loved it that she had a perfect body. He loved it that she was socially so adept. He loved it that she was so good at her job. He loved it that she was independent. God knew he didn't want some woman clinging to him and whining that he was never home. Sally had never seemed to mind, except when it came to his not showing up for her business functions.

"I come to yours," she had said indignantly one night when she confronted him in the bedroom. "This was important to me, Cliff, and you said you'd come. And you forgot! Forgot! Heaven help me if I'd ever forgotten one of your stupid hospital functions, kissing up to the big brass. You don't really care about me, Cliff."

He had thought, at the time, that he did. After all, he had lived with her for five years. That was no small matter to him. And yet he had never asked her to marry him. He had told himself that he was being cautious, that they were too young to marry, that she had never pushed for marriage. Oh, but when she told him she was leaving, she gave him an earful about that, too.

"And then there was the matter of your never respecting me enough to want to marry me," she'd insisted. "Oh, I was good enough to live with, and I was good enough to sleep with, and I was good enough to share your meals, but you couldn't quite bring yourself to marry me, could you? And do you know why, Cliff? It's because you don't really think much of women. You're of the 'if you can have the milk without buying the cow, why bother' school. I've known it, God help me. Why the hell I stayed with you all this time, I'll never know."

"I think it was because you loved me," he'd suggested rather hotly.

"Oh, love, schmove," she'd countered. "What is love after all? Yes, I loved you. And it's a damn shame you don't even know what love is. It's a lot more than sex, Cliff."

He had made a joke at that point. Bad mistake. She had really torn into him then, accusing him of sexism of the most heinous kind, of being a male chauvinist of impressive credentials. And then she'd told him she'd accepted a job in Boston and that she was leaving the next day. The next day! That was the kind of person she was, informing him of her departure without giving him any notice at all.

Cliff had not known for months whether he most resented her leaving him on such short notice, or her accusing him of sexism, or her inconveniencing him when he'd grown to rely on her, or because he sincerely missed her as part of his life. After meeting Angel he had come to suspect that he had been more hurt by Sally's being the one to dump him than his genuine feeling for her, but that was hindsight. If his relationship with her had not had much depth, it had certainly had longevity. Didn't that say something for him? He wasn't sure what, and decided not to consider the matter too closely.

The further down the peninsula he got, the warmer it became. Sun shone on the golden hills around him, and he rolled down his window to catch the breeze. Summer had passed so quickly, he'd hardly noticed it was there, except for the weekend in the mountains. Now here was the tag end of the season, with autumn right around the corner, and he'd scarcely been swimming or played tennis or gone windsurfing. His turn in the mountains was here again, and he couldn't even think of going there. He'd have to remember to offer the time to

Jerry or Roger. Not if Roger would take Angel there, though. That was not something he could contemplate.

He swung up and over the hill, down to San Mateo Park. He'd never understood why someone would want to live outside the city, except for the weather, of course. And maybe for raising kids in a safer environment. And having an altogether calmer way of life. But cities were exciting, damn it! They had things to offer that suburbs didn't. Escaping them was like escaping reality. Which was understandable, he decided as he drove down the tree-draped streets of his sister's community.

Most of the houses had wide expanses of green lawn, with trees and winding drives and a flash of swimming pool to be seen between the hedges. Your kids would never get street smart here, he decided. This was where the upper middle class lived, where kids were protected from the harsher aspects of life. Not from drugs, of course. They weren't protected from drugs anywhere. But from an excess of crime, and the daily ordeal of seeing ragged homeless people wander the streets.

Catherine's house was a two-story French villa of sorts, attractive but a little pretentious. Cliff knew the house had been Mark's choice, but Catherine's touch had warmed things up inside without making it cutesy. The front door was open, and he wended his way through to the back where he could hear voices. Catherine's paintings hung on the walls of several of the rooms, and Cliff stopped in some surprise before one of them.

There was power here that he hadn't noticed before. The colors were vibrant, the textures rich. Though it was an abstract painting, there was something boldly familiar about it, something insistent in its voice. Cliff's brow furrowed as he stepped back farther to get a more comprehensive view of the canvas.

"What do you think?" Catherine asked from the doorway of the kitchen. "It's a new one."

"It's really compelling. I feel like I've seen it before."

"That's because it's you."

"Me?" Cliff cocked his head to consider the whorls of paint. "Obviously I should have recognized myself. Did Mom and Dad?"

"No, but they don't take my painting seriously."

Cliff caught the wistful note in her voice. "Sure they do," he protested. "This is terrific. Would it be egotistical of me to ask about buying it from you?"

"Trying to save us single-handedly?" she asked. "You should have heard Dad's ideas for Mark."

"Not too helpful, huh?" He moved over and kissed her cheek. "I warned you about doctors and business matters."

Catherine reached up to smooth down a stray windblown lock of his hair. Her own hair was worn casually pulled back to the nape of her neck with a multicolored band that matched her culotte skirt. She looked slightly strained, but wholesome and healthy. It was always a little difficult having their parents stay with her, Cliff knew, though he didn't understand why. When the elder Lenzinis stayed with him, he scarcely noticed their presence, they were such undemanding guests.

"Everyone's out back," she said, turning toward the rear of the house. "Go on out. I have to check on the food."

Cliff walked through the open sliding door onto a redwood patio that clung to the left side of the house, stepping down into a landscaped yard with a pool off to the right. His parents were talking with a couple he didn't know, standing on the flagstone path by towering sunflowers and hollyhocks. Catherine also had a way with plants.

His mother was the first to see him. Her smile broadened, and she waved him over to them. She was an attractive woman of fifty-five who was dressed a little more formally than his sister. Seeing her there, Cliff realized that his mother had the same kind of elegance that Sally had. His mother was the perfect hostess, the perfect guest, the perfect wife and mother. She exuded competence more than warmth, though Cliff certainly thought of her as a loving mother. Hadn't she always been there for him when he'd needed her help?

His father hadn't noticed him yet, so Cliff watched him unobserved as he approached through the garden. Howard Lenzini had a distinguished silver mane that was almost classic. This was everyone's idea of a doctor: tall, broad-shouldered, mature, capable, concerned. And he was a good surgeon. Cliff had always known that, had always borne well the half-jocular admonitions of his father's colleagues: "You have a way to go to match your old man, Clifford."

Cliff had chosen not to compete with his father in the same specialty or the same area, but he had no doubts of his own capabilities. His father, pontificating now on the need for doctors to maintain control of their own practices against the rising tide of federal regulation, looked both earnest and enlightened. The couple to whom he spoke were young and entranced by his authority.

"Hi, Mom," he said, bending down to kiss her on her cheek, as he had his sister. It was a family tradition, he supposed. They didn't hug, or spread germs by kissing on the lips, or carrying on the way some families did. They were subdued, sophisticated, and slightly awkward with each other.

"Cliff. How wonderful to see you!" she exclaimed in her lovely, modulated tones. "It's been months. You should get down to San Diego more often."

"I've been busy, Mom."

She smiled ruefully. "I've heard that excuse for any number of years, dear boy. See if you can get your father to let these poor people go refresh their drinks."

Howard Lenzini had already turned toward his son, offering his hand for the hearty shake he was famous for. "Catherine said she'd roust you out of your hospital, and by heaven, she's done it," he said jovially. "All work and no play and all that, son."

"*You* should talk," his wife teased. "You'd think he'd start to slow down a little, wouldn't you? But no, he's sailed right past sixty without blinking or looking back." It was obvious that she was proud of him for his commitment and energy.

"Hi, Dad. How's the broken bone business?"

"Not bad, not bad. They're doing some great new imaging. But you probably know all about that at your center. Fielding's been getting a lot of publicity lately. I think you're in the right place at the right time, Cliff."

"I hope so." Cliff was reminded of the continual cuts that his department had been subjected to. Though he knew his father would sympathize, he also knew that his father would automatically calculate how this was going to affect Cliff's future, and Cliff wasn't interested in that kind of discussion. "I haven't had as much time for research as I'd like. There are some intriguing wound-healing possibilities we've been working on."

"Good for you, good for you!" His father clapped a hand on his shoulder. "One of these days I'll be reading about you in the paper. Damn shame you didn't go into neurosurgery, though. Those guys are getting all the press."

Cliff had long since learned to shrug off his father's pet peeve. With mock disappointment he said, "Nobody wants to write about diseased colons and gallbladders. But don't you love this laparoscopy? We're pushing the boundaries further and further. Do you suppose . . ."

"Now don't get started," his mother protested. "Catherine didn't invite us here to have you two discuss the wonders of modern medicine in the middle of her barbecue. Cliff, I don't think you've even had a chance to speak to your brother-in-law."

So Cliff found himself passed off to his brother-in-law, who was acting chef at the Weber grill. "God, I haven't had a chunk of steak like that in months," Cliff confessed. "I want the biggest one you've got."

"Hello to you, too, Cliff," Mark said. "We always

save the biggest piece of meat for you, old man. If you're a giant, you get giant portions."

"Thanks. Medium rare. With lots of macaroni salad."

"That's Catherine's department. But she made it the way you like it, with pimientos."

"Good for her. She's a woman of remarkable discrimination." Cliff leaned against the corner of the house and considered Mark. No one else was around, so he said, "I hope my father didn't drive you nuts with his business suggestions. Unless he's doing orthopedic surgery, he doesn't necessarily shine in the advice department. The best move he ever made was letting my mother handle their investments."

"And the best thing she ever did was buy San Diego real estate." Mark turned a piece of steak and grinned. "She told me once, in confidence, that the only reason she'd done it was because a cousin of hers sold commercial real estate. And the rest is history."

Cliff nodded. Mark didn't sound jealous, only a little bemused. It was difficult for Cliff to know what to say to his brother-in-law. He wanted to tell him to lay off Catherine, to let her just be an artist and a wife, but that really wasn't his business. And he wanted to offer to help the two of them financially, but he was afraid he'd insult Mark. Instead he said, "Your garden's looking really great, especially this late in the summer. My gardener quit, and I haven't had the time to look for someone new. I'm afraid all the fuchsias will die."

"Do you water them?"

"Now why would I do anything reasonable like that?" Cliff retorted. "Yeah, actually I do remember to water them. They look so great pretty much no matter what you do that I like to reward them with a little moisture, even a little plant food now and then. You haven't been up in a while. I have a few more varieties."

"Catherine said she stopped by a few weeks ago."

There was a pregnant pause, and Cliff waited to see what would follow it. Either Mark knew about why Catherine had come by, or he knew what had happened with Angel. It was hard to tell which, and Cliff wasn't actually keen on talking about either.

"She said she met a woman there, but that she seemed to precipitate a breakup between the two of you. I told her I thought it was highly unlikely it was her fault."

Cliff could hear the question in Mark's voice, but he was reluctant to answer it. His brother-in-law was a good-looking man in his late twenties, blond and built like a runner, who usually kept strictly out of Cliff's affairs, so it was surprising that he was prodding here. Cliff shrugged. "Things usually run the course they were meant to run."

But Mark was not satisfied. He jabbed the steak with a knife to test its doneness, and shifted it to a plate. But before he handed it to Cliff, he said, "Catherine has been concerned about you. She thinks maybe you blame her."

"Of course not. I'm sure I haven't said anything of the sort."

"But then, you wouldn't, would you?"

"I'll speak with her," Cliff said, reaching for the plate Mark still kept at his side. "It isn't anything she should worry about. Thanks for the steak, Mark. I'm going to find the macaroni salad."

He sat down at a redwood table laid with flatware and red napkins, with bowls of salad and fruits and baskets of breads in a row down the center. There were already three people seated at the table. Cliff sat down, introduced himself, helped himself to the food, and proceeded to socialize with these people he'd never seen before. It was a gift everyone in his family had, of being able to talk to complete strangers without difficulty. Cliff had learned to find a common basis, sometimes medicine, but as often movies or cultural events. He was curious about what people had to say and listened with an intensity that seemed to flatter them.

One couple was in their forties, and their chief topic of conversation was the trouble their teenage son managed to get into. The husband told amusing if nerve-wracking tales of high schools where children came with weapons, where drugs found their way to even the straightest of students, and where learning seemed by far a secondary matter.

Cliff asked questions of the man and probed for information about their city life, never allowing himself to reveal through any delicate reference that he was a doctor. Once you did that, they turned their curiosity on you, and he was not interested in sharing his professional life with them at this point. Sometimes, when he really didn't wish to be identified as a doctor, he told people he was a scientist, which was true, but certainly not the whole truth. But then, at a social gathering, you weren't taking an oath as to the veracity of your statements.

The father of the teenager was Mark's partner in his computer firm. The other man was an associate professor of biology at Stanford. The woman, married to the computer partner, really said very little. Cliff had sat there taking in the conversation and contributing encouraging questions for some time when his sister sat down beside him. He smiled at her and motioned to the spread in front of them. "Nice work, Catherine. And Mark does a great steak."

"Thanks. Have you met everyone?" When he nodded, she said, "Anne did that sculpture in the side garden that you like so well."

"Really?" Cliff was almost shocked. The sculpture his sister spoke of was an intricate fountain of figures and animals that he'd admired for years. He would have commissioned something for his own yard, except that he hadn't gotten around to it yet.

Cliff turned to the woman now, and realized he had hardly noticed her. Her husband had done most of the talking, and Cliff had naturally assumed that this woman was "just his wife." He felt a sinking in the pit of his stomach. "I love that fountain," he admitted to this bright-eyed woman. "Could we talk sometime about your doing something for me?"

"Sure. Catherine has my number."

Catherine, Cliff realized, was just Mark's wife to a lot of people. His own mother, sharp as she was and as self-denigrating, was "just" Howard Lenzini's wife.

This woman opposite him, Anne, was a very well-known artist in the Bay Area, and he wouldn't even have known who she was if his sister hadn't mentioned it.

With his usual ease, Cliff now conversed with her, but his mind was running a second line of thought past him that disturbed his equanimity. He *did* make assumptions about women that didn't accord them the same status as men. That was the way his world had always been shaped, and that was the way he accepted it. In his family his mother was not as "important" as his father. It had nothing to do with his love for either of them, but with the interactions he had observed from childhood, and in the way their world valued them.

After a while he excused himself to return to the house, where he stood for some time in front of his sister's painting of him. And he realized then that her work was commercial. He wandered through the house where various paintings hung, three others, and knew that they would easily sell in a gallery. So why had all of them—Catherine, and Mark, and his parents, and himself—believed that they weren't salable?

Catherine, perhaps because of her lack of confidence, or her unconscious wish not to outshine her husband. Mark, well, he might not have relished being upstaged, or it might have been his unconscious need to keep Catherine in their private world. Who knew what would happen to her if she became a known artist? And their parents simply didn't expect as much of their daughter as they had of their son.

They didn't believe in her talent the way they believed in his. How unfair for Catherine.

"They're good, aren't they?" his father said beside him, but not with the conviction Cliff was feeling.

"They're remarkable. We've been letting Catherine hide her light under a bushel, Dad. Colluding in her fear of going public with them."

"Artists are a dime a dozen," his father reminded him.

"So are surgeons," Cliff retorted. "Catherine deserves some recognition."

"Along with recognition comes criticism. There will always be people out there who trash anyone who dares to declare their work good enough for exhibition. You can't shield her from that."

"No, but we can prepare her for it." Cliff raked energetic fingers through his dark hair. "It's how you grow, remember, Dad? Moving from the dog lab to the operating room. Being in the full light of day. It broadens your mind and challenges your skills. You wouldn't have been content to dissect cadavers all your life."

"It's not the same thing, Cliff."

"Maybe it isn't. But there is some parallel. Catherine deserves a chance to grow."

"She's going to have other responsibilities one of these days." Howard Lenzini grinned. "Kids make you grow, believe me. When I was your age, your mother and I already had two kids. I'm betting it won't be long before Catherine and Mark start their family. This is just a temporary financial setback for him. Computers are today what plastics were, right?

And you should be looking around for the right woman to settle down with, Cliff. It can do your career a world of good."

Wouldn't Angel love hearing that, Cliff thought with a grimace. *Is that what I think? Is that why I was with Sally for so long? And if it was, why didn't I marry her?*

"I have a feeling my career is about to take a new direction," Cliff said out loud.

His father looked interested. "Really? You haven't said anything. What's happening?"

"I may leave academic medicine."

"Leave academic medicine?" His father was stunned. "That would be crazy. You were made one of the youngest associate professors of surgery at Fielding. You have a wonderful reputation there. You can't be serious."

"Well, it's far from certain," Cliff admitted, wishing he'd said nothing. *After all, what did he really mean? As things stood, Angel wouldn't even take a call from him.* "I'm just a little restless, I guess."

"Get married," his father advised, with a wink. "That will take care of the restlessness. A good steady source of sex, especially in this day and age, is the perfect solution. You young men spend too much time searching for something you could have waiting for you at home."

You hear that, Angel? Cliff thought, but with a sadness that weighed on his chest. "I just don't know what's happening right now, Dad. It's something I have to work out for myself."

Howard Lenzini shook his head. "Things just

aren't the way they were in my day. I don't envy you, son."

Cliff glanced once more at the painting on the wall before turning back toward the party. "Just wish me luck, Dad. I'm going to need it."

Chapter Sixteen

Angel didn't understand why the pain didn't diminish. When she had insisted on not seeing Cliff anymore, she had assumed that she would be upset for a few days, a few weeks. But more than a month had passed and she still felt miserable. It was painful to see him, and painful not to see him. Once she'd almost run right into him when she was hurrying around a corner, and he'd steadied her with his large, capable hands. She had felt like bursting into tears. Instead she apologized and hurried on.

Cliff's friend Jerry, the psychiatrist, had said something cryptic to her one day when they were leaving a patient's room. "You can't control other people's behavior, only your own. But sometimes that's enough." Since this had had nothing to do with the patient on whom she'd called him to consult, Angel assumed it was a comment on herself and Cliff. Fortunately, Jerry had disappeared into the room off the nurses' station before Angel could question him further. She had no idea what she would have asked him. And by the time he'd finished writing his note in the chart, she was already busy attending to another patient.

Angel moped around the flat when she was home. Nan couldn't even convince her to go out to a movie.

"I just don't feel like it," Angel would say. "You go without me."

"I'm only going because you need to get out of here," Nan would protest. "A little fresh air, a change of scenery, a little nonmedical stimulation. I know what would help. Let me fix you up with someone nice."

Angel cringed at the thought. What was the sense of it? She still dreamed of Cliff, and had to remind herself that she had no control over her dreams. When she woke up in the on-call room, she was invariably disoriented and always somehow expected Lenzini to be there, whether it was the middle of the night or early morning. It took a great deal of effort to reconcile herself each time to being alone.

As September progressed, Angel could feel autumn in the air, and in the changing quality of the light outside the medical center. Her sadness seemed to be echoed in the changing season, a touch of melancholy tingeing everything around her. Though she continued to love her work, she didn't get quite the satisfaction from it because something seemed to be missing. Like people who quit smoking kept reaching for a cigarette, Angel found herself meaning to tell Cliff something, to share her thoughts with him, or ask him a question.

Always there was that feeling that she had lost something important. And yet, she continually scolded herself, she'd only known him a short while. Not long enough to form some permanent attachment. That didn't happen in a couple of months. Did it? Surely not with someone whose chauvinistic mind-set she couldn't accept. You couldn't love someone you didn't approve of. Could you?

When all was said and done, it didn't really matter, though. She'd ended the relationship, and Cliff had accepted her decision. Now she had to get on with her life. Angel decided this about four times a day, in those odd moments when she wasn't literally too busy to see straight. Or too restless to fall asleep.

One of her favorite distractions was her continuity clinic. While she was on the obstetrics rotation, she still had her clinic three half-days a week, with more and more families she had followed now for several years. From sturdy infants to frail elders, she welcomed the challenges of primary care for this growing group. She had seen Ellen, newly confirmed pregnant with her second child, just the day before, so she was surprised to have a page from the emergency room after midnight when she was on call.

Various possibilities raced through her mind as she hurried to the ER. There was the possibility that Ellen was having a miscarriage, or that something other than her pregnancy was causing her problem. But just as likely, given the reported symptoms, was an ectopic pregnancy, with the fertilized egg trying to grow in the fallopian tube instead of the uterus. Very dangerous if not taken care of immediately. Angel increased her pace.

Ellen was in the gynecological examining room at the end of the emergency department. Even from the doorway, Angel could see that her patient was in a good deal of pain. She moved forward and reached to take the young woman's hand. "Tell me what's happening, Ellen," she said, as the nurse handed her notes made by the first doctor who had seen Ellen.

"The pain has been getting worse all day," Ellen said softly. Her face looked pale and pinched, not at all the radiant oval it had been the previous day. "I didn't want to have to come in, but I couldn't stand it anymore. What's happening? Am I going to lose the baby?"

"I can't tell yet." Angel drew on gloves from the box on the wall. "I'll need to do an exam, but I think we'll probably need an ultrasound, too."

On examining the young woman, Angel found that the pain was not decidedly localized to a spot on one side, but if the embryo was lodged in the tube close to the uterus, that could be deceptive. An ultrasound was definitely indicated, so she and the nurse took Ellen down the hall to the sonography suite. Since it was the middle of the night, Angel set everything up for herself, including the long, thin vaginal probe that would give her a better view of the uterus.

"This won't be comfortable, but you'll be able to handle it," Angel assured her patient. Each step of the way she explained what she was doing, feeling a growing sense of urgency as Ellen's pain obviously continued to grow. "This is a view of the uterus," she explained to Ellen, who couldn't really see the screen very well. "What I'm looking for is a sign of the embryo here. It would already be at least a half centimeter long."

But there was nothing to be seen. No evidence of the fetal pole, of the fetal heartbeat. Angel moved the probe to change the picture, but there was nothing. And yet a test the previous day had confirmed Ellen's pregnancy. It was possible that she had already miscarried, but Ellen was adamant that this had not happened, and her pain continued to escalate. Ellen was moaning softly, her head moving back and forth to help her cope.

"I'm sorry," Angel said gently. "There's nothing here. Chances are, Ellen, that the embryo has lodged in the fallopian tube, what is called an ectopic pregnancy. It can't stay there, or it will burst and cause bleeding."

"There's no way to save the pregnancy?" Ellen asked unhappily.

"Not if it's an ectopic. The embryo can't develop in the tube. We're going to have to take you to surgery to find out for sure what's happening and take care of it." She looked to the nurse for information. "Who's the attending OB on call?"

"Williams, but he's already in surgery with an emergency, and Jacobs is assisting."

Oh, great. Angel picked up the phone and asked to be connected with Dr. Williams' OR suite. She was put on a speaker phone and explained the situation. Williams said, "Get hold of the general surgeon, Dr. Crawford. I'll send Jacobs out as soon as I can, but this is tricky. Lenzini's on call. He'll be able to handle it."

Terrific! Angel almost dropped the phone into its cradle. Just what she needed. Well, she could handle it. She was a mature, competent woman. She picked the phone back up and had Cliff paged.

Within minutes the phone rang, and she heard his familiar voice say, "Lenzini here. What's up?"

"This is Dr. Crawford . . . Angel."

There was a moment's pause. "Oh, um, I thought this was a medical call."

"Well, it is. Dr. Williams said to call you because he's in emergency surgery with the senior OB resident, and I have a patient here from my continuity clinic who has presented with pain and vaginal bleeding. An ultrasound shows nothing in the uterus. There's no localized one-sided pain but every other indication that it's an ectopic."

"But it's a surgical abdomen?"

"Absolutely. I think she needs surgery immediately. I don't want her going into shock."

Angel was afraid he was going to argue with her, to make her spell out exactly why this was so urgent. But he merely said, "Okay. Meet you in the operating room in ten minutes."

With a shaky breath, she hung up the phone. "Everything's all set," she said to Ellen. "Dr. Lenzini is a fine surgeon, and he's ready to take you straight to the operating room."

A tear slipped down the young woman's cheek, but she nodded. Angel explained exactly what would happen in surgery. The consent form was signed. Transport arrived to take Ellen up. And Angel left to scrub. It was 1:23 A.M.

At one-thirty, Angel found herself at a sink next to Lenzini, unable to keep her eyes off his large soapy hands. They both already had their masks, scrubs, and caps on. Angel was doing the necessary ten-minute scrub herself and managed not to meet his gaze. He was talking to her, though, and she listened intently because what he was saying surprised her.

"I'm going to let you do it," he said. "Have you ever shelled out an ectopic before?"

"No. And I've only seen it done a few times. Maybe you should do it yourself."

"Do you think you couldn't handle it?"

"No, I'm sure I could handle it. But I've never done one before."

"Well, it's the sort of thing you might have to do out in the wilds," he teased. "Not that I mean on a kitchen table. But you might be the only one around at some small community hospital. You wanted experience in gynecologic surgery, as I recall."

"Yes," she agreed, standing a little straighter. "We'll use the laparoscope, of course."

He grinned. "Yes, ma'am. Anything else I should know?"

"She has a history that includes chlamydia. There may be some scarring on the fallopian tube. She has one child. This was her second pregnancy, and she wanted it."

Lenzini nodded. He tossed the scrubbing pad in the wastebasket and backed into the operating room. Angel followed close behind him, her arms lifted so the water dripped down her elbows. The circulating nurse dried Angel's hands, slipped on her surgical gown, and snapped her gloves in place. Cliff was already standing over the patient, who was about to be anesthetized.

"I'm Dr. Lenzini. And Dr. Crawford is right here. We're going to take good care of you."

Angel smiled at her patient, but realized Ellen

couldn't see her encouragement. "By the time you wake up, everything should be fixed. We'll talk again then."

"Okay," Ellen murmured, sleepy from the sedative she'd been given. "I can still have another baby, can't I?"

"I hope so." Angel wanted to say that she definitely could, but she was not in the habit of lying to her patients, even when they were about to undergo surgery. If the fallopian tube had to be removed entirely, Ellen's chances of becoming pregnant would be reduced, but not gone. "You're going to do fine," she added as the anesthesiologist began his work.

Within moments, Ellen was unconscious. Then movement in the OR became faster paced but orderly. The patient was draped for laparoscopic surgery, the screen on which the doctors would watch the surgery was pushed into place. Angel made several small incisions in Ellen's abdomen. The abdomen was injected with carbon dioxide to inflate it, and the laparoscope was inserted through an incision near the navel. Through the other incisions specially designed surgical instruments such as scissors, clamps, and suturing devices could be inserted through tubes as wide as a drinking straw.

The laparoscope's fiber-optics shined bright light on the organs inside the abdomen, and a series of magnifying lenses with an attachment that connected to a tiny television camera projected the image on the screen with amazing clarity. Angel was grateful that she'd misspent many hours of her youth playing video games. Much of the manual dexterity and timing she'd learned had come in handy.

"So, what have we got here?" Cliff asked, observing the screen from behind her shoulder. "Definitely swollen there on the left tube near the uterus."

Angel agreed. What worried her was the amount of scarring above the swollen portion. But obviously, even with the scarring, Ellen had become pregnant this time. There was no reason to believe it couldn't happen again. Removing the tube might cut her chances of pregnancy in half.

The senior resident in OB bustled through the door, allowed a new pair of gloves to be slipped over the ones he was already wearing, and trotted up to the operating table. He nodded to Lenzini, but barely seemed to notice Angel.

"I can take over here now," he informed them. "Dr. Williams has his case under control."

"This is Dr. Crawford's patient from continuity clinic," Lenzini explained. "She'd like the chance to remove the ectopic, and I'm happy to oversee her."

"But she's a family-practice resident!" Jacobs protested. "She isn't even in OB/GYN."

"I've done a number of gynecologic surgical procedures," Angel informed him. "My program has helped me get experience."

Angel continued to maintain control of the instruments, though she made no move to further the procedure. Lenzini regarded Dr. Jacobs with mild amusement. "I'm not in OB/GYN either, but I'm in charge of this operation," he said mildly. "Tell us what you think should be done, Dr. Jacobs."

Jacobs considered the screen for several minutes. "There's too much scarring to save the tube," he finally proclaimed. "Besides, she's got the other one, right?"

"Yes, but we don't know if it's functioning perfectly," Angel said. This was true. There was no reason to believe that it wasn't, perhaps, but it was a consideration.

"From the scarring on this one, I'd guess she's had a venereal disease," Jacobs said. There was mild distaste in his voice.

"So?" Lenzini asked.

"So, nothing. I was just observing. Has she had a venereal disease, Dr. Crawford?"

"Chlamydia, ten years ago. So the other tube may have scarring, too. I'd like to keep this one if we can, in case."

"Does she have any children?"

"One," Angel told him. "But she'd like to have more."

Jacobs shrugged. "It would be easier to just remove the tube."

"But not very professional," Lenzini remarked. "If the patient were awake to be asked, I'm sure she'd opt to have the tube saved if possible. Wasn't that your understanding, Dr. Crawford?"

"Definitely," Angel agreed, blinking at him in surprise.

"But then," Lenzini mused, "she's a woman, and we don't always bother to give women what they want, do we, Dr. Jacobs?"

"I beg your pardon?" Jacobs stared at Lenzini as if he were mad. "Of course we give women what they want, when it's feasible. I don't think there's a necessity to save the tube. She probably has a perfectly good right tube that will make another pregnancy possible."

"I don't think I'd want someone to throw away one of my testicles on that basis," Lenzini mused. "But then, it's not the same thing, is it?"

"Not quite!" Jacobs insisted. "Look, if you want to try to save the tube, do it. I thought you might need my help here, but it appears you have everything under control."

The sarcasm only made Lenzini grin more widely. Even under his mask, Angel could tell. His eyes danced with amusement. "Well, we'll give it a shot. You can hang around if you like, but there's no need."

With a sound very close of "Harumph," Jacobs departed.

"So, let's get on with it," Lenzini suggested. "I trust you don't have to work with Dr. Jacobs very often."

"I've never even spoken with him before," Angel admitted. "Of course, I'd better not now."

Even as she spoke, she began manipulating the laparoscope so that it perfectly lit the swollen portion of the fallopian tube. "I'm going to cut right here," she said, indicating with the tiny scissors.

"Go for it," Lenzini said. And as they both watched her delicate movements on the screen, he added, "You probably should have gone into surgery, Angel. Not a flicker of hesitation. Not a tremor of the fingers."

"You're trying to provoke me," she retorted, without pausing for a moment. She maneuvered the clamps to stem the bleeding. Then, cautiously, she began to shell out the lodged embryo.

Lenzini watched the screen intently, but his stance was one of easy unconcern. "If you want me to help you get more time in the operating room, I'd be happy to do it. People in the wilds of Wisconsin deserve a family practitioner who can do some surgery. We don't want them bleeding to death on their way to the medical center in Madison. Where I'll probably be next year, by the way."

There was a sudden attention in the OR that quite outdid the concern with the picture on the screen. The anesthesiologist glanced up sharply from his instruments, but could read nothing from Cliff's eyes. The nurses turned toward him, one of them saying, "I hadn't heard you were leaving, Dr. Lenzini."

Angel's heart had stopped. She knew it had because there was obviously no blood getting to her brain. Her instrument seemed to have a life of its own. Even as she felt her body stiffen, her hand continued to maneuver its tool.

"What did I tell you?" he said. "Not a quiver. You're good, Angel. You're very good."

"You are not moving to Wisconsin." Angel continued to shell out the tissue. "There's nothing in Wisconsin to interest you in the least."

"Now, there you're wrong. I've already talked with the head of surgery at the university hospital. He feels certain they could make a place for me in their department. In fact, he'd be really pleased to help get my research grant renewed."

The other members of the operating team were

regarding the two of them with outright curiosity, but neither Cliff nor Angel seemed to notice. Cliff pointed to a spot on the screen. "That scarring may give you a little trouble. Can you feel it? With the instrument, but your fingers will understand where it is. Right, like that. Two things. Make sure you've gotten everything from the inside, and when you sew it, you'll have to remember that it's sort of pleated when you appose it to the other side. Good."

Angel, confused, excited, and fascinated, felt suddenly that she was so intimately connected with Cliff that she could do anything. She understood everything he was telling her about the operation, even if she refused to understand what he was telling her about himself. "The university in Wisconsin," she said firmly, "does not have the same reputation as Fielding. You would destroy your chances of being a star."

"Hell, they're offering me a full professorship," he responded, his eyes dancing. "I'm only an associate professor here. And people get diseased in middle America just as much as they do on the West Coast, Angel. You probably haven't noticed that."

"It wouldn't be the same." She had stopped shelling out tissue and was checking now for anything more she should remove before trying to repair the tube. "What would you do with your wonderful house? You couldn't possibly leave it."

"I wouldn't sell it," he admitted. "But I'd rent it out. Because someday I might come back here, and I'd want to live in it if I did."

"Well, exactly," she said, though she wasn't quite sure what she meant.

"There's plenty of room in that house for a couple of kids. Some kids, even raised in Wisconsin when they were little, might not mind moving to San Francisco. A lot of people like living in San Francisco. You like it, don't you?"

"Five years wouldn't be long enough. The kids would still be too little."

"Now, Angel, we all have to make compromises. Seven years, say. But the kids would have to start coming pretty soon."

Angel glanced around the operating room at all the people staring at her. A flush suffused her face, which was obvious even under her mask. She deliberately began suturing the opening in the fallopian tube, taking special care with the scarred area. "It's probably even easier to be a chauvinist in Wisconsin than it is here," she said.

"I'm a reformed man. Couldn't you tell?"

"Oh, it's easy to do one or two things right to prove a point. It's a lot harder to change a lifetime's mentality."

"I realize that, Angel. I'd need someone to remind me."

She concentrated for a moment on getting the two sides of the opening to appose properly. As she patiently adjusted the sutures, she commented, "It's like this scarring, Cliff. One side doesn't quite match the other. They aren't a perfect fit."

"They don't have to be a perfect fit," he insisted. "They'll accommodate to each other. They'll heal together. If there's a bump here or there, well, nothing's perfect. They'll both be trying to mesh, not just one side."

Angel sighed. The nurse handling the carbon dioxide inflation of the abdomen asked diffidently, "Do you want more gas in here?" The anesthesiologist wagged his head sagely and remarked, "There's already plenty of hot air in here, if you ask me."

Once again Angel and Cliff ignored them, except for Angel shaking her head no to the nurse. Her suturing was nearly complete now. The operation had gone so smoothly, she almost hated to see it end. Ellen's chances of getting pregnant again had not been appreciably reduced, and the dangers of the ectopic were now eliminated.

And Angel seemed to have been proposed to.

Chapter Seventeen

Angel had been relieved when Cliff was beeped from the OR just as they were completing their work. He had, with his usual flair, remarked as he backed out the door, "Thanks, everyone. Hope you've all enjoyed yourselves as much as I have." And, blowing a kiss at Angel, he'd disappeared. "Don't ask *me*," Angel had insisted, to forestall any questions. "The man is obviously crazy."

"The man," said her circulating nurse with a big grin, "is obviously in love."

The hospital buzzed with gossip about Angel for the second time that year. She refused to answer anyone about what was going on. Even when her roommate Nan called, she said only, "I don't know what's happening. I don't know when I will know what's happening. In the OR, Nan, in front of all those people, he decides to carry on a discussion about our future. What future? I don't know when I'll be home, either, because—um—he's headed toward me right now with a very determined look on his face. Bye."

Within the hour, Angel found herself at Cliff's house. He had bullied her chief resident, a wholesome, worthy fellow, into letting her go at a reasonable hour and had insisted on their stopping at his favorite Chinese restaurant to get takeout. "You can choose what you want, as long as it's Chinese," he'd said. "They probably don't have decent Chinese food in Wisconsin, and I want to get my fill before I leave here."

"We have perfectly good Chinese food in Wisconsin. And no one said you had to come there, either."

Lenzini had ignored any protests about peripheral matters. "We're just going to sit down and discuss how this is all going to work out," he'd insisted.

"How what's going to work out? Cliff, I think you've forgotten that we broke up."

"Well, I did decide to forget that for the time being. You know, Angel, I've learned some things in the last few weeks. Ask Catherine. She can tell you. I'll call her, and you can talk to her."

"That won't be necessary." Angel climbed out of the car in his garage and reached down for the paper bag of food containers. When he attempted to take it from her, she glared at him and he laughed.

"Okay, so you're strong enough to carry a paper bag," he said. "I was just being polite."

"I realize that. But for now it makes me a little nervous, Cliff."

"I like the presumption that there will be a later on." He held open the door into the kitchen. "This is okay, right?"

"I'd do it for you if you had your hands full."

"Hmmm. Are you giving me clues here?"

"Something like that."

Angel set the bag on the table and began to take

out the wire-handled white containers. Cliff opened cabinets and began setting out plates, wineglasses, flatware, and napkins. Angel loaded it all on a tray, and indicated that he could be the one to carry it into the dining room.

"See?" he said. "We're a great team."

Over the green onion pancakes with peanut butter sauce, he tried to convince her that he had seen the light about women. "It was my father, Angel. I've always patterned myself after him, and he's from the old school."

While spearing the special garlic shrimp, he admitted that it wouldn't be easy to change something that deeply embedded. "But it's like quitting smoking, see? You know smoking isn't good for you, and that it's a habit you have to break. So you do it. I'll go see 'Thelma and Louise' again."

After a thoughtful bite of oyster-sauce beef, he suggested, "You could remind me when I was being a jerk. Even in front of other people."

"I don't want to remind you. I don't want to change you. You can't build a relationship on that kind of shaky ground," Angel said.

"You're not asking me to change. I *want* to change."

"Oh, Cliff, that's today. Next week when some woman, probably someone with a great deal less status, ticks you off, you're going to behave just like you always have."

He regarded her seriously. "I don't think so, Angel. You know why?"

"I can hardly wait to find out."

"Because I wouldn't want someone to think of you

that way. Or my sister. Or my mother. But even more than that, Angel, I don't want someone to treat our daughter like that."

Angel felt the familiar prickling at her eyes. "Sometimes you get to me, Cliff. I don't know what to say."

"Oh, just say you'll marry me, and we can get on to other stuff."

Angel helped herself to the chow mein. "Then there's the matter of your living in Wisconsin. I can just see how you'd hold that over me. 'Well, since we're living here, you should make a few concessions to me.' Not a good start, Cliff."

"Who knows? I may fall in love with Wisconsin. I may not want to come back to San Francisco. You never know."

"Oh, sure. When this house will be sitting here waiting for you."

"By then the tenants will probably have trashed it," he said sadly. "There'll be graffiti on the walls, and gouges out of the floor where their dogs have dug. It will be totally uninhabitable."

Angel couldn't help but laugh. "At the rent you'll be charging, you'll have only the very nicest people here, and they aren't going to destroy the place." Then she frowned. "Cliff, I appreciate your attempts to find a place in Wisconsin, but, well, even if you were at the University, that's not exactly where I had in mind to practice. Madison's a real city. That's not why I went into family-practice medicine."

"I know that." He reached around to the sideboard and produced a map of Wisconsin, which he spread out at the other end of the table. He had marked it up with red pluses. Tapping one spot where there were two pluses, he said, "This would work for both of us. Not too long a commute for me, and, going the other way, you're almost in the wilds. And yet we'd be close enough to your folks so you could see them when you want."

"How do you know where my folks are?"

"Because I listen to you, Angel. I've listened to you since the day we met. And I'll tell you all about Sally if you want to know, but it's kind of boring. She'd have made a good wife for me if I'd *really* been my father's son. But I'm a different person, and I couldn't really fall in love with someone like her. I thought I could. I think I thought I should." He shrugged. "But I didn't fall in love with anyone until I fell in love with you. Because you're the right person for me."

"Maybe I'm just a challenge to you."

"I've thought of that," he admitted. "Proud surgeon rejected by second woman in a year, won't let it happen. But that's not the way it is, Angel. I feel rotten when I'm not with you. I need you in my life. Mostly, I need you to love me."

Angel reached out to touch his hand. "I do love you, Cliff. I just don't know whether it would be harder to live with you or without you."

"I have a good side," he said persuasively, wrapping his fingers around hers. "I'm actually very easy to live with, mostly because I don't much care about little things—whether you put the toilet paper on upside down or not, or when I run out of beer. I'm a good improviser." He cleared his throat. "And I do watercolors when I'm in the mountains. You may have seen them in my bedroom."

"I thought they were your sister's. They were delightful. You're a man of many talents, Cliff. And I want you to be happy. Honestly I do. But maybe being with me wouldn't make you happy. I hate to think of us a few years down the road, miserable because we couldn't resist each other, but turning out to be too different to get along."

"It's not going to be that way," he protested. "Read your fortune cookie."

Angel gave him a questioning look as she cracked it open. " 'With this person your happiness is assured,' " she read.

"Right." Cliff split open his and read, " 'With this person your happiness is assured.' See? What more could you ask for?"

"How long have you been patronizing this Chinese restaurant?" Angel wanted to know.

"A couple years. They keep a few special ones on the side. You may not want to eat the cookie. It's probably stale." He grinned. "Hey, I don't believe in counting on chance. I wouldn't be a good surgeon if I did."

"And you're a very good surgeon." Angel allowed him to draw her hand to his lips.

"Roger thinks we're right for each other." He kissed the back of her hand. "So does Jerry, I think." And the tips of her fingers. "You're the only one who seems to have questions, Angel." He turned up the palm and kissed it lingeringly.

"With good reason," she grumbled, taking her hand back.

Cliff reluctantly began to eat again. "Oh, I don't know. We have a lot in common. We're both doctors. We both want to start a family."

"How do you know that?"

"I just know. You've loved this obstetrics rotation. The way your eyes shine when you talk about the babies. Hell, you can't miss it. The fact that you chose family practice, the way you're determined to get to Wisconsin, the playground of wholesome American families."

"You see, you're mocking it. You just don't belong there, Cliff."

"I imagine Wisconsin has something to teach me, and I have something to teach Wisconsin," he said, coaxing her with a smile. "I'm not an unreasonable man."

"Of course you're an unreasonable man. Somehow I don't think I'd love you if you weren't."

"Do I sense a little confusion here?"

"I have to be honest with you, Cliff." She set her fork aside and sighed. "It's alarmed me, my falling in love with you. How is that possible, to fall in love with someone who doesn't value women properly? I don't understand it."

"I doubt if there's any logic about who we fall in love with, Angel. It has a lot to do with sexual attraction. And who could resist me?" He frowned at his own joking dismissal of the subject. "Or maybe you have doubts that I tap into. Jerry would know that kind of stuff, I suppose. All I know is that you really are the most special woman I've ever met. And I love it that you fell in love with me. And I'll do everything I can to keep you in love with me."

Angel let it drop. Not that it wasn't important, but she realized it was her own problem. She would have to keep watch over her own principles. Cliff had come to love her, despite himself, for possessing them. She would have to protect them, for his sake, and her own, and their hypothetical daughter. What was it Jerry had said to her? "You can't control other people's behavior, only your own. But sometimes that's enough."

"You okay?" he asked.

"Yes, I'm fine."

"Want to see the sunset?"

Angel glanced at the west-facing window and saw the sky alight with deep reds, oranges, purples, and pinks. She nodded and followed him into the living room, where they sat down close together on the sofa. He drew her back against his chest, his arms around her waist. "Sometimes in the autumn you see the most incredible harvest moons here," he said. "And I'd be perfectly willing to have you live here with me so you can see them for yourself. But, Angel, I think it would be even better if we got married. Then we'd feel more comfortable starting a baby."

"Would we?"

"You know we would." He stroked her wrist with a seductive finger. "Of course, if you want to wander around the medical center big as a barn and not married . . ."

"Hmmm. September, October. Nice month for a wedding, October."

He kissed the top of her head. "Do you think so?

Where would you want to be married, if you were going to get married in October?"

"Well," she said, looking around her, "this isn't a bad spot. It would limit the number of people who could come, which is good, and there would be this incredible view in the background."

"I like the way you think. And then, because it was the place we were married, it would always be special to us."

"So that we'd come back from Wisconsin to live here some day, you mean?"

"In seven years," he suggested.

"We wouldn't want to be too rigid."

"Well, some rigidity is good."

"I wasn't talking about that kind of rigidity," she said, shifting slightly on his lap. "We were talking about our wedding, weren't we?"

"Yes, but since that's settled, we can go on to other things."

"You've been wanting to get on to other things all evening."

"So what's your point?" he asked. "Haven't you?"

His hands wandered up to her breasts, and Angel caught her breath. "There are probably a lot of other things we should be discussing, Cliff. But, no. All that can wait. Men think with their dicks."

He laughed. "I know. I'm thinking. I'm thinking."

Don't miss Elizabeth Neff Walker's
Rising Temperatures,
coming soon from Signet.

Jerry had been very impressed with Rachel's handling of the ethics consultation. She had used all the strength she'd accumulated as an attorney to guide the discussion and point out aspects of the issue that each side had overlooked. She gathered together the necessary information as though she'd been conducting this type of meeting for years, made sure everyone agreed to it, and with consummate skill, led the participants to the best solution. Yes, he was impressed with her.

And he seemed to be seeing Rachel with new eyes. First, there was her irritation at him, which came as a surprise. He had always known her as an even-tempered woman and had in fact sometimes wondered if she wasn't just a little *too* even-tempered. The fire he'd seen in her eyes tonight had been missing before, or perhaps he hadn't noticed it in the past. Then there was her ability to compromise, to apologize, to accept his own apology. He had been in the midst of too many power struggles not to appreciate the grace with which she conceded some of her personal power for the sake of the situation.

The participants in the conference had been handled carefully, not allowed to place themselves in a position from which they could not retreat. That was perhaps the most impressive feat of all. Half a dozen egos the size of California seated at one table and she'd managed to keep them all balanced. A truly remarkable accomplishment. No wonder the attending had complimented her. Jerry felt very much like hugging her.

As they walked side by side through the hospital, Jerry saw her smile to herself and asked, "What's that about? What are you thinking?"

Her eyes flashed with excitement. "God, wasn't that fantastic! I've never had quite that kind of experience before—where everything worked. Everything! It was like magic. I felt like I was pulling the strings, you know? Not in a bad way, but as if I could do no wrong. Oh, I know it won't always be like that, but hell, if it happened even once a month I'd probably expire from euphoria!"

"You'll get a reputation for being high as a kite," he teased. But he found her excitement moved him both emotionally and sensually. "We could have a drink in the hot tub at my place."

"I'm not as comfortable with my body as you are with yours, Jerry," she protested. "I know people sit around in hot tubs naked without thinking a thing of it, but I'm not like that."

"We could find you a suit."

"Oh, great! Then I could sit there covered and try not to look at you."

"I wouldn't mind you looking at me. Remember, I'm comfortable with my body." He held the outside door open for her and they walked out into the cold November night. "The hot tub is especially invigorating at this time of year. The outside air is cold and the water is hot, and your body just tingles with the difference. Steam rises off your flesh like you're cooking. Come on, Rachel. There's never going to be a better time for me to convince you to try something different."

"I know," she admitted, stopping beside her car, an older minivan from when the children were younger. "I'm almost high enough to agree."

"Live dangerously. I'm never going to hold it against you."

"I know you wouldn't." She unlocked the car and hesitated, but her eyes were still echoing the excitement she felt, and probably her need to talk about it. "All right. Just be a little patient with me."

"Promise." He closed her door behind her and patted the side of the car as though it were a horse's flank. "See you there in five minutes."

He could understand her hesitation. She was a woman he might be working with more frequently at the hospital. Not every woman was comfortable with nudity, certainly not Rachel. But they'd been friends forever, and he felt sure he could help her, and indeed himself, maintain the proper distance in their personal and professional lives. Jerry was not being completely honest with himself, perhaps. He was refusing to acknowledge that recently he had twice felt quite sexually drawn to Rachel—during the swimming episode and this evening. As a naturally potent man he frequently felt sexual stirrings for the women who passed through his life.

But Rachel wasn't passing through his life, and that made the situation different. Jerry had no doubt, however, that he would be able to behave in an entirely appropriate manner, no matter what his feelings were. He was, after all, a psychiatrist, and he knew how reasonably well-adjusted and socialized people were supposed to act. He imitated them whenever he felt in the mood.

Rachel was parking her car on the street outside his building when he pulled into the garage. He met her in the foyer and could tell she'd lost a little of her enthusiasm for the projected adventure. "Don't flake on me now," he urged. "You're going to love how relaxing this is. You'll probably order a hot tub for your house the minute you get home."

"No doubt," she said dryly, but she followed him into the elevator.

Jerry never precisely apologized for his condo, but he had a way of looking at it each time he entered that gave any visitor some idea of how he felt about the amorphous unit. "Let me turn the heat up in the tub, and I'll be right back," he said, leaving Rachel in the living room. On the way back from the balcony through the bedroom he checked in several drawers and the closet in hopes that someone had left a woman's swimming suit. He didn't really expect to find one, but it was possible. Barbara might have left one here when she visited with her new husband (whom Jerry found infinitely boring), or one of his son's various women friends might have left one, mightn't they?

He returned to the living room with a kimono and a towel. "I'm afraid you'll have to make do with this," he said, indicating the blue towel. "You can just wrap it around you and get into the hot tub with it."

Rachel regarded him skeptically but accepted the two items. Jerry felt it was time to remind her of her excitement from the meeting. "I almost laughed when that surgery resident tried to question Mr. Paras about his medical condition," he said, his eyes dancing.

Rachel grinned. "There was a certain justice to it. Mr. Paras has one of the finer baseball reminiscences I've ever heard and the 1961 World Series scores sounded a little like Mr. Paras's lab values. And you have to admit the surgery resident is so full of himself he deserved to be taken down a notch or two."

"Really, Rachel, I never knew you had it in you. You've always seemed such a 'good' woman. It's shocking to find out that you harbor all sorts of vengeful fantasies."

"Hardly." But her eyes shone. "Still, didn't you think it was particularly subtle, the way I handled him? He left there thinking I found him a very skillful diagnostician."

"Well, didn't you?"

"I suppose so, but so stuffy. It was great to see him loosen up a bit."

"And all because of you."

She grimaced at him. "You're trying to flatter me so I'll go in your stupid hot tub." But she couldn't be distracted for long. "Imagine. Every one of them was ready to have me walk them through the process and not be defensive or dawdling. That's not going to happen all the time, you know. It was like being an actress or something. Like I was just doing something that had already been written down. Like everybody followed their parts and they were just what I would have wanted them to be."

"That's because you were the director," he said, shepherding her toward the kitchen. "Tell me what you'd like to drink. I have wine and beer and hard liquor and mineral waters." He opened the refrigerator and pointed to a row of bottles on the door. Rachel chose one, and he took it from her to screw off the top. "Now go undress in the spare bedroom and wrap the towel around you, and I'll let you keep talking about your triumph."

"Smart-ass."

"Hey, I'm just trying to be helpful."

When she had disappeared he carried their drinks through to the balcony and set them beside the tub. Since he felt certain she'd be more comfortable if he was already in the water, he returned to his bedroom and stripped quickly. For his exit from the water he brought along the kimono robe he usually used and laid it on the redwood boards. Naked, he climbed into the hot tub and turned on the jets. The water was still not as hot as he liked it, but it would continue to heat even with the bubbles going. It was several minutes before Rachel appeared at the sliding glass doors from his bedroom.

She looked adorable in her blue towel, tucked in modestly over her breasts. It turned out not to be the best place to tuck it in, however, because when she sat down on the underwater seat, the towel had a tendency to spread apart. Rachel kept tugging it together with her hands, looking a little chagrined.

She studiously kept her eyes off Jerry's naked body—or at least the most significant parts of it.

Jerry reached over to check the thermometer. "Good. It's just about there now. Doesn't it feel great?"

"Yes," she admitted. "It's heavenly."

"It's even better if you're naked."

She gave him a quizzical look. "I'm sure it is."

"I suppose not all doctors are comfortable with nudity, either. They see naked bodies all the time, but often bits and pieces—identifying the surgical abdomen or doing a breast examination. It's just a body, after all. Nakedness comes to be associated with a lack of power in some way. The caregivers are clothed and the ones taken care of are unclothed. Sometimes I think that's why I like shedding my clothes. It's like dropping out of that phony power game."

"Only doctors see nakedness like that."

"Hmmm. Is that really true? Certainly most people view nakedness as vulnerability. You, for instance. You'd feel vulnerable if you were naked. Now why do you suppose that is?"

"I haven't the slightest idea," she muttered, once again drawing the towel back over her stomach.

"Do you think I would see you as a sexual object? Or that I would take your nakedness to mean that you were sexually available? You know neither of those things is true. Not with me."

"Oh, you're a saint," she grumbled, twisting sideways so that she could let go of the lower end of the towel and still be mostly out of his line of vision.

"Not at all. I'm like every other man, except that

I'm used to nudity, professionally and personally. I could easily be a nudist, you know."

"Yes, I'm sure you could."

"Clothes have always seemed constricting to me, especially suits and ties. I mean, what's the point? It's such a rigid, uncomfortable form of dress. I imagine if we all went around naked it would be a little distracting at first, but people would get used to it, like they do at nudist camps, and think nothing of it."

"Have you ever been to a nudist camp?"

"No."

"Then you're just talking through your hat."

He winked at her. "You know very well I'm right. If everyone were naked, it wouldn't be any big deal."

"Well, everyone isn't naked. Some people are modest."

"What's to be modest about? I've seen naked women, Rachel. Hundreds of them. Probably thousands of them, even though it's not as common with psychiatric patients. Do you think I'll judge your body?"

"Of course you'd judge my body."

"No, I wouldn't. I'm not a judgmental type."

"It doesn't matter. You're human. You'd think to yourself, well, her breasts aren't very big, and her hips are a little wide, and her legs aren't very shapely."

Jerry shook his head. "Nope. I'd say to myself, 'How great she was able to let her hair down and enjoy herself.' *That's* the sort of thing I'm likely to make a comment about, not whether your legs are crooked."

"Not crooked," she protested. "Shapely. Like model legs. Everyone expects model legs."

"I don't."

"Of course you do. And besides, it's not even that, really. My body feels private. I don't share it with other people. I don't walk around my house naked and I never have. You probably do."

"Sure."

"See? It's just a difference of viewpoint. You don't need for your body to be private, and I do."

"Why do you suppose that is?"

Rachel, perhaps unwisely, snapped, "I suppose it's because all too often women don't have a *real* choice about what to do with their bodies."

"Ah. Now we're getting somewhere. Give me an example of what you mean."

"I don't feel like giving you an example."

"I see." Jerry closed his eyes for a moment, resting his head back against the redwood decking. Without opening his eyes, he began to speculate. "Choice. When I think about choice I think about freely making a decision. That would mean that I didn't feel coercion of any sort. Not by someone else expecting something of me, or even me expecting something more of myself than I wanted to give. For instance, if I were married and my wife wanted to make love, I might not feel, on every occasion, that I had a free choice of saying no."

"Yes, but that probably seldom happens with men."

"I wouldn't say seldom. Men do seem, all hype aside, to take a greater interest in sex than women do. Sex meaning sexual intercourse. Women on the other hand probably take a greater interest in physical affection, cuddling, hugging, that sort of thing."

He had continued to keep his eyes closed. Rachel asked, "Do you know that from your patients?"

"You mean anecdotal experience? Mm, partly. And partly from reading, and partly from personal experience."

"In what way 'personal experience'?"

"I've known women to give themselves unwillingly because they thought it was expected of them."

"But you let them do it."

Jerry opened his eyes and studied her in the dim light. "Well, it's hard to know all the time why someone is doing something, Rachel. Sometimes they're giving you a gift, and it would be unkind not to accept it."

"I suppose."

"It's not an easy thing to unravel, the relationship between a man and a woman. There are all sorts of factors at play all the time. There are men who do the same thing: have intercourse because they think it's expected of them, though I think it's far less likely for a man than a woman. It's not a subject people can be very open about."

"You're pretty open about it."

"I don't know whether that's my training or my personality, but yes, I think I'm a little more able to talk about it than most people. It's not always comfortable for the other person, though."

"No."

"My openness sometimes can seem like an invasion of privacy."

"Yes."

"It's not meant to be. Like my urging you to just enjoy the hot tub naked. That's not for me; that's for you. But if it doesn't feel right to you . . ." He shrugged his bare shoulders and smiled at her. "You have to do what you feel comfortable doing, Rachel. If you do something because you feel intimidated or rushed into it, you're going to be resentful."

"Tell me about it," she muttered, letting her legs float in the stream of bubbles. "Can we get back to talking about how brilliant I was tonight?"

He laughed. "Sure. You were smashing. You were powerful and capable and clever and charming. Tom Washburn is probably going to call you in on all his cases now."

"You certainly know how to flatter a woman," Rachel retorted.

But she went on to ask his opinion on a number of questions and to share some exciting thoughts she'd had about the evening and the prospects for her career. Jerry willingly fell in with her enthusiasm and introspection. Her animation was more than a little stimulating. When she at length fell silent he felt so close to her that he wanted very much to hug her, or kiss her. But the hot tub was not the appropriate place. Especially when he'd been assuring her that there was nothing *personal* in his wish to have her naked. Jerry found at this juncture that he was quite mistaken about that. He would very much have liked to be there with her naked, and to see if anything sexual developed between them.

That, of course, would be the height of folly, after what she'd said. And because they'd been friends for so long. Any sexual relationship between them could ruin that friendship for good, and Jerry valued her friendship. Rachel was a mainstay in his life and had been since Barbara left him. When Dan died, he had been there to comfort her, and she had been extremely grateful for his help. Their closeness had been platonic all these years, which had not previously bothered him very much. When he looked at her now, though—relaxed yet vibrant—he wanted there to be something more between them. Obviously it was time to call it a night.

"You're exhausted," he suggested, realizing that indeed she was. "I'll go in to change, and you can dry yourself here with the towel and put on the robe."

"Thanks, Jerry."

Surprisingly, she didn't turn her head away as he climbed out of the tub but regarded him with an unreadable expression on her flushed face. He stood there for a moment toweling himself off before donning the kimono-robe. Even when he walked back to the sliding glass doors he could feel her gaze on him, and he was tempted to look back. But then she'd suspect that he was going to watch her while she left the hot tub, and he didn't want her to think anything of the sort. It was hard for him, though, to obey his conscience and not try to catch a glimpse of her naked body, since he could so easily have done it.

After a while he heard her pass quietly through the room and out into the hall. His own body, turned away from her, was even more aroused than he had expected. He forced himself to relax. Where was all this disinterested enjoyment he'd been talking about? No wonder she thought he was full of it.

She could probably feel his arousal two rooms away. Jerry dragged on a pair of blue jeans and a Yale sweatshirt. He ran his fingers through his hair to tame it, not bothering to go to the bathroom for a comb. That seemed, at this point, just a little too studied.

On the redwood deck he found her blue towel, wrung out and hung over the railing. He gathered it up along with their bottles and took them inside, wanting to be seated in the living room when she came out of the second bedroom. He drew the beige curtains and turned on a standing lamp. Its light on the ceiling threw the rest of the room into weary shadows. Why hadn't he spent more time making the place look presentable? The only real touch of color was a bright red pillow on the floor that he used when he watched TV on his back there. One black wood sculpture of a tall, slender hunter that his son had sent him from Africa stood on an end table, almost invisible in the poor light. Jerry was about to pick it up when Rachel returned to the living room.

She looked sleepy now, and her skirt was just slightly off center. She smiled and sighed. "Back to the real world now, eh? That was great, Jerry. I could fall asleep on my feet."

"You look like you're about to. Do you think I'd better drive you home?"

"No, no. I'll be fine. It's just a bit soporific, your hot tub."

"Mm." He walked with her to the door, where she hesitated, looking around. "Forget something?"

"Probably not. I've got my purse. It just seems like there should be something else."

No wonder, he thought. "Well, if I find anything, I'll bring it in tomorrow."

They stood in companionable silence in the descending elevator. Jerry walked her out to her minivan, still half aroused by her presence. When she had unlocked the car door he placed a chaste kiss on her cheek and gave her a friendly hug. "This has been a great start for your new career, Rachel. Best of luck with it."

"Thanks, Jerry." She climbed into the vehicle and rolled down the window. "I'm still steaming. I'll probably have the windows fogged up before I get home."

"Sure you don't want me to drive you?"

"I'll be fine." She started the engine and gave a little wave as she pulled out from the curb. Jerry stood there until her car was out of sight.

"Taut, highly literate ... Barbara Parker is a bright new talent."—Tony Hillerman

"Superb . masterful suspense ... hot, smoldering, and tangy."—*Boston Sunday Herald*

SUSPICION OF INNOCENCE

by Barbara Parker

This riveting, high-tension legal thriller written by a former prosecutor draws you into hot and dangerous Miami, where Gail Connor is suddenly caught in the closing jaws of the legal system and is about to discover the other side of the law. . . .

"A stunning, page-turner!"—*Detroit Free Press*

"A fast-moving thriller . . . charged Florida atmosphere, erotic love and convincing portrayals make it worth the trip."—*San Francisco Chronicle*

Available now from **SIGNET**